KEEPING HIS MATE

ALIENS OF OLUURA

IVY KNOX

AUTHOR'S NOTE

If you don't have any concerns regarding content and how it may affect you, **feel free to skip ahead to avoid spoilers!**

This book contains scenes that either reference or depict abduction, human trafficking, graphic violence, threat of sexual assault, as well as drug use, which may be triggering for some. If you or someone you know is in need of support, there are places you can go for help. I have listed some resources at the end of this book.

CHAPTER 1

BRUVIX

hlvo rattles off the details of how he will trade the sack of halu leaves, the jug of sap from the da'koi trees, and the crate of shilmashi petals we brought from Oluura, and I nod, pretending to listen. It is not that I do not care; I am just distracted. My mind is not on Nu'Piix, or the tasks we must complete here. It is not even on Oluura, though I am eager to return home.

My focus is on the white med tube I spotted outside of Bzzsil Chi's brothel not long after we landed and had a drink at the tavern. It looked like the med tubes human females are put into when they are bought and sold at places such as this.

After all, this is where Varrek and Ahlvo found their mates, and Bzzsil Chi is the smarmy slaver who held that very auction. I have no plans to place a bid, however. Because I refuse to line that wretched pvorki's pockets any more than they already are.

I have…another idea.

"Are you listening to me?" Ahlvo hollers, waving the cane Nalba made for him in my face.

"Of course, brother," I reply automatically. "That sounds like a splendid plan. I shall meet you here as the timekeep strikes three then?"

"Very well," Ahlvo says, his tone wary. "What will you do? Spend a few credits at the brothel?" He wags his brows and gives me a sly grin.

"No, no," I tell him. "I have no interest in that. I shall…uh, check in with my contacts. Nee-roh suggested we get a heat scan detector for the village but has had trouble locating one. I will try to track one down."

It is a lie, but only because I am certain Ahlvo would not approve of my true plans.

He nods, seemingly convinced. "Ah, good, good. Meet you here at three." He limps away on his cane, pulling his wagon of goods behind him. Though his leg has improved and gets stronger every day, he likes the cane and the support it provides. And I am pleased to see him accepting his body as it is, a challenge I was certain a stubborn male like him could never overcome.

I glance at the timekeep on my screen pad before tucking it into the pocket of my vest. I have a short time to complete my task. There is none to waste.

Strolling casually around the exterior loop of the Nu'Piix Enbalo Post, I take a visual tally of the guards. I count twenty-seven concentrated around the exterior of the brothel and a few huddled together behind the large building next to the brothel. This must be the auction facility where Varrek bought Cloh-ee, Aye-vah, and Kay-teh. It matches their description perfectly: a decrepit structure too large for the land it occupies and out of place next to the brothel.

But if everyone knew that Bzzsil Chi dabbled in human trafficking, it would look right at home there.

I cut through the center of the post, just watching people as they make their way from the tavern to the trading stalls, or to the brothel, or back to their ships. That is the extent of activities to engage in here, so it makes observing people an easy endeavor.

I pull out my screen pad to appear busy as two flixiel guards wearing bronze armor over drab yellow jumpsuits pass by.

Twenty-eight minutes left.

Turning my back toward the dock, I take the time to study the words on the crates and packages being hauled from the ships near the brothel and the auction facility. The language is alien to me, but what I'm really looking for are med tubes. White ones. And I see several being rolled out of a large shipping vessel and into the back room of the brothel by five flixiel guards in the same hideous attire.

Are these all human females?

Or are there males too?

What if there are females of other species among them?

I ask myself these questions, despite not having the answers, as I formulate my plan. I must get to them, these unconscious beings that were taken from their homes, and free them before Bzzsil Chi sells them to slavers and predators. But there are at least a dozen med tubes that just arrived, and I am but one male.

How am I to achieve this?

Three guards enter the building, the heavy door slamming shut behind them, leaving two outside.

I drop into a crouch and slink closer, so I can hear the guards unloading the tubes. I hide behind a black crate the size of my ship as they chatter away in their native tongue—a language I have stored in my language chip, luckily. They make a few repulsive jokes about human females, and my knuckles crack as my fingers curl into fists. I will enjoy breaking their necks.

"What does he want with this one?" a flixiel with an eye patch asks.

The other one with a long greasy mane pulls a sheet of paper off the top of the med tube that sits between them and reads it silently. Then he laughs. "It is a return, apparently. It says this female was awoken and immediately attacked her owner and bit his nose. She was then drugged and promptly returned to stasis."

"Ah, a fighter. Those are the most fun to take," Eye Patch says with a croaking laugh.

"You are right," Greasy Mane says. Then lowers his voice. "I doubt Bzzsil even wants this one. He won't be able to sell her."

Eye Patch leans in. "Do you think he would notice if we had a little fun?"

I have grown tired of seeing these males alive. I slip behind the crate closest to them, directly behind Greasy Mane. Launching from my feet, I leap over the crate and slam an elbow into the side of his head, knocking him to the ground.

Eye Patch has a dagger to my throat before I land, but flixiels are as slow as they are hideous. I knock the dagger from his hands, and it clatters to the ground. He thinks I crouch to steal his blade, but that is because he is stupid. As I sweep my foot in a circle, knocking him off his feet, he comically flies in the air for a moment before landing in a pile on the ground.

I grab Eye Patch's dagger while I'm down, and before a now-angered Greasy Mane can charge me with his sword, I hurl the dagger in his direction, and it lands with a wet thud into his neck. Bright green blood spurts like a fountain from the wound, and I smile as he gurgles with panicked eyes for a heartbeat before he collapses into a pool of green.

But my work is not done. Eye Patch is back on his feet, shaking the dizzy from his skull as he reaches for a pistol holstered at his side. A bullet will not kill me, but it will slow me, interfering with my mission. There is also no guarantee that what is inside his pistol is a simple metal projectile. After Varrek's father was able to coat a bullet with flesh-eating bacteria, causing the infection in Ahlvo's leg to spread and decay at a frightening speed, I no longer underestimate the lethal power of weapons pointed at me.

But I can certainly pretend to be unbothered.

I wait until his pistol is aimed at my heart, giving him a false sense of confidence, then I reach for a wide steel disk, a common shipping component, which lies to my right on the ground. I toss it in front of me and it distracts Eye Patch's one good eye long enough for me to roll toward him and throw myself into his gut, shoulder first. The air leaves his lungs with a satisfying "oof" as he falls to the ground, pistol dropping from his hand and skidding away.

Pinning his hands beneath my knees, I straddle Eye Patch and revel in the look of fear that flashes across his face. "What is wrong, little flixiel?" I ask as I pull my dagger from my vest and rise over his face.

"I thought you liked fighters..." then I drive my blade through his good eye and into his brain, sending him into eternal darkness.

I take a moment to admire my work before pulling the dagger free and wiping it on my tunic. Then I check my screen pad.

Two minutes remaining.

This seems like an opportune time to depart anyway.

I get to my feet and drag the rolling med tube behind me. I can only save the one female, the biter that Eye Patch and Greasy Mane wanted for fun. I quicken my pace, running past the other med tubes, wishing I could save more, but there is no time. Passing some of the larger ships, I know there are several more before I reach ours.

"What is that?" I hear Ahlvo ask accusingly behind me. I turn and his eyes widen when he sees the blood on my shirt. "Bruvix...wha–"

"You there!" a flixiel guard yells.

"Run," I tell Ahlvo as I break into a sprint, pushing the med tube in front of me. Ahlvo goes as fast as he can, but stays behind me, and fires an occasional shot from his laser gun over his shoulder as we make our way around the docks.

"How many guards are left?" I shout.

"I do not know!" he replies, irritated. "How many were there to begin with?"

"Just keep shooting," I tell him. I suppose the number doesn't matter as long as we make it out of here alive.

The door to our ship opens as it registers our heat scan, and I shove the med tube up the ramp as I run inside. Ahlvo fires off another shot and then curses after a click sounds from his gun where a red beam of skin-melting radiation should be emerging. "O fah! I did not remember to charge this."

I put the med tube behind the command chairs and join him by the door to finish the job. But I am too late because as soon as I reach him, Ahlvo is slicing the gilded sword that was once his cane through the neck of a single flixiel guard. The guard's head lands next to Ahlvo's foot.

"Are we clear?" I ask him, looking down at the blood that covers more of his tunic than mine.

"For now," he replies as he searches the dock. "Let us go before more arrive."

Once I secure the med tube inside the room Varrek typically sleeps in, I join Ahlvo on the bridge. We have taken off, safely, and are well on our way back home.

"That was fun," Ahlvo says with a smirk. "I enjoyed that very much." His tone is that of someone who has just received a thoughtful gift.

I dip my chin once, unsure how to reply.

"Now, are you going to tell me why we slaughtered those flixiel guards, inevitably leaving a trail for Bzzsil Chi to come after us, endangering our clan?"

I swallow. I did not think this through at all. "We saved a human female," I tell him.

He holds my gaze for a moment, then nods. "Good," he says with a sigh. "That is good. We will figure out the rest later."

* * *

After two days of travel, we reach home, our skin free of blood and wearing clean clothes. We receive many questions when we stroll onto the main path of the village while carrying a med tube, but we answer none and head straight to Kaiva's.

Varrek follows the moment he sees us, as does Cloh-ee.

We stand in the med room, huddled around the tube as Kaiva begins the process of waking the human female from stasis.

"I heard she attacked her owner and bit his nose the moment she awoke, so we should be careful," I warn them. Varrek, Kaiva, and Ahlvo back up a step while Cloh-ee's and Aye-vah's feet remain planted as they laugh.

"That's awesome," Aye-vah says.

"Yep. She already fits in nicely," Cloh-ee adds.

"It is almost complete," Kaiva notes as she looks up from her screen pad. The glass top of the tube opens with a hissing sound, and as the sleeping human female comes into view, Aye-vah and Cloh-ee both gasp.

"Ohh shit," Cloh-ee mutters.

"What bothers you?" I ask as I look down at the female who is about to join our clan.

"Her hand," Aye-vah says, pointing. "See the ring? She's married."

CHAPTER 2

ELEANOR

*D*o these women know how creepy they look right now? I'm guessing not. I could tell them, but I can't seem to get the words out. Being pulled in and out of stasis for I don't even know how long is bound to make one's throat a little scratchy.

I've got to do something though, if only to get them to stop smiling at me like they're about to slather me in butter and chop me up into bite-sized chunks. "Hi," I say, the word coming out in more of a whisper.

Their eyes widen with excitement as they look at each other and then back down at me. "Hello!" the one with wavy reddish-brown hair, porcelain skin, and big brown eyes says. "Eleanor, right?"

I nod, offering a meek smile. *Please be normal. Please don't kill me.* I silently pray. I have no idea where I am, but the presence of humans is a good sign. I hope.

"This is Chloe, and I'm Ava," the one with the glowing brown skin and curly hair tied in neat twists adds as she places a hand over her heart. The creepy smiles have vanished, thank god, and I have a hunch these two are trying to make me feel comfortable. I appreciate the effort, regardless of the dreadful delivery.

"Um," I mumble before releasing a hoarse cough. I clear my throat before continuing. "May I have some water, please?"

"Oh god! Of course!" the one named Chloe exclaims as she scurries out of view and whispers something. She's back within seconds, and I take the cup from her hand and greedily swallow the contents in two gulps. "More?" she asks with a softer smile.

I take a deep breath, mentally compiling a list of the questions I need answered. "No, thanks. The date. What is the date?"

Ava chews on the inside of her cheek for a moment, eyes on the ceiling. "Right. Well, since Earth time is similar to Oluura time, we estimate it's early February. But we might be off by a week or two."

February. That means I've been floating in space for three months. I've been woken a handful of times, only to realize that I'm somewhere new, and I've been sold to a new alien. Then the scenario plays out the same way each time. I try to get my bearings, figure out where I am and how to escape, and I realize there is no escape, that I'll never return to Earth, to my job, to Frank. I scream internally for about a minute straight, and then I focus on the fact that I'm still alive, and there are only so many things I can control.

"Three months," I mumble aloud to myself, still struggling to accept how long I've been gone.

"I'm sure you have a million questions," Ava says softly, breaking through the whirlwind of confusion in my mind. "And we're happy to answer all of them. But first, I'll give you the basics."

"Okay," I reply, my voice still cracking, but now with emotion I'm trying to hide.

"So, you were kidnapped from Earth by aliens. We were too," she says, pointing between her and Chloe. "Along with another woman you'll meet later."

"You ended up in the hands of Bzzsil Chi, who is a terrible dude. Like, Uncle Scar from *The Lion King*-level evil," Chloe adds.

"Luckily, Bruvix got you out of there just in time," Ava continues, "and now you're on a planet called Oluura. The majority of our clan is from Trovilia. They settled here years ago. You're safe in our village, and you'll be fed and clothed and given shelter, and nothing bad will happen to you."

Okay. That sounds nice. Certainly better treatment than what I've endured since I was taken. But a few of those words aren't registering. "Bruh-vix? And… who is a terrible dude?" I ask.

"Right, right, right," Chloe says in a rush, waving a dismissive hand. "Let me tell you about the clan…"

She continues talking, but I struggle to remain focused because what I really need right now is to get back to Earth. Specifically, to Frank. He needs me. I pull myself into a seated position inside the sterile white tube thing I'm in and notice there are others in the room.

"Gah!" I shout. Pinching my eyes shut, I briefly wonder if I'm hallucinating. When I reopen them, I know I'm not.

There are four of them—creatures with golden skin, all over seven feet tall, and all extremely wide. They present as three males and one female, though I'm not sure how they identify here. Two of the males have silky silver hair. The one with long silver strands holds his chin high and his shoulders back, indicating an impressive level of confidence, or that he holds a position of power among the group. Although both could be true.

The one with shorter silver hair has the opposite posture of the leader. His head is bowed and tilted to the side like he's entranced by the floor beneath his feet. His wide shoulders are hunched, and his thick arms are crossed over his chest. If I had to guess, I'd say this guy wears shame like a coat he never takes off. But I have no guesses as to why. He's rather beautiful in a rugged kind of way.

The other two golden beings look alike. One is a male leaning on a steel cane in his hand, with long black hair in tight braids, and the other is a female with the same bright eyes and kind smile, just with streaks of white in her hair.

"Sorry," Chloe says, gritting her teeth. "We should've warned you about that."

"No, it's all right," I reply, sitting up taller inside the tube, so the others can clearly see and hear me. "I apologize for my reaction. All the time inside this tube has made me a bit loopy," I say with a chuckle, trying to gauge their temperament. These giant gold people seem terrified of me, which is laughable considering I'm barely five-foot-two.

"This is Varrek," Chloe says as she drags the one with long silver hair toward me by the hand. "He's the leader of our clan, and the daddy to this half-alien baby inside my gut!"

His striking green eyes hold mine as he bows slightly. "Greetings, Elle-noor," he says with a strange pause in the middle of my name. I find it charming. "It is my honor to welcome you to Oluura."

"Nice to meet you, Varrek," I reply. "Did I say that right?"

"You did, yes," he says with a proud grin. Then his gaze drifts to Chloe at his side as he puts a hand over her protruding belly. A grunt sounds behind him, and Varrek's focus snaps back to the other golden ones. "Ah, yes. The members of my clan that I trust the most. Elle-noor, this is Ahlvo, my second-in-command," he says as he points to the male with black hair and the cane.

"Also my mate!" Ava adds with an enthusiastic hop.

"And his mother, Kaiva, who is our resident healer," Varrek continues, gesturing to the older female at Ahlvo's side. "Ava helps her care for our clan."

I knew they were related. I knew it.

"And, of course, Bruvix, my cousin, who has many talents, but who also rescued you from Bzzsil Chi," Varrek adds, pointing to the only person left in the room. The one who still won't lift his gaze from the floor. This is the one who saved me from the "terrible dude," who I'm guessing is Bzzsil Chi.

Why won't he look at me?

"You know," Ava says, moving closer to my side. "I'm not sure this is the right moment to get into the whole Bzzsil Chi mess. Perhaps, let's help her get settled in her new home first?"

"Yes," Varrek mutters with a dip of his chin. "I misspoke, Elle-noor. I am sure Bruvix would be happy to provide those details another time."

I'm...frustrated by the mention of my rescue and lack of information surrounding it, but I'm having trouble leaning into that frustration when Bruvix still won't meet my eyes. What is his problem? I did scream at the top of my lungs when I first saw him and his buddies, but how else am I supposed to react after being woken up in a room full of aliens? "I look forward to that, Bruvix. Nice to meet you, by the way," I holler, since his back is still pressed against the far wall.

He grunts. That's it. Just a single grunt before pushing off the wall with his foot and striding quickly toward the front door. Seven steps are all it takes for his long, tree-trunk legs to take him out the exit. "Something I said?" I ask the girls once the door slams shut behind him.

"Don't mind Bruvix. Happy is not an emotion he's familiar with," Chloe says with a laugh.

"He is a miserable fellow indeed," Ahlvo adds.

Despite the harsh words, the familial love for Bruvix shows in Chloe's expression, and in Ahlvo's. Maybe he's just the town grump.

"Just so you know, I'm here to listen anytime you want to vent or discuss your experience since being taken… if you want," Ava says softly.

Chloe nods emphatically. "She's great! Ava's our resident therapist."

Ava scoffs. "I was in school to become one, back on Earth, but then I was taken. Anyway, I'm here if you want to chat."

I smile in response because I'm not sure what to say. My head is still spinning from the fact my unconscious body has been bouncing around space for three months. I just hope Frank is okay. I know my ex, Olivia, probably has him now, given that we were sharing custody. But it kills me that I may never see that goofy smile of his again.

"Here, let us help you," Ava says as she takes my arm. Varrek rushes to my other side and guides me out of the tube. Once I'm on my feet, I take a few moments to stretch the numbness from my limbs and shake my muscles awake.

"So, how far are we from Earth?" I ask, pulling the elastic from my hair and retying it into a low bun.

Chloe and Ava give each other a look that's a blend of panic and sorrow, and it makes my stomach drop. Then I catch Ava eyeing my left hand as she bites her lip, and when I look down, I see what she sees. The slim yellow gold band my grandmother left me. Her wedding ring which I'm wearing on my ring finger.

"I'm so sorry, Eleanor," Ava says, her hand covering her mouth as she shakes her head. "I wish there was a way we could help you get back to Earth. But we can't."

Chloe bites her lip before adding, "There are several galaxies between ours and the Milky Way, and we have no means of safe travel from here to there. I–I'm sorry."

"Frank" comes out of my mouth as a croaked whisper. They rush to wrap me in a hug, and as I stand there, sandwiched between them, the warmth of the embrace breaks something within me. The tears fall, and as they stream down my cheeks, a pained cry falls from my lips and I collapse on the floor. Ava and Chloe continue to hold me as I let it all out.

I haven't spent more than twenty-four hours awake and in the same place since I was taken, so it stands to reason that I haven't even had time to process the fact that I was abducted by fucking aliens.

This place, though, Oluura, feels different. Chloe and Ava feel like people I can trust. Not just because they're human, but also because they were abducted too. They understand. I want to trust them. I want to believe I'm safe here. It's the only positive aspect of this whole nightmare.

"Come on, girl," Ava says as she wipes the snot from my nose with a cloth. "Let's get you some food, clothes, and put you to bed. Plenty of time for tours and clan introductions tomorrow."

"Okay," I mumble through wobbly lips. I notice once I'm back on my feet that Ahlvo and Varrek have left, and Kaiva is the only one who remains. In her hands is a pile of clothes that look similar to what the girls are wearing.

Chloe takes the clothes from Kaiva and leads me up the stairs.

"You may stay in Ahlvo's old room, Elle-noor," Kaiva says in a soft voice. "My room is right above it. You let me know if you need anything at all."

I try smiling as I nod, but I'm still crying, so I'm sure I look ridiculous.

Ahlvo's old room is pristine with not much in it but a wide wooden chest, a bed that could fit a soccer team, and a side table. A handful of glowing orbs are scattered in the corners of the room on the floor, creating a cozy ambiance I didn't know I needed. I haven't slept in an actual bed since the night I was taken, and I sigh at the sight of the massive one in front of me.

Chloe puts the stack of clothes next to me on the bed as I plop down on the edge. "Here," she says, "you get changed, and Ava and I will go grab you a plate of food so big, you'd think it's Thanksgiving."

I wipe the wetness from my cheeks and let out another sigh. "Okay."

They pat my shoulder before they offer me a final smile and leave. Then I'm alone in what is apparently my new home, dozens of galaxies from where I should be.

Chloe and Ava clearly think I'm married, and that my breakdown is the result of learning I'll never see the love of my life again.

They aren't totally wrong.

I need to tell them I'm single and only wearing this ring on my ring finger because I was at a bar with friends the night I was taken and didn't want random white guys with an Asian fetish hitting on me. And I should tell them the love of my life is Frank, my four-year-old spaniel/terrier mix. The one who has my heart is a dog who barks at plastic bags on the street and refuses to poop outside when it's raining.

I should tell them all these things. But not tonight. Tonight is for food and sleep. My next round of weeping can wait until tomorrow.

CHAPTER 3

BRUVIX

I let out a grunt as my bare back slams into the dirt. Varrek hops to his feet and peers down at me with a triumphant gleam in his eyes.

"Where is your head this day, Bruvix?" he asks, wiping blood from his forearm where my claws tore through his skin. He offers me a hand and pulls me to my feet. Brushing the dirt from my face, I take a moment to find the answer to his question because he is right. I am not focused on the training session. Varrek has bested me the last four times in hand-to-hand combat, and I lose more interest in this practice with each defeat.

It may be the knowledge that a new human female is among our clan, Elle-noor, and I cannot stop picturing her face. Her kind eyes. Her scent. Fuck, her scent was hypnotic in its unique sweetness. My mind flashes back to the moment the med room blurred around her, and she was the only thing my eyes could see clearly.

The tether. I felt it the moment she awoke.

Her high-pitched scream fills my ears, and I am reminded of the moment her eyes first landed on me. She sat up inside her med tube, and when she noticed me, Varrek, Ahlvo, and Kaiva, she shrieked. But her eyes were on me first, the acrid scent of her fear thick in my nose, and I am certain the scars covering my face were what caused her such intense horror.

I should not have been surprised by this reaction as it is one I have received many times. That, or staring, or whispers, or a curled lip of disgust. These are all quite common when people first encounter me. My face is not pleasant to look at. The mit'xcruul that attacked me when I was a young male saw to that. It was intent on killing me, but short of accomplishing that goal, it made sure I would never be the same. It is because of that gruesome beast that I am one too.

Elle-noor quickly recovered from her fright, and pretended her reaction was due to our unexpected presence in the room. But I know better. It is why I left shortly thereafter. That, and the pull of the tether toward a female who has a mate on Earth. She has been through enough trauma since being taken from her home. She does not need my ghastliness to heighten it.

"I am not at my best, I admit," I finally tell Varrek.

His head tilts to the side and takes me in before nodding and patting me on the back. "Go," he says. "You need not return for the rest of the session. You shall be better tomorrow."

I should be disappointed by his dismissal and angry at myself for causing it. However, my mind has drifted to the bed of piloi flowers on my roof garden and how they are just beginning to bloom. It rained through the night and into the morning, which means many of them will be opening soon, and I wish to follow that progress closely. The pilois are a hardy flower, the only one that flourishes during the cold season. When the surrounding greenery withers and dies, the pilois remain. It takes a great deal of destruction to keep them from blooming. Their thick, pink petals are almost impossibly soft to the touch, especially considering how much they can weather. I must acquire more piloi seeds from the falls to plant alongside the newly bloomed pilois.

Anything to keep my mind off Elle-noor and her captivating dark brown eyes.

Heading off the training grounds, I stomp through the damp soil toward the falls where the largest patch of piloi flowers exists, and around it, I will find scattered seeds to plant in my garden. I am covered in dirt and sweat and bruises from today's session, but I will not come across another soul out here. The falls are typically vacant this time of day. The clan is still waking, or busy with morning chores, or eating their first meal at the food hall.

As I push through the brush and make my way past the tall, lush trees of the Ga'Nvi forest, I let the collective sounds of nature settle the adrenaline still coursing through my blood. The drip of rain falling from the leaves, the creak of a branch as a small creature jumps from one to another in search of sustenance, and the squelch of my boots as they sink into the mud. It is quite peaceful here, just outside the village.

It is a shame the only safe time to enjoy the depth of the forest is while the sun sits in the sky. Once darkness emerges, the wretched tr'gorys follow. They lurk within the shadows of the night, seeking blood and flesh however they can get it. Despite making this territory our own, the tr'gorys remain, circling us in the darkness, only returning to their dens when the sun rises. Tr'gorys killed one of our clanmates not long after we arrived here on Oluura, so we know to avoid the creatures.

Even when I witness a tr'gory from afar, I shudder. I would rid this planet of the whole lot if I could. Useless, vile monsters, they are.

Once I reach the falls, I allow myself time to take in the tranquility of the falls and the pool of water it spills into. Tucked away, but within a short walk from the village, it is the ideal spot for escaping the constant bustle of the clan. Though, ever since Varrek was attacked by a tr'gory the day he brought Cloh-ee here, most of the clan has not ventured to this spot.

I have no concerns I shall come face-to-face with one on this day, however, as the sun is still high in the sky. So, I will collect the seeds I require and return to my home, my garden, where I am safe and surrounded by quiet.

Locating the cluster of piloi flowers by the far corner of the pond, I collect the seeds that have fallen to the ground beneath. Many are broken or turning from the vibrant orange color of a newly fallen seed to a dull brown, so those I leave in the dirt. I crawl around the flowers until my pocket is filled with the seeds, and the knees of my pants are wet and stained with soil.

I smile as I run a hand over the seed haul in my pocket, knowing this should create at least forty new blooms in my garden. Spending the rest of this day carefully planting these seeds, tending to the newly bloomed pilois, pruning dead leaves from the patch of vakopurri that is starting to grow—that will certainly erase the disappointment from my horrid performance on the training grounds.

No one in the clan knows I have a garden on my roof. Few members have seen the inside of my home at all. It is my private space. A silent, hidden oasis. It is just for me, and I plan to keep it that way.

Before I depart the falls, I decide to scrub this dirt and grime from my skin. I will have a proper wash when I return to my dwelling, but for now, I wish to feel the chill of the water on my face and chest. To remove the remnants of this morning from my body and feel energized as I move on to the next part of my day.

Climbing up onto the ledge of the pond, I sit sideways with my knee bent and my other leg dangling, so I am able to keep an eye on anything that would approach while I am here. I use both hands to scoop the water and pour it over my head, then my chest and back.

A contented growl rumbles in my chest as I let the water run down my skin, eventually soaking the top of my pants. Not that it matters much since I will change as soon as I return home. Bending over, I shove my face beneath the surface of the water, gritting my teeth as the chilling temperature sends bumps over my flesh. Plunging deeper, I dunk my entire head, scrubbing the dirt from my hair.

When I return to the surface, I let out the breath I was holding beneath the water, and flip my head back, letting the excess water fly behind me.

It is then that I hear a squeal of surprise. When I turn, I find Ellenoor, the mated human I saved, who is also, quite possibly, my inara. She is...here.

And she has been watching me.

CHAPTER 4

ELEANOR

I am absolutely not watching Bruvix. I was not peeping on him as he splashed his heavily muscled chest and arms with water from the falls, and then flipped his wet hair back like some god-like model in a cologne ad.

Nope.

That's not what I'm doing.

But the way Bruvix is looking at me right now, it's clear he thinks I've been ogling him like a supreme perv.

"I'm sorry. I didn't mean to sneak up on you," I finally say in a quiet, embarrassed voice as I wipe the water he splashed me with from my eyes and hair. It's also all over my shirt, under which I'm not wearing a bra, so as an unfortunate bonus, my nipples are now hard and poking through my tunic.

"Why are you here?" he asks, his tone gruff as his gaze scans my body. When they land on my breasts, I feel my nipples harden even more to the point of aching. "You were...watching me? Why?"

"No, it wasn't like that," I quickly reply, holding my hands up in surrender and averting my gaze. "Ava was giving me a tour of the village, but Kaiva called her back to the med room. Something about Chloe's cramps...I'm not sure."

Bruvix continues staring at me with those incredible navy-blue eyes, and for a moment, I forget what I'm trying to say. The blue is so dark, they're almost black, but there's also a shimmery quality about them. Even though he's standing about five feet away, I can see several silver flecks in his irises catching in the sunlight as he continues to scowl at me.

He's trying to intimidate me, but it's not working.

Okay, maybe a little.

But he's more intriguing than intimidating. I get the sense that he carries every painful memory he has on his back. He seems like a kind soul, but a lack of confidence forces him to keep a wall between him and everyone else. Maybe I'm way off, but that's the vibe I get, and I've always been good at reading people.

"Um, so anyway," I continue, babbling on in nervousness. "She told me there was a nice waterfall out this way, so I just followed the sound of the water, an–and here you are. I just got here, like, two seconds before you splashed me."

"Why do you have this?" he asks, tugging at the corner of his eye with his finger. Did he? Is he seriously making fun of my eyes right now? Even in fucking space, Asian eyes are mocked, apparently. Unbelievable.

"Just because my eyes are a different shape doesn't mean you can fuc–"

"No," he interrupts. "Not the shape. The dots."

"The…dots?"

"You have two brown dots, right here," he says, pointing to the corner of his eye again.

Oh. Okay, so he's not racist. That's good. I lift a hand to the outside corner of my right eye, feeling the parallel bumps. "They're just freckles. Tiny moles."

Bruvix mouths the word *freckles*, still looking puzzled. "But why do you only have two when Kay-teh has many?"

"I don't know. We all look different," I reply with a shrug. Is he bothered by my lack of freckles? What a weird thing to notice. "My dad always said it's a beauty mark, and that because they're near my eyes, I have a sensitive soul."

"Beauty mark," he repeats, then huffs a breath, like the term is some kind of joke to him. He turns away from me, facing the falls, and leans his hands on the stone ledge of the pond. "You should not be in the forest alone. It is not safe." His accent is so odd. All of them have it actually, but his seems more pronounced, maybe because his tone is always gruff. It's like a French accent mixed with a Scottish accent with a dash of Boston mixed in. It's not pretty, but part of me is desperate to keep him talking, so I can hear it.

"You're alone," I point out as my eyes trace the scars on his shoulders.

In a flash, he straightens to his full height and stomps toward me, being careful to tilt his head down slightly and to the left, most likely to conceal his facial scars.

"You are right. Neither of us should be here," he says. Roughly grabbing my arm, he pulls me along behind him toward the village. "The tr'gorys could be lurking despite the early hour."

"Hey!" I shout, trying to break free of his grasp. "Let go of me, asshole!" His urgent touch reminds me of before…of my previous owners and the way they touched me. Panic rises, my calm vanishing. He ignores the insults I spew at him, but when I thrust a knee into his gut and duck my upper half beneath his arm, twisting his elbow, he lets go with a pained grunt.

Then Bruvix and I stand there, him bent over at the waist, and me leaning against a tree as we both try to catch our breath from our brief tussle. "So," he says as he rests his hands on his knees, a rigid smile lifting one side of his mouth, "that is why your previous owner returned you. I understand this now."

Scoffing, I cross my arms over my chest. "Because when someone touches me without my consent, I fight back? Yeah. I suppose that would bother your average shitgibbon."

"Is that what happened?" Bruvix asks, straightening to his full height. His smirk is gone, and in its place is a hard, grim line. I feel his anger from where I stand, and I'm confused. "He touched you?"

"What the fuck do you care?" I reply skeptically. Suddenly he's worried about me?

He jerks back as if I've slapped him, which I'm still somewhat inclined to do. Then he clears his throat and places his hands on his hips. "You are right. It is none of my concern."

We stand there, saying nothing for what feels like an eternity, before I blurt, "Okay, fine. The moment I woke up the last time, this feathery monster with a bulbous black nose was poking me. I told him to stop, but he continued to poke, poke, poke, like I was some kind of science project. When he leaned in closer and poked my tit, I bit a chunk of his nose off."

I watch as Bruvix's eyes widen, his mouth slowly stretches into a mischievous grin, and then he starts howling with laughter. It's a rich, rumbling sound that makes me think of a thunderstorm in the middle of summer.

"And how did he react?"

"He squawked like a chicken the moment he noticed his own gooey blood all over his shirt," I reply, smiling at the memory of him hopping around, clutching his nose like it was about to fall off.

Bruvix continues to laugh, clutching his stomach.

"I, um, I'm assuming that's why he returned me," I add with a chuckle of my own.

His laughter finally fades. "I am saddened I was not there to witness such an event."

"Well, grab me like that again, and you'll get the full reenactment."

He nods and clasps his hands together behind his back, then looks away, his eyes scanning the depths of the surrounding forest. "I shall not repeat that mistake."

I take this opportunity to really look at this mysterious male who rescued me. He hates how he looks, clearly, which I find baffling. He has scars, tons of them, in fact, but when I look at them, I don't find them unappealing. I wonder where they came from. I ache for the pain he must've felt. The ones on his face are extremely deep. A long, jagged mark slashes through his brow, all the way down to the middle of his cheek. He's lucky he didn't lose that eye. Then there's the scar that cuts through the left side of his mouth, making his smile crooked. The third scar is a short line that forms an L shape along his jawline.

His chest is also covered in them. Long silver stripes that cut through his gold skin, leaving uneven, raised, and puckered skin on either side.

He catches my eye, and quickly lifts a hand to the scarred side of his face, trying to cover them in a nonchalant way, and I instantly feel like a jackass for allowing my gaze to linger. I want to tell him it's not what he thinks. That I was envisioning his pain and feeling sorry for what he went through.

But would that admission actually make him feel better? It's probably best to not say anything at all. We need a change of subject. That'll fix the mood. "I wanted...I just, um... Thank you for rescuing me."

He lets out a quiet grunt, turning on his heel and striding for the tree line at the edge of the village. "It was no trouble." As he's about to step onto the main path, he says over his shoulder, "I am sorry you cannot return to your mate." His gaze softens as it travels down to my grandmother's wedding ring, and then snaps forward as he strolls away.

I'm left speechless, standing in the mud as I process everything that just occurred. I resist the urge to chase after him and tell him the truth about my situation because he still seems wary of me.

Is it his wariness that draws me to him? Like a moth to a strong, silent, emotionally ambivalent flame? It would certainly explain...well, all my past relationships.

No, I tell myself. *I can unpack that later.*

Pushing through the tree line, I make it back onto the main path a few minutes behind Bruvix. I'm about to grab a bite at the meal hall when a whirling mass of fiery red hair steps in front of me, blocking my path.

"You must be Eleanor!" she hollers, her green eyes wide with delight. "I'm Kate."

She's shorter than me by a few inches, but with curves everywhere. Freckles cover her nose and cheeks, her skin is so light, it's almost translucent, and her red hair is long and curly, reaching her chest. Kate's the first member of the clan I've seen that isn't wearing a gray tunic and black leggings. She's wearing a black velvet dress with subtle white pinstripes that hits just below her knees.

"Yes, hi," I reply with a smile. "Nice to meet you."

"May I call you Ellie?" she asks.

"Um, Eleanor is good," I tell her. Kate's smile falls briefly before she widens it again with a nod. She wasn't expecting that from me. And maybe giving someone a nickname is a way for her to bond with them. "It's just...There was this girl in my high school named Ellie and she was a colossal twatwaffle when I came out as bi. So now that name just makes me cringe."

"You're bi?"

"I had a poster of Dana Scully on my wall and wore my corduroy overalls so many times that my parents paid me $20 to stop, so yeah," I reply. I spare her the details of growing up queer with conservative Korean and Filipino parents, and the complex history of the LGBTQ+ movements in my parents' native countries, because that'll just bring the mood down.

She laughs, then says, "That's cool. Well, yeah, fuck that Ellie chick. I hope she develops a salted caramel allergy." Then she grips my forearm, her expression turning serious. "Wait. That's too mean. Jo said I'm not supposed to hex anyone this early in my training." She lifts her gaze to the sky. "I take it back!" she yells, tracing a hexagonal shape over her heart.

I have so many questions. "Wait, what?"

"Oh, I'm a witch. And I'm thirsty for vengeance, but Jo, my teacher—you'll love her—is trying to help me channel that into something 'more productive,'" she adds finger quotes to the last part as if it annoys her.

I tilt my head to the side. "You're a fascinating one, Kate."

Then she clasps her hands together with an excited look in her eye. "True story. And get excited, because I've got a big day planned for us, Eleanor."

"Do you now?"

"Oh yes," she replies with a wicked smirk. "Chlo is on bed rest for the day. Doctor's orders. And my mate, Niro—who is a dragon, but not scary at all, by the way, you'll meet him later—anyway, he's busy at our caves setting up a camera in the nursery. But I thought it'd be fun to have a girls' day at Chloe's. Just us humans."

I let her lead me back to Chloe and Varrek's house as she chatters on about how Ava and I can get drunk since we're not pregnant. How she's extremely jealous because she and Niro have been busy decorating their house here in the village, and it's stressing her out and she would love nothing more than to throw back some of Bruvix's "terrible ale."

By the time we reach Chloe's house, she's filled me in on how she felt totally out of place amongst the clan until Niro kidnapped her. She explained her strange dream link with Niro, and how she broke the link when he got too possessive at her birthday party.

"So, wait. He was worried you were going to cheat on him with Bruvix?" I ask when she's done telling me about how she ended up forgiving him.

"Yeah, Bruv and I have an… interesting friendship. He once offered up the use of his dick when I couldn't sleep," she says with a laugh.

Huh. "How thoughtful of him" is all I can say because now I'm picturing Bruvix and Kate together and it's making me feel weird in a way I wasn't prepared for.

"Seriously," she adds as we climb the steps to Chloe and Varrek's bedroom. "It was probably the least sexy pickup line I've ever been on the receiving end of."

Once we make it to the top floor of the house, we find Ava sitting at the foot of Chloe's bed as Varrek sets up a table with countless bowls of food, alongside two jugs of a frothy orange liquid and three jugs filled with a creamy white liquid.

"Well, hello, ladies," Kate says to Ava and Chloe. "You doing okay, Chlo?"

"Oh yeah," Chloe says with a dismissive wave of her hand. "Totally fine."

Varrek clears his throat as he stands. "She is not fine. She has had some bleeding and will need to stay in bed until tomorrow."

"Varrek, I've got this," Ava vows. "I'm not gonna let Chlo get nuts tonight. Don't you worry."

He purses his lips, but then sighs, realizing nothing will stop this girls' night from happening. Then he leans down and gently kisses Chloe's forehead, whispering, "I shall be close by at Ava and Ahlvo's. If you need me, yell for me, and I will run across our branch. I will be here in a heartbeat."

I look away because the interaction seems too intimate for my eyes. But also, incredibly sweet. If I had any reservations about how humans are treated by these males, they've been wiped away now.

"Go already!" Kate groans dramatically. "This is a no-peen zone, Varrek. Sorry, I don't make the rules."

"You do, though," he replies. "That is a rule you just made."

"Potato, tomato," Kate says in a bored tone.

Ava giggles. "Yeah, that's not the phrase."

Holding up a mug full of the orange stuff, Kate ignores Ava. "Ale, Eleanor? Or would you like some tibbi? It's a non-alcoholic juice."

Since it's not even lunchtime, I opt for the tibbi. I'm not against day drinking, but I don't know these people well enough to let my guard down that much. Not yet anyway.

* * *

Hours of snacking and chatting later, I feel much more at ease. Kate, Chloe, and Ava are all lovely in their own unique ways, and they've had each other's backs since they were shoved into Bzzsil Chi's glass cage on the planet Nu'Piix. Each of them struggled when they first arrived here, but having a specific duty, a way to contribute to the clan on a daily basis, seems to have helped immensely.

Plus, they've all fallen in love, which clearly plays a big role as well. Kate took the longest to find her place, but thanks to Niro's grand cave palace and penchant for gadgets, Kate spends most of her time creating pieces of clothing for the clan.

"So, Eleanor, your turn," Chloe says as she nibbles on another piece of junasii bread. "Top three things you miss about Earth. Go."

And just like that, my mood sours, and I'm hurled into a black cloud of depression at one hundred miles an hour. "Um," I choke out, gritting my teeth to hold back the tears. But when I feel one slip down my cheek, it's like a gate opens and suddenly they're rushing out.

"Oh, honey. I'm so sorry," Chloe says as she leans forward and wraps me in a hug.

"Chlo, what the fuuuuck?" I hear Kate whisper to Chloe. She's trying to be quiet enough that I can't hear, but my hearing has always been exceptional, and I hear it all. "Obviously she misses her husband. Let's not make it worse."

"No, no," I say as I pull back from Chloe to look at the three of them. Sighing heavily, I decide this is as good an opportunity as any to tell the truth. "I'm not married."

I was expecting a collective gasp, but they just sit there staring blankly at me, so I continue. "This is my grandmother's wedding ring," I say as I take it off my ring finger and put it back on my middle finger where it's usually worn. "She left it to me."

"So, who is Frank?" Ava asks, resting her cheek on her knee.

I use my sleeve to wipe the last of my tears away. "Frank's my dog, and my best friend, really."

"Oh, shit," Chloe mumbles. "I'm sorry, Eleanor. Of course, you miss him. I get it. I mean, I've never had a dog of my own, but I've always wanted one."

I let out a chuckle as a montage of memories flip through my mind. Frank doing zoomies on the bed every night after I feed him dinner, him wiggling and turning so much during the night that I'd often wake up with his little paw in my face, or that time he ate an entire baguette and kept farting so loud, I couldn't sleep.

"Yeah, he was the greatest," I say after a long pause. Playing with the frayed edge of my sleeve, I let the reality of my situation finally sink in. I'm never going to see Frank again. "I know he'll be okay without me. My ex and I were sharing custody of him after we broke up, and Liv is a great dog mom. I just hate that I didn't know that the last time I snuggled with him was going to be the last time, you know?"

"Good-byes are the absolute worst," Ava says with a somber nod as she takes a sip of ale. She talked about how she lost her mom earlier, and I know she's thinking of her now.

I take her hand and give it a comforting squeeze. I've been hesitant to mention or even think of Frank because I knew I'd have to face the pain of losing him. Now that it's out in the open, I do feel a bit lighter. Not better, necessarily, but not as burdened. "They sure are."

Interlacing my fingers, I press my hands away from me, stretching my arms. "Three things I miss about Earth... Well, now you know that number one is Frank," I say with a sniffle. "Number two would be my mom's hobakjuk."

"Is that food?" Ava asks.

"Yeah, it's a Korean dish. My mom's Korean and my dad is Filipino. My mom moved to the Philippines when she was a teenager, met my dad, and they came to the U.S. not long after they got married. I grew up in St. Louis, Missouri. Anyway, hobakjuk is basically a pumpkin porridge, and her recipe is to die for. She always made it for me when I was sick," I reply, my mouth watering at the memory. "Ooh, and watching K-dramas with her while my dad was working nights. That was the best. And number three is my boss, Dr. Valdez at the animal hospital where I worked. So kind and generous. She paid for me to go to school to become a registered vet tech. She said I had a gift and wanted to invest in it, so she could keep the most talented people on her staff," I tell them as I cross my legs in front of me, smiling at the memory. "I passed the exam two days before I was taken."

"That's amazing!" Chloe cheers. "That's the equivalent of a nurse, right? In animal terms?"

"Yeah, pretty much," I reply. "Vet techs are trained to administer anesthesia during surgeries, perform dental cleanings, take x-rays, draw blood—things like that."

"You prefer animals to humans then, eh?" Kate asks.

"Ha! Yes, absolutely," I practically shout. Animals never have an agenda, and they can't bore you to death with small talk. They follow their instincts to survive, that's it. And if you're lucky enough to get a creature with such a pure and honest heart to trust you…there's nothing in the universe as rewarding as that. Nothing.

I hadn't considered that those moments were behind me now that I'm here. This is the only thing I'm good at. The only thing I truly know how to do. Maybe I can put these skills to use somehow? "So, if you know of any alien pets that need medical treatment, I'm happy to provide."

"Hmm," Chloe says, her brow furrowed. "Not unless you're looking to get your arm bitten off by a tr'gory, I'm afraid."

"A tr'gory? What's that?" I remember Bruvix mentioning them in the forest, but I was too distracted by his presence and wet chest to ask.

"Oof," Ava mutters at the same time Kate makes a clicking noise with her tongue and Chloe lets out a dramatic sigh.

"It's a massive wolf-like creature with blood-red eyes and curled white horns," Chloe tells me.

Well, that sounds scary. But looks can be deceiving.

"And when I say massive, I mean fucking *massive*. Like, the size of a car," Chloe continues. "One attacked Varrek at the falls. I thought maybe it wasn't afraid of me because it didn't get growly until it noticed Varrek, but that was probably all in my head."

I certainly don't want to be eaten by a wolf the size of a car, that's for sure. "I'll pass."

CHAPTER 5

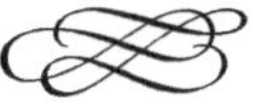

BRUVIX

I enjoy sleep, but it evades me this eve. Is it because of my encounter with Elle-noor by the falls? Possibly, I suppose. But why is she consuming my thoughts? There is a chance she is my inara, but she can never truly become my mate. She is already mated.

Unavailable.

Not for me.

Never for me.

I let those words repeat as I trim the empty stems of the piloi flowers in my garden, the few flowers that were unable to bloom, willing her face to leave my mind. I do not need to wonder what those two brown spots are doing next to her right eye. Why are there just two? Why does Elle-noor have fewer of them than Kay-teh? And why does her long black mane look so soft to the touch? Where are the snarls and knots that my mane is constantly riddled with?

She looks different from the other humans, this is true, but also similar in many ways. She is small in stature, and her skin seems dangerously delicate like the others. I have concerns about their ability to breathe through such compact noses, but somehow, they manage to do so. Overall, they are fragile. That seems to be a standard component of their race.

But Elle-noor… she moves with elegance, as if her feet do not touch the ground. Her wide dark brown eyes can see beyond what is in front of her. When she looks at me, it feels as if she is peering inside my head. It is unsettling. Her skin is darker than Cloh-ee's and Kay-teh's, but is still light, and there is a soft glow about it that makes me want to feel it beneath my fingers.

Her mane smells of flowers and crisp morning air. The sharp point of her chin when her smile stretches across her face—it dazzles me, especially when that fascinating indentation appears beneath her lower lip on the right side of her mouth. Her belly and arms are soft and rounded, and her legs are thick and muscled. How could such a stunning combination appear on one human frame? Down to her short blunted claws, every part of this female entices me, which is cruel because she can never be mine.

But maybe this torture was meant for me. Maybe I deserve it for those I have wronged. For the lives I have taken. For the occupants of the med tubes that I left behind at Bzzsil Chi's brothel. Maybe, to the goddess, my soul is as gnarled as my body.

I let the latter thought take root, sink into my brain tissue, and allow it to reframe recent memories as well as give it the power to influence the moments ahead of me. Part of me wishes this is merely a dejected concept created by shame, and I should bat it away, dismissing it as such. But a bigger part of me is certain it is truth, and it makes a great deal of sense with the way my life has turned out.

I am alone.

I shall remain alone, just as I have always been.

The tether between Elle-noor and me will continue draining my energy, the longer I deny its existence, but I can persevere. I must.

My hands dig into the soil as I create small holes for the piloi seeds. Once I drop five seeds into each hole, I fill it back in and spread out the dirt. These seeds should take nicely, I tell myself as I repeat the task over and over until I have no seeds left.

I remove the brown wilted leaves of the huutra vines that climb the inner walls of the roof garden until there is nothing but bright yellow. Next, I harvest a pile of red bozpa stems to mix into my next batch of ale. After that, I water the blooming buds of the vakopurri, a flower foreign to Oluura that I bought long ago on Nu'Piix. The stems are said to have a rich, savory taste to them, which I suspect will be a grand addition to my ales.

But a quick inspection of the eternally wild branches of the qam shrub leads to a disappointing discovery: several of the light purple leaves have circular holes in the center. That can only mean one thing: niimi worms. These little buggers continue to gorge themselves on my qam shrub, despite how often I spritz the leaves with soap and water to keep them away.

"Ah, there you are," I say to the long, hideous, white-and-brown-speckled pests when I find a group of them huddled under a thick branch. Carefully, I extract them from their snack zone and place them in my palm. Once I have all six, I put them on the roof ledge near a huutra vine. They do not like the taste of the huutra, and I know they will eventually make it back to the qam shrub, but with their tiny feet, it will take days. That should give the qam leaves enough time to heal from the niimi's destruction.

It would be much easier to kill them, but I do not see a need for that. They are merely trying to eat. I can play this game with them forever as long as they do not cause me harm.

Standing, I brush my dirty hands on my pants and survey the progress of my garden. The piloi flowers—if the seeds I just planted grow—will border the garden on all sides, encasing my other plants, herbs, and vegetables in a wide rectangular shape. A divine embrace in various shades of pink, much like Elle-noor's soft lips.

Stop thinking of her, I tell myself.

"You will grow tall," I whisper to the seeds that lie beneath the soil. "I know it." I look forward to the pride I will feel when that day comes.

Though I wish I could spend all my waking hours in my garden, I have other responsibilities I must see to. I give the plants one last look as they rattle in the wind, and head back inside to clean up.

Following a quick wash, I change into my night attire, which is nothing, unless it is particularly cold outside. Tonight, it is warm enough for my skin to be bare. There are few things more infuriating than feeling constricted inside a layer of scratchy fabric as you try to rest.

I climb the stairs to the second floor and check my security system for the village. Scanning through the last day, it appears we are clear on all sides, aside from a small pack of tr'gorys that lurk through the forest near the falls and emerge past the tree line under the cover of darkness, nothing has crept inside our peaceful hamlet.

The tr'gorys, as much as I abhor them, do not bother us when they wander through the village at night. The clan is safe as long as they are inside their homes. The tr'gorys do not mess with the meal hall, or attempt to sneak inside our food storage shed, and they do not leave their droppings on our main path. What their interest is with the village, I do not know, but when the night comes, they do too.

Luckily, they seem to be our only trespassers at the moment.

It is a relief as we are still anticipating some kind of retaliation from Bzzsil Chi for stealing Elle-noor and killing his guards. We do not know when he will act, or how, or where, but if he chooses to show his face here, we must be ready.

I would love nothing more than to be the one that slices him from jaw to pelvis, ending his reign as scum king of the Nu'Piix Enbalo Post, but we are not sure how far his reach stretches across the galaxy and with whom he does his dubious deals. We know there are high-ranking officials, kings, queens, and officers that dabble in the slave trade, but what we do not know is how many of them have a tight connection with Bzzsil Chi.

The answer to that question, or lack thereof, is what has kept him alive. Because with Bzzsil Chi's wrath comes the wrath of all he does business with, and we do not want to put our safety in jeopardy.

If I were smart, I would have considered this before I stole Elle-noor's tube and killed his guards. But clearly, I was not thinking that day. I was letting my thirst for his blood guide my hand.

"Cousin." My screen pad buzzes beside me. Varrek's face fills the screen as I go to respond.

"I am here," I reply. "Why are you awake?"

He rubs a hand down his face, looking run down. "Cloh-ee is not feeling well this eve. She is sleeping soundly now, but I must keep an eye on her."

Varrek has made mention of Cloh-ee possibly being close to the end of her pregnancy. The clan is certainly excited, but it is earlier than Kaiva expected, and that has turned Varrek into a mess of nerves, worrying that something will go wrong.

I am envious of Varrek and what he has with Cloh-ee. That he has someone to lose sleep over is a gift. "And who is looking after *you*?"

His eyes roll, a human reaction he has no doubt picked up from his inara, and he sighs. "I shall be fine. How do our borders look? Any sign of him? Or anyone?"

"None," I reply, checking through the perimeter scans once more. "The same pack of tr'gorys, but that is all."

Varrek growls low in his throat. "Why do they feel entitled to roam our land? Just because they do it while we are slumbering does not make it acceptable."

"I do not know, cousin," I tell him. "Would you like for me to inquire?"

He chuckles at that. "Yes, please arrange a summit so I may speak to the pack leader about this series of indiscretions."

"Certainly. I shall make it my top priority."

He rubs his eyes for a long moment before letting out a yawn.

"Go to sleep. You cannot lead the clan if you suffer from severe sleep deprivation."

"Very well, you petulant beast," he says in a light-hearted tone. Then the screen turns black.

Suddenly, I am in a vexatious mood. "Contact the kidnapping drax-ilio," I command my screen pad. Within moments, Nee-roh's haughty glower fills the screen.

"What do you want?" he greets from his workroom in the caves. His hair is disheveled between his horns, but he does not look tired.

"Have I interrupted your slumber?" I ask innocently.

His lip quirks up in a proud grin. "Not at all. I was busy pleasing my female."

And he just...stopped? What a fool. If I were Kay-teh, I would be furious. "Yet you chose to speak with me instead?"

"You need not worry about my mate's satisfaction, I assure you. Now, what is it you want at this late hour?"

Right. There is more to this discussion than my petty mockery. "Have you discovered anything in your atmospheric scans? Or the local nav logs?"

"Nothing," he answers quickly. "You are still anticipating a counterattack from that brothel slug?"

"Yes. There will be something. We just do not know when."

He nods as he scratches his chin. "I shall keep a watch on this and will alert you should I find anything."

"Good."

"Get some sleep. You look terrible," he jeers.

I respond with a fake chuckle, and he smiles just before the comm is disconnected.

I continue to look through perimeter logs, saving them to the appropriate folders and manually checking that each system is current long after the communication with Nee-roh ends. While we may have been adversaries not long ago, Nee-roh and I have since developed a comfortable alliance. I care for Kay-teh, but only as a member of the clan, and a close friend. And he keeps her happy and safe. As long as that continues, he is part of our clan too.

As my vision starts to get fuzzy, I realize I must rest. It seems I have completed enough tasks that my mind is ready to sleep. I climb to the third floor of my home and collapse onto my wide, heavily cushioned bed. Hauling my tired body beneath a layer of furs, I turn onto my stomach, resting my head on its side, so I may peer out the window into the trees.

I am drifting into a deep sleep when a horrifying, strangled bellow echoes through the forest.

CHAPTER 6

ELEANOR

*W*hat in the galactic fuck is that noise? Did I imagine it? Was it part of a nightmare?

Just as I turn onto my side in an attempt to go back to sleep, I hear it again—the strangely high-pitched shriek of a creature clearly in pain.

An animal.

A tr'gory? Possibly.

A creature I can help? Definitely.

I peek out the window of Ahlvo's old room, and I see lights turning on in neighboring houses as the rest of the clan grows as curious as I am.

Grabbing the top fur blanket from the bed and wrapping it around my shoulders, I rush downstairs into Kaiva's med room, wiggle into my boots by the door, and head out into the night. I'm met with sleepy faces and wide, worried eyes as the clan gathers on the main path. The moment I see Chloe, I rush to her side.

"Chloe, hey! Any idea what that was?" I ask as more clan members spill from their homes and huddle around us.

"No clue," she replies, shaking her head as she looks around. "I've never heard anything like that before. Varrek hasn't either, apparently."

It didn't sound like a fight between two animals. More like a dying creature, suffering alone. Or maybe it was attacked or giving birth. I don't know. But I can't just stand here and do nothing. "It sounded like an animal in pain. Which direction did it come from?"

"Hold on," Chloe says, holding up a finger. Then her eyes go unfocused for a moment like she's on a phone call without a phone.

Varrek makes his way through the crowd and arrives at her side. "We think it came from there," he answers as he gestures toward the direction of the falls.

"Wait, how did–what did you–" I mumble, looking between them.

"Oh," Chloe says with a laugh. "Because we're mated, we can communicate telepathically."

"Wow. Okay then." This place gets more fascinating by the second. Speaking of mates, I lean in close to Chloe's ear so I can ask a question that's been on my mind all day. "Um, I'm not expected to become someone's little alien wifey right this second, am I?"

"Oh no!" she whispers back. "I mean, if you find someone you're interested in, by all means, pursue it, but no one is expecting you to lock down a mate and start pushing out babies."

I nod, feeling relieved. "Cool. Cool."

Her eyes search my face, as if she's looking for some sign of... a lie, maybe? I'm not sure. "What?"

Chloe chuckles, waving a dismissive hand. "Nothing! I just wasn't sure if there was anyone you had your eye on. Male," then she pauses, "or female?"

Ah, there it is. "Am I your first bisexual friend, Chloe?"

Her cheeks and neck turn bright red. "No!" she scoffs. "Well, possibly. Sorry, am I being an ignorant dipshit right now?"

I laugh, letting her know she's off the hook. "Nah, it's fine. Don't ask me if it's just a phase, like my mom did when I came out, or demand that I list the women I've been with as proof of my bi-ness, and we should be fine."

She lets out an exaggerated sigh as she covers her heart with her hand.

"And no, there's no one I'm currently interested in," I finally answer. It's not the whole truth, but it feels like a safe answer to provide. Bruvix has certainly caught my eye, but I'm more curious about what's going on inside his head than anything else. At least I hope that's all it is.

Ahlvo and Ava find us in the crowd, and Ahlvo whispers something to Varrek as the girls chat about Chloe's pregnancy. I try leaning closer so I can hear what Ahlvo is saying, but the noise from the clan drowns it out.

"Where are Kay-teh and Nee-roh?" Ahlvo asks.

"At the caves for the night," Chloe replies.

"Um, guys?" I say, waving a hand in front of Varrek. "I'd like to investigate. That creature sounded like it was in excruciating pain. I can help. I just need to borrow some medical supplies from Kaiva. I know the woods aren't safe at night, though. Can someone come with me?"

Varrek and Ahlvo exchange a wary glance before Varrek's eyes land on me again. I wait longer than I normally would, letting the silence get almost too awkward because I know Chloe is talking to him through their mental portal, or whatever, and I stay quiet.

Eventually, Varrek says, "I understand that you are trained as a healer for Earth creatures, but the only ones in this area of Oluura are tr'gorys, which are extraordinarily dangerous."

"If one is dying, or dead, it is a good thing for all of us," Ahlvo adds.

I know I'm new around here, but that seems unnecessarily cruel. "Okay, I get that," I begin, trying not to sound combative, "but if it's suffering. It's probably not in a position to attack me. And if it's beyond saving…" I swallow the lump forming in my throat, "I'd like to put an end to its pain."

Just as I finish speaking, the howl rips through the damp night air once again, and it's so achingly pitiful that I have to pinch my eyes closed.

"Please," I beg. "I can help."

Ava puts a hand on my shoulder. "That's really kind of you, Eleanor. I realize it's the humane thing to do, but it's too dicey. The clan lost a member to a tr'gory attack not long after they settled here.

Then there was the incident with Varrek and Chloe at the falls…" she trails off, looking at Chloe with concern furrowing her brow as if reliving the memory.

"The risk is too great, Elle-noor," Bruvix says in a low rumble from right behind me. I whirl around to face him, and his gaze is unyielding and intense like it usually is. His silver hair is a messy mop that curls around his pointed ears, his pants are untied at the top, and his tunic is on backward. It's almost cute how disheveled he is. Did he get dressed in the dark?

Focus.

"A look. Just let me take a look. Please. If it's surrounded by other tr'gorys, or looks too angry to approach, I'll haul ass out of there," I promise as panic rises in my chest. They're not going to let me do this, are they? They're about to let that poor thing die out there, all alone. "I just need to see it."

"I told you how big they are, didn't I?" Chloe asks. "Like a fucking minivan, Eleanor."

I'm not concerned about the size of it, but if that's the issue, shouldn't that indicate how badly it's injured? Thus, how incapable it is to attack anything right now? "I know, bu–"

"Girl, this is not like helping a Labrador that's been hit by a car," Chloe interrupts. "It's like… like helping a rabid fucking polar bear that's been attacked by I don't even know. Something even bigger!"

"Okay, I hear you," I reply, quickly losing my composure, "but I've treated everything from a hamster to a horse. I can handle it."

Varrek sighs, his shoulders falling as he offers me a sympathetic smile. "I am sorry, Elle-noor. I cannot allow it."

Huffing a breath, I rub circles into my temples, trying my hardest not to lose my shit. I'm hanging on by a thread though, and if that poor creature screams again, they'll have to physically hold me back from running toward it.

"But," Varrek adds, and hope fills my heart, "if you wish to check the area in the daylight, I will have one of my warriors accompany you. Just not while the skies are dark."

It's not ideal. Not even a little. The thought of that creature unable to move and lying there in pain through the night is enough to send me to my knees. However, if this is the only way I can help it without putting the clan or myself at risk, I'll take the win. "Okay. Deal," I reply. "Thank you, Varrek. I really appreciate it."

"I will go with her," Bruvix offers immediately.

Varrek tilts his head as he looks at his cousin. "Bruvix, are you certain you wish to—"

"Yes," he interjects, clearing his throat. "I am certain."

Varrek and Ahlvo exchange a glance that almost looks like a shrug before Varrek says, "Very well. At first light, you will accompany Elle-noor to the falls to investigate. I shall have the crew waiting at the tree line should you need assistance," he says with a nod. Then he takes a deep breath. "But should you feel that anything is off, or that this creature poses a threat, do nothing and return to the main path at once."

"Understood," Bruvix replies. Then he looks down at me, expectantly.

"Oh, yes. Agreed. Uh-huh," I add, nodding enthusiastically.

Ahlvo looks down at the screen pad in his hand then gives Ava the telepathic-conversation look. A moment later, Ava says, "The sun should be up in about three hours, so you won't have to wait too long, Eleanor. Maybe try to get some sleep while you can."

"Yeah, okay," I reply, trying to sound convincing. There's no way I'll be able to sleep knowing there's a hurt animal out there, but I appreciate the concern for my well-being.

Varrek turns, and waves his arms above him, trying to get the attention of the clan. Then he begins speaking in his native Trovilian, which the translator chip Kaiva installed behind my ear translates to "Clan! We must remain cautious of this creature we are hearing until we have the sun at our backs. Until then, it is not safe to venture off the main path. Return to your dwellings. Resume your slumber. We will seek the source of this noise in the light."

Everyone nods and murmurs their agreement as they disperse. Ava and Chloe give me comforting pats on the arm before they leave, and then I'm left on the main path with Bruvix, and no one else.

We stand there, staring at each other long enough that it gets uncomfortable, and then his eyes dart away first.

"Right. Well, I'll be up waiting for the sun to rise," I say, looking up at the inky black sky. "Want me to come wake you when I'm ready to go?"

He doesn't reply at first, just stands there, brushing his hands together as if there's dirt on them. I follow the movement, tracing the length of his long, calloused fingers. His hands are strong, I notice, with little silver scars crisscrossing over his wide knuckles. Then he narrows his gaze and then finally says, "This is a terrible idea. It is not safe."

"I'm aware," I tell him, nodding. I don't need to be reminded of this. "Look, you don't have to come with me. I can ask Varrek to find someone else to–"

"No. I will go," he growls, his tone resolute. "I shall meet you here when the sun is up."

"Okay," I reply, confused by his willingness to do something he clearly wants no part of, and also stunned by the low, rich timbre of his thickly accented voice. Such a puzzle, this one.

He storms off with a final grunt, and I can't help but watch him go. When his wide back and thick, juicy snack of an ass are out of sight, I stumble back to Kaiva's, kick my boots off by the door, and make my way upstairs.

Flopping down on the bed, I lie there, staring at the ceiling as I count the minutes until the sun comes up.

When another long yelp meets my ears, starting off low and growing into a piercing wail that cracks by the end, tears fill my eyes. We lie there, this unknown creature and I, crying together as we wait for the darkness to fade into light.

CHAPTER 7

BRUVIX

"Morivikka, Elle-noor," I greet her as she stumbles out Kaiva's front door on wobbly legs. Her tunic is wrinkled, and little hairs stick out around her forehead. She lifts her chin mid-yawn as an acknowledgment of my presence and passes by me onto the main path. The dark smudges under her eyes tell me that she truly has not slept at all since the creature's cries first began. Cries that continued until the darkness faded. "The torture you are inflicting upon yourself is a waste of time." It is just a tr'gory. A violent monster intent on slaughtering anything in its path. Why does one in pain bother her so?

"A living thing dying a slow, agonizing death in our backyard is a waste of time?" she asks dryly, slinging a small, stuffed pack over her shoulder. "Good to know." Then she turns to face me and begins walking backward. "Hey, if I ever end up injured in the middle of the forest, please make sure you're not in the rescue party, okay? Send someone else. Preferably, someone whose chest isn't a hollow tin can." Turning, she resumes facing forward, but now with a sour expression on her face.

"You assume I would not care if you were hurt merely because I feel no sense of urgency to save a tr'gory?" I ask, catching up to her and walking at her side. She does not answer me. She keeps her eyes on the path in front of her as she takes long strides toward the falls. "You are wrong," I finally reply. "I would do whatever was in my power to save you, just as I did everything in my power to save Dokai, a hunter who came with us from Trovilia, and who was killed by a tr'gory not long after we arrived."

That gets her to meet my eyes. She stops walking, and her chin dips. "You were there when he died?"

"No, he was dead when we discovered him at the bottom of Nee-roh's mountain. His blood was soaked into the path beneath him, his left foot was ripped from his body, and his stomach was slashed open," I tell her. "Varrek and I attempted to revive him, but he was already lost—his soul taking its final rest."

Elle-noor sucks in a breath. Her dark eyes glisten with unshed tears. My fingers flex at my side, desperate to catch any tears that spill onto her smooth cheeks—marring the exquisiteness of her skin.

"I carried his body home."

She pinches her eyes closed, and I know I have hurt her soft heart. It was not my intention, not initially. But I cannot comprehend how someone could have more concern for a brutal beast than a member of the clan. She must know what they are capable of before she puts herself in danger like this.

"Look," she mutters quietly as her gaze drops to a clump of blue moss on the ground. "I'm really sorry. I know you don't understand why this matters to me, but it does. I've always had a bond with animals. An intimate, instinctual connection that I can't explain. Strays have followed me home since I was a kid."

She is right. I do not understand. I am not inclined to try, either, given the behavioral similarities between tr'gorys and the mit'xcruul, the colossal carnivorous predators of Xelai, a vast prison planet on the edge of our galaxy. That was where my first mission took place as I was training to become a warrior. It is where a mit'xcruul attacked me under the dark of night with its massive green tusks and leathery brown skin. Its eyes were red, much like a tr'gory's, its claws were twice the size, and just as sharp.

I was not meant to survive that encounter. Incredibly, I did, and here I am now, willingly putting myself between a small human female and another bloodthirsty behemoth.

"It is nice that you feel a kinship with creatures of your world," I tell her. "But you are not on Earth anymore, Elle-noor. Tr'gorys are not like the docile balls of fur you are accustomed to."

Her pink lips quirk up on both sides before she resumes walking. "We'll see" is all she says. As if this is a challenge she is eager to take on.

When the rest of the crew comes into view, lined up in front of the trees, I straighten my spine and grit my teeth. Now is not the time to dwell on pain from the past. I must be alert. I must protect Elle-noor from her own tenderness. Her kind heart will not be the death of her. I will not allow it.

"Greetings, Elle-noor," Varrek says when we approach the path leading to the falls. "Bruvix," he adds with a stiff nod.

"Morning, Varrek," Elle-noor replies warmly. "Thanks for letting me do this. I know it goes against multiple clan safety rules, so I really appreciate it."

"You will enter the falls, check the surrounding area, and then you will return," he commands as he clasps his hands behind his back. "This is not a lengthy excursion. We do not know what is out there, and you could both be in a tremendous amount of danger by seeking out the source of those cries."

"Understood," Elle-noor says. "At the very least, I'm hoping to learn about the tr'gorys, so we can get a better idea of their hunting techniques, pack hierarchy, and physical behavior so we can keep everyone safe."

Varrek's brow lifts, a curious look spreading across his face. "Very well. That is information we shall certainly benefit from having."

Then he glances at me, his expression skeptical. "You are certain you desire to do this?" I understand he is no longer acting in his role as clan leader but as a member of my family. He knows the pain I endured and how difficult this will be for me. Surely, he is surprised I volunteered for this task.

"All will be well," I reply as I put a hand on his shoulder. He mimics the gesture and gives my shoulder a squeeze, and I know he is praying for our safe return.

Varrek steps aside, giving us room to enter the forest.

I take the lead onto the narrow path with Elle-noor following close behind. Pulling my sword from its sheath, I keep it in front of me, my dagger in a tight grip in my other hand, and my laser pistol strapped to my thigh. Elle-noor wraps a hand around the back loop of my vest, and I cannot resist the shudder that racks my body at the contact.

"It's quiet," Elle-noor whispers. I immediately turn and shake my head, putting a finger to my lips to indicate she must not speak. Not yet. Not until we know what lies ahead.

She is correct, though. There have been no strangled howls since the sun rose. It is quiet in the forest. Too quiet considering the uproar of the previous eve. I was expecting to hear a tussle between the creatures seeking to devour the tr'gory corpse. Or at the very least, the victor of said tussle gleefully tearing the tr'gory's meat off its bones.

I hear none of that.

There is only the hushed buzzing of insects and an occasional chirp of the plukki birds. But even they seem to be unsettled this morning.

The heavy flow of water fills my ears as we edge closer to the falls. I can feel Elle-noor's grip tighten with each step, though her fear scent does not fill my nose. It is as if excitement is driving her forward, whereas my fear is doing everything possible to push me back. Back toward the main path. Back toward the clan. Back toward safety.

This is something Elle-noor needs, and for that reason, I carry on. I can deny her nothing.

When we enter the clearing, I let my eyes, ears, and nose scan the area. I do not see movement or even the still remains of a tr'gory long dead. There are no scraping or heavy footsteps in the distance. I do find the scent of a tr'gory, perhaps more than one, but it is faded.

There is nothing here.

How can that be?

"It is vacant, somehow," I tell Elle-noor. She steps around me and stands at my side, letting her own senses investigate the scene.

"The hell?" she whispers, her small nose scrunched up tight in confusion. She places her hands on her waist as she stomps around the clearing, kicking up clumps of moss and piles of leaves. She is angry, and I am finding it difficult to focus on my duty to protect her when she looks like this. There is a spark of determination in her eyes, and a hardness in the way her shoulders are set. She does not give up easily, this one. "I don't understand," she finally says, walking around the edge of the pond.

I strive to conjure an explanation, something to ease the furrow in her brow. "It is a good sign, is it not? Without remains of a tr'gory, it is possible that tr'gory survived." I do not agree that this outcome is good because it means there is an injured tr'gory that is probably still close by. We could be in for many more eves with obnoxiously loud howling keeping us awake. I do not say any of this to Elle-noor, though.

There is another explanation. One I certainly prefer. "Or perhaps the tr'gory did not survive, and the body was dragged away by pred—"

Elle-noor's horrified gasp sends adrenaline coursing through my body as I race to her side on the outer edge of the falls. I find her kneeling in the dirt, leaning over a large pool of blood.

"What is...that?" I ask, sheathing my weapons and pointing to a long string of yellowish-white floating in the center. The end of it is attached to a mass of dark red I cannot identify.

She shakes her head, her hands pressed into either side of her face. "Some kind of tissue. It could be anything."

My eyes scan the ground surrounding the blood, and I discover a subtle trail of blood droplets leading to a hole in the ground in front of a cluster of boulders. Slowly, I pull out my blades once again, and keep my feet light as I approach. The hole is wide enough for me to crawl into, but smaller than I would expect for a pack of tr'gorys.

Placing my dagger in my sword hand, I reach into my pocket and pull out a douku orb. Throwing it onto the dirt at the entrance of the tr'gory den, the palm-sized orb cracks upon impact and light beams out. I wait for movement, weapons at the ready.

Elle-noor creeps behind me and pokes her head around my arm but remains quiet. It pleases me to see her taking this seriously.

After a few moments, I toss in two more pebble-sized douku orbs and peek inside. It is empty. Elle-noor and I release simultaneous sighs as we stand back. When I turn to face her, she is chewing on the inside of her cheek, and her gaze is hard with frustration.

"Do you have a theory before we return to the village?" I ask, secretly thrilled I did not have to lay my eyes on a tr'gory this day.

She huffs a breath and looks down at the tissue in the puddle of blood. "Yeah, I do, actually."

"And?"

"I think a tr'gory gave birth here."

A female tr'gory? Why did I assume the nearby pack was all males? If it was a birth, what does that mean for the safety of our clan with a growing litter of tr'gorys close by?

"I'm worried about her though," Elle-noor adds, cutting through my string of concerned thoughts. "This is a lot of blood. I know tr'gorys are big, but still."

"Well, she is no longer here, and neither are her pups, so she cannot be that weak," I reply.

"Yeah, I know, but if she has trouble nursing, her babies might not survive."

That is the least of my concerns at this moment. If Elle-noor's theory is correct, then we have a tr'gory mother in the area who is even more aggressive than the average tr'gory because she has new pups to protect. We need to get back to the village and ensure that no one leaves the main path for the foreseeable future. "This is not our responsibility, Elle-noor," I tell her. "Come. The clan is waiting for our return."

The look Elle-noor gives me is scathing. "I can't just leave them out here!"

"You do not even know where they are!" I shout back. I was tasked with keeping Elle-noor safe, not the tr'gory she heard cry and that tr'gory's pack of pups. I gesture for her to follow me back to the main path, and she shakes her head as she crosses her arms across her chest. Does she think I would truly leave without her? Or that her stubborn expression would deter me from protecting her? She has no knowledge of what I am capable of and the lengths I would go to in order to keep her safe. "If you do not come willingly, I will not hesitate to throw you over my shoulder and carry you back."

Her mouth drops open, and her eyes sparkle with defiance, which makes my cock pulse beneath my pants.

"You wouldn't."

I give her a wicked grin and take a step toward her. "I would. Happily."

Elle-noor's eyes stray to the blood again, and her mood visibly shifts. There is no fear in her scent, but when her chin dips and her lips wobble, I can feel her devastation and powerlessness from where I stand. "But…"

Suddenly, I know how I can help her. She must regain control of this situation, even if she cannot find the tr'gory in need of medical attention. "Come with me," I say, holding out my hand. "I have perimeter footage of the tr'gorys coming in and out of the village each eve for the last three moon cycles. Watch them. Study them. I am certain you will feel better once you observe them."

She sniffles quietly. "Really?"

"Really."

"Okay," she mutters with a small smile as she walks toward me, placing her hand in mine. Her skin is warm, smooth like the finest Trovilian silk, and when she gives my hand a single squeeze, my body prickles with awareness. It is as if I could measure the distance between our bodies without even looking. And every drop of my blood seeks to close that distance as if my survival is dependent on it.

It is the tether, reminding me that not only does my inara exist, but "she is here! Right here!" and that I must make her mine immediately, and eternally.

Since I cannot accomplish this goal, I break the contact between us, dropping her hand. Briefly, she looks down at her palm, searching for something. Then lowers her gaze and continues walking at my side. Once the path becomes narrow, I guide Elle-noor in front of me, in case the mother tr'gory is closer than we think. We reach the tree line and Varrek sighs as we emerge onto the main path. "Well?" he asks.

Eleanor straightens her spine and gives Varrek a quick summary of our findings. "I think the sounds we heard were a female tr'gory giving birth. We didn't see her, or her pups, but there was a pool of blood left behind near the falls, and I think it's her placenta."

"The clan should not veer off the main path until we have more information," I add. "She may be close by and will be protective of her pups."

Elle-noor nods as she pushes her mane behind her ear. "Bruvix is going to let me watch the footage he has of them, and I'll see if I can get a better idea of their pack dynamics and where this new mother could be hiding."

"Is that so?" Varrek asks, narrowing his eyes at me. "Bruvix allowing a guest into his dwelling? Interesting."

Elle-noor looks at me, then at Varrek, then at me again. "Is that a rare occurrence?"

"No," I reply quickly.

In the same moment, Varrek says, "Yes."

I clear my throat and change the subject. "There is quite a bit of recording to look over. We should be going."

"Keep me apprised of any patterns you find significant," Varrek hollers as Elle-noor and I start walking.

We stop at the meal hall, and I fill four plates with junasii bread, roasted kuhnypa meat, and berries, handing two of them to Elle-noor to carry. Waldric tells Elle-noor he is looking forward to getting to know her better when she begins dish duty the following day, an arrangement Aye-vah set up for her.

Elle-noor is quiet as she follows me to my home, and I know it is because the unknown location of the tr'gory and her pups weighs on her. Perhaps the new mother is fine and healing nicely following the birth, but since Elle-noor does not know for certain, she assumes the worst and carries that burden inside her kind heart.

I kick the front door open with my foot since I do not have a free hand, and we put our plates on the shelf by the water spigot so we may remove our boots. Then I guide her to the second floor where my security system is located and offer her the comfortable seat at the center of the table. I take the creaky wooden chair with uneven legs, and Elle-noor begins eating as I ready the recordings.

I start with the perimeter camera view from the earliest known date the tr'gory pack started entering the village at night, a little over three moons ago. Between bites, I share any information I think she might find useful about them: what a particular stance indicates, how fast they run, where the view is being captured in relation to the meal hall. Though I am unclear which tr'gory is the alpha of this pack, I show her how to identify each of the adults by markings in their fur. She asks questions and jots down notes on the screen pad I gave her.

"You may keep that one," I tell her, nodding to the device in her small hands. I am constantly upgrading my equipment and have at least three or four that are not currently in use.

"Oh no, I couldn't," she says, blood rushing to her cheeks and turning them that captivating pink color.

"It is not the generous gesture you think it is, I assure you," I promise her as she tries to return it to me. "I will not use it. Truly, it is yours."

She holds it against her chest and smiles when she thinks I am not looking and warmth pools in my chest at the sight.

Eventually, I compile the views from the dark vision cameras and link them, so they play continuously from one eve into the next, skipping the daylight footage entirely. She scribbles and scribbles as the vid plays, and I turn my chair slightly away from her, so I can check the recording from near the falls during the previous eve. We work like this for a long time, silent but focused on our tasks.

I growl in frustration when I discover the camera we have positioned near the falls is not facing the area in the location of the blood. I find nothing that shows a tr'gory existed there.

"What is it?" Elle-noor asks as she stretches her short arms and legs and lets out a loud yawn.

"This mysterious tr'gory seemed to position herself out of view as she gave birth," I grumble, slapping at the keyboard as I rewind the recording. "I have no view of her."

"'S okay," she mutters, yawning again.

"Do you wish to resume this work tomorrow? You should rest," I tell her, rising from my chair and stacking our empty plates.

"No, I'm good," she replies, shaking her head. "Promise. I just need to stand up for a sec."

She follows me down to the first level of my home and looks around at my entryway, which is not much more than a spigot, a compact fire pit, a cold box, a few shelves with mugs and plates, a deep wooden basin filled with the casks of the different ales I have brewed, and a small washroom off to the right. Above the basin is a shelf lined with glass jugs filled with the various seeds and petals I add to my ales to give them flavor. "This is so cool," Elle-noor exclaims as her gaze lingers on the more colorful piloi petals.

They remind me of your lips, I almost say. But I do not. Elle-noor has a mate, so I cannot say the things I wish her to hear.

"I wish to show you something," I tell her. Knowing how to keep that wide smile on her face, enhancing that indent beneath her lips. If she were anyone else, I would be tired of her company already, and would tell her it is time to leave as I gave her a nudge toward the door. But Elle-noor… she looks as if she belongs here, in my home.

I guide her to the top floor and open the door to the roof where my garden is located. If anyone will appreciate this place as much as I, it is Elle-noor. And I am proven right when she steps out from behind me and lets out a gasp as she looks around. The breeze hits her skin, pushing the little hairs of her mane off her forehead, and I watch as she inhales deeply, taking in the many scents of my garden.

"This is so lovely, Bruvix," she says when her eyes finally open. She bats her long lashes in my direction, and I am no longer a fierce warrior. I am merely a boneless puddle of a male who lives for the smiles of a human female. What is happening to me?

Is this how Varrek felt when he first met Cloh-ee? Or Ahlvo with Aye-vah? Is this merely the tether, telling me I must tie myself to this human? Or do I feel this way simply because Elle-noor has been kind to me?

Kindness, conversation, trust, long looks lacking in fear—these are not things females often give me. I assume it is because of the way I look, but it could also be due to my surly demeanor. I must be careful not to confuse Elle-noor's warmth with genuine interest. I must–

"Oh my god, you have blackberries here?" Elle-noor shouts from across the garden. I had not even realized she left my side. "These are my favorite!"

When I reach her, she is plucking a handful of plump dark purple berries from the pistil of the newly bloomed vakopurri flowers. "Berries?" I mutter to myself. "I did not realize this flower contained berries at all. I purchased the seeds based on the sweetness of the stems."

She pops one in her mouth and moans when her tiny teeth sink into it. "H-holy cripes, this is even sweeter than an Earth blackberry."

A muffled grunt escapes my lips and I quickly turn away. I adjust my hardening cock, tucking it beneath the waistband of my pants. If she is going to continue moaning as her eyes roll back in her head, I am certain I will spill my seed all over myself. And soon.

"Here, try one," she says between bites, tossing one to me. I catch it and pop it in my mouth, and the flavor explodes on my tongue. Tangy and sweet, but not too rich. It is divine. I eat another, and another, and as the juice slides down my throat, I wonder if Elle-noor's cunt tastes this good.

"Ah, man!" she says with a pout as she scans the vakopurri flowers once more. "All gone."

"No more berries?"

"Nope," she replies after a long pause, then suddenly drops to her knees. "Whoops!" she yells with a loud chuckle. Then she rolls onto her side, a long vakopurri stem still clutched in her left hand. Flopping onto her back and letting go of the torn stem, her mouth falls open as she stares at the sky.

This is odd. Though human behavior is famously difficult to predict. "Elle-noor, are you well?" I ask.

She rubs her eyes with her purple, berry-stained fingers, then blinks repeatedly before her gaze lands on me. "Know what, Bruvix? I'm really not."

My heart speeds at her words. "What is wrong?" I ask, panic rising in my throat. "Tell me, and I will fix it." Then another Elle-noor appears, not next to the first Elle-noor, but sort of on top of her, and I worry my Elle-noor is being crushed by this new one. Who is she? What does she want from us?

"Wellllp," my Elle-noor mutters, patting my arm. "I'm definitely tripping, and pretty soon you will be too, if you aren't already."

"Trih-ping? What is this word?" I ask, the translation chip indicating it is another form of falling which does not make sense as Elle-noor and I are both perfectly still.

"Drugs, my fine friend," she replies, her words now coming out at an alarmingly slow pace. "Weeeee arrrrre ooonnn druuuuuugsssss."

I rub a hand down my face, concern twisting my insides when my face feels as if it is covered in a thick layer of mud. But when I pull my hand away, there is nothing on it. "How many did you eat?" I ask, looking around at this part of the garden. I do not like the energy coming off the plants over here. It feels dark. Ominous. I must find another corner to huddle in while I wait for the drugs to leave my blood.

"Ummmmm thhhhhrrrreeeeeee, mmmmaaaaayyyyyybbbbbeeee?"

That is not good. I have eaten five.

CHAPTER 8

I am tripping my ovaries off right now.

Pretty sure Bruvix is too, though I'm not sure where he is at the moment. As soon as I told him we were high, he crawled away on his hands and knees to the other side of the garden. Meanwhile, I'm surrounded by a group of lanky flowers with yellow stems and black and pink petals that keep whispering to each other and giving me dirty looks. When I hear one of them whisper something about how I should invest in a skin-lightening cream, I fight the urge to rip these judgmental twits out of the ground.

"What?" I finally say to them. "I introduced myself, and you all just stood there. I even offered to get each of you a glass of water. But somehow I'm the rude one?" I don't know what the fuck their problem is, honestly. I could not have been nicer.

"Elle-noor!" Bruvix shouts from where he lies on his back in the section of the garden where the hot pink flowers are the tallest. "Come see this!"

I crawl over to him, shooting the stink eye over my shoulder at the lanky flower in the middle that I suspect is the ringleader of the group, and find him staring up at the purple clouds that float overhead.

Flopping down on my back next to him, I watch as he tilts his head to the side, his pupils so blown out that his eyes are almost completely black. Then I follow his gaze to the sky and suck in a breath. "That one looks like The Rock!"

"What rock?" Bruvix asks as he stretches his legs out next to me.

"No, no. *The* Rock. There is only one, and he's outstanding," I explain.

He makes a clicking sound with his tongue that reminds me of a "tsk" and says, "I do not see this rock. I see two warriors in battle. But it is not a fair fight, because one holds a sword, and the other holds his cock."

I let out an undignified cackle as I search for this warrior who took his dick out at a sword fight but come up empty. Bruvix points to what he says is the warrior's hand wrapped around his dick and pointing it at the other guy, but I don't see it.

"It is not an impressive cock, anyway," he says with a low chuckle, waving a hand in front of him.

Then I turn onto my side, propping up on an elbow. "You should know that those flowers over there aren't very welcoming."

He gasps and then looks over at them. "What did they say to you?"

"Nothing!" I tell him. "They refuse to speak to me but have no problem talking shit right in front of me."

"Uh, uh, that is unacceptable behavior," he replies, his tone stern as he pulls himself up onto his knees. "Do not worry, Elle-noor. I shall remedy the situation."

He starts to rise, but I grab his arm, pulling him back down. "Noooo, you have to crawl. So the trees don't see how messed up we are," I explain. We don't need those gossipy trees telling the whole clan about our misguided consumption of hallucinogenics.

Bruvix nods. "Yes. That is wise." Then he crawls around the shrubs, past the white vines, and over to the cliquey flowers. I lie on my back, waiting for him to scold them for how they treated me. But when I hear a rustling sound followed by a muffled grunt, I get curious.

I crawl back the way I came and come upon Bruvix lying on top of them, face down in the soil. "What happened?"

He slowly rolls onto his side, his face caked in dirt, and shoots me a lazy, crooked smile. "They raised some valid concerns."

"Oh did they?" I ask, incredulous. Those little bitches.

"But when they suggested I remove you from the premises, I got quite angry," he explains, wiping the clump of soil deeper into this vest, rather than brushing it off. "I struck first, and then they hit back..." he pauses, lifting his hand close to his face and staring intently at his fingers. "And now I am here."

I focus on him as his gaze is locked on his claws. He's so cute like this. Carefree. Almost happy, even. Has anyone in the clan ever seen him this way? Maybe he should get high more often.

On the other hand, his grumpy, growly, *I hate everyone so leave me alone* vibe is also appealing in its own way.

"Come on," I say, offering my hand to pull him up. He takes it, and I am instantly reminded of how much bigger he is as he pulls me down on top of him. I let out an "oof" as my face smacks into his hard chest, and then we're both laughing as he wipes dirt off my cheek.

The laughter fades at some point, and I'm left staring at his wide, soft mouth. His lips are a darker gold than his skin, just a shade or two. I study the scar that cuts through the left side of his mouth, and suddenly I'm angry at whoever or whatever took it upon themselves to mar such perfectly kissable lips.

Then again, that silver slash is such a striking contrast to the dark gold that it really draws the eye. And I could stare at that crooked smile all damn day if he'd let me.

I feel myself leaning closer, my chest pressing more and more against the hard planes of his. I close my eyes just as the distance between us disappears, and I press my lips to his. He doesn't move at first, his lips frozen against mine, but after a moment, he responds. He's a clumsy kisser, his mouth eager to devour mine, but maybe he hasn't kissed anyone in a while. Perhaps I caught him off guard, this rough and beautiful warrior. And maybe it's just the berries feeding my boldness, but the urge grows to deepen the kiss, to show him with my lips and tongue just how intriguing I find him.

Then, in a heartbeat, Bruvix lifts me off him by my arms and plops me on my butt in the dirt. With a reluctant look in his eye, he releases me, and backs away until he's leaning on his heels, his chest heaving slightly. "We cannot," he says in a low rumble. "What would your mate say?"

My mate? What is he talking about? Then he looks down at the ring on my hand, no longer on my ring finger, and it clicks. He thinks I'm married. "I don't have a mate," I tell him.

"But your ring," he protests, pointing at it now. "Aye-vah and Cloh-ee said–"

"Yeah, my grandmother's wedding ring. I was wearing it on that finger when I was taken," I admit. "It's a decoy, for when I go to bars and don't want to be harassed by creepy guys. To make it look like I'm taken."

He furrows his brow as he tries to understand my words. "Why would you need to trick males into thinking you are not available to be courted?"

I let out a bitter chuckle. "Because they seem to respect that more than the word no."

"I do not understand the rules of your home planet," he replies, shaking his head.

"It's okay. I don't either."

A drop lands on my forehead. Then on the tip of my nose. Soon, rain is pouring down on us as we rush to crawl to the door. We squeeze in close under the narrow cloth awning and giggle as we try to make ourselves as small as possible. The rain splashes onto my bare toes that peek out from beneath the awning, washing the dirt away. I wiggle them as they get clean, and soon I'm mesmerized by the feel of the fat, warm droplets as they hit my skin. My eyes close as I lean against Bruvix's side, and I drift off within moments.

Much later, my eyes flutter open to find the sky several shades darker than before. I would guess it's around dusk. I look over and find Bruvix's body slumped down and curled into a ball with his head in my lap as he snores like a freight train.

The rain has stopped, which is good, but the plants closest to us look like they've grown at least three feet since we fell asleep, so we're definitely still tripping. I am, at least.

"Thirsty," Bruvix mumbles in his sleep, his lips smacking together. "Thirsty!" he yells this time as he snaps up to a seated position. He looks around, bewildered, until he sees me and then his eyes soften a bit. "Elle-noor," he greets with a nod. "I have been informed that the qam shrub needs a beverage. I shall grant its wish."

He crawls over to a bucket in the corner that's filled with water. But before he reaches it, a deep sense of dread fills my chest, turning my stomach into knots. "No! Stop, Bruvix!"

I scurry over to him and use my arm to block him from getting any closer to the bucket.

"Elle-noor, the qam is suffering. I must care for it."

"No. No, no, no, no."

"What is wrong?"

I know that what's about to come out of my mouth won't make any sense, but I feel the truth of it in my bones. "What if we see our reflection in the water, but it's...the old, wrinkly version of us. From the future. Are you ready to face that?"

His hands drop to his sides, and he considers this for a moment. "What if," he begins, "it is our reflection of how we are now, but we see those who have died hovering behind us."

That's definitely much scarier. I want no part of that.

Simultaneously, we shake our heads and back away. After a minute, or possibly an hour, the fear of the water bucket passes, and we sit in comfortable silence as the sky grows dark. It's hard to know how long this high will last, but I feel safer being in the garden with Bruvix than I would anywhere else.

A high-pitched mewl reaches my ears, and immediately I turn to Bruvix to see if he hears it too. He whips his head around when it happens again, and that's how I know it's real. We race to the side of the roof garden, and peer down at the ground below, seeking the source.

"There," he says as he points to a bush nestled against the corner of his house. I wonder briefly if he got it wrong, or is hallucinating, but then the branches begin to shake and we hear a low, halting cry coming from that exact spot.

"Come on," I yell as I throw the door open and race down the stairs. I hear Bruvix's heavy steps as he hurries close behind me. When we reach the bush, Bruvix parts the branches slowly before dropping a douku orb to the ground. The inside of the bush is instantly illuminated, and the little red eyes of a tr'gory pup blink up at us.

CHAPTER 9

BRUVIX

ot breath fans my cheek, and I wonder where I am. Confused but comfortable, I decide to push my worries aside and deal with them later. When a paw swipes against my face and the little pointed claws dig into my skin, my dread returns tenfold.

On my bare chest sits a tr'gory pup, and its long bushy black tail wags against my thighs as I lift my head. Next to me lies a slumbering Elle-noor, and as peaceful as she looks, the need for answers has me shaking her shoulder until she awakens.

"Tell me this is not reality," I beg quietly as the pup lies on my stomach, tilting its wide head side to side with each word. Elle-noor looks around my bedroom for a few moments before her eyes land on the tiny monster in the room. "Ohh fuck. Oh fuck, oh fuck, oh fuck," she squeals as she hops out of bed and covers her mouth. "We stole a tr'gory puppy. This is bad," she whimpers as she rubs a hand over her lush bottom.

"When, Elle-noor? When did we do this?" I demand as the pup slides off my body and curls up into a tight ball on the pillow Elle-noor used.

"Last night. You don't remember?" she says in a rush as she begins to pace back and forth. "We were still high, and we heard something crying in the woods, so we looked down from the garden, and you saw a bush moving, so we ran downstairs and found this little guy hiding just outside your house."

None of that sounds familiar. "I remember not wanting to look at the water in the bucket," I tell her, searching my memories for a moment in time when I would have willingly taken a tr'gory pup inside my home. "I do not recall anything after that."

"Okay. Okay," she murmurs in a panicked voice. "This is okay. We can handle this. We'll just put it back where we found it, and *nanay* tr'gory will never know."

"Who?"

"Huh?" she asks, pausing her frenzied pacing to look at me.

"That word you used… before tr'gory…"

Her eyes light up. "Oh! Nanay, right. It's Tagalog for mom or mama—an archaic term, but it's a nickname my dad gave to my mom once I was born. Or 'Nay, for short. Sorry, I didn't even realize I used it."

"How do you say this word?" I ask. If it is something that comes from her past, I am eager to learn it. "Repeat it for me."

"Nah-naye," she replies, moving her pink lips slowly so I may follow.

"Nah-naye," I repeat, giving her a questioning glance at the end.

"Yup! Well done!" she says with a smile, causing her chin to form that sharp point I am so intrigued by. "My dad was always trying to get me to speak Tagalog at home. Korean was harder for me to pick up, so we spoke mostly English, but I know some Tagalog words." She sighs, her smile fading. "I'm never going to see them again… It just sort of… hit me."

I do not know what to do. Elle-noor is sad, and I long to comfort her. Would my embrace be acceptable to her? Would she welcome my touch? Before I can open my arms to her, the pup releases a yawn that ends in a howl, and then promptly sneezes all over my bed. A layer of sticky white mucus covers my right arm and my pillow, and despite my obvious disgust, it crawls toward me with its tail wagging behind it.

Elle-noor, on the other hand, is not at all deterred by the pup's eagerness to spread bacteria via its snout, and rushes over to examine it. "Aw, poor baby," she croons as she uses my shirt to wipe the mucus off its face.

The pup wiggles and wags as she pokes at it, checking its abdomen, and dropping her head down to its chest to listen to its heart-beat. "Hmm," she mutters to herself as she picks it up and places the pup on the floor. Its legs shake before it collapses. When I hear a loud squelching sound followed by a horrid stench, I realize how much trouble we are truly in.

"I think he's sick," she says.

"It is male?"

"Yeah, I just checked."

"How do you know he is ill?" I ask, deeply concerned about what that means for us.

"Well, there's the alarming amount of snot he got all over your bed, the diarrhea on your floor, and his heartbeat sounds irregular to me, but he's not an Earth dog, so maybe that's normal."

I survey the mess and have never been so eager to do anything as I am to drop this pup in the bush where we found it, but I am starting to worry that is no longer the plan. The odor that fills my nose, the bodily fluids that are scattered across my bedroom—it is utterly disgusting. And unacceptable.

"That could be why he was alone," Elle-noor says. "His mother might have abandoned him if she didn't think he was going to survive."

I am not fond of tr'gorys, vile, ruthless creatures that they are, but that seems needlessly cruel. "Why would she abandon him when he needs her the most?"

Elle-noor shrugs. "It happens sometimes. If the mother is sick, or just too weak to nurse her entire litter, she'll leave the runt or the sick one behind. It's sad, but it's about survival."

"So we are to let this pup die because its mother chose not to care for it?" I ask, incredulous. I am partially irritated at the mother's callousness, but also at my sudden interest in how this beast fares.

"No way," she replies, aghast at my suggestion. "I can nurse it back to health. When he's strong enough, we can reunite him with Nanay."

She makes it sound like such an obvious, simple plan. I suppose I am to be the one paying attention to the logistics of it all. So be it. "And how do you plan to nurse it back to health without anyone knowing? You are going to remain holed up in Ahlvo's old room with a tr'gory pup?"

"Well," she replies, and then pauses as if she did not consider anything beyond the mucus covering my bed and the feces on my floor. "We don't have to keep it a secret," she says. "I'm sure...Kaiva, um, wouldn't mind."

I laugh. The sheer lunacy in her words is too humorous to ignore. "You do not know Kaiva well, but I assure you that she would very much mind, as would Varrek and the rest of the clan when they learn that a tr'gory pup, of all things, has been rescued and that clan resources will be used to aid in its recovery."

She stares at me, blinking several times as she mulls this over. "Well," she finally says as she clears her throat. "We could keep him here, with you."

I am about to unleash the loudest and most passionate protest ever spoken when she adds, "I'd stay here too, of course, and I'll handle everything: the cleanup, the daily feedings... everything."

Elle-noor.

Here.

With me.

In my home.

Sharing my bed.

"Very well," I reply, suddenly remembering our conversation from the garden about how she is not, in fact, mated. Her heart does not belong to another. She is free to choose a mate. Perhaps... me.

The moment the thought enters my mind, I shut it down. Of course, she would not choose me. I am far too hideous to stand at Elle-noor's side for the rest of our days. She is luminous and soft, where I am grizzled and rough.

But having her offer to share my bed until we return the tr'gory pup to Nah-naye is not something I am capable of refusing, not when the tether grows stronger each day. She does not know she is my inara, and she does not need to know. That is a secret I must keep, just like the presence of a tr'gory pup in my home.

I envision lying next to Elle-noor and feeling her soft curves pressed up against my aching cock when an impatient knock sounds at the front door.

"Shit," Elle-noor mutters as she begins using my tunic to wipe up the pup's waste.

"You handle this," I tell her. "I will handle that." The easiest compromise I have ever made.

I shake my arms out, trying to compose myself before I pull open the door and quickly pull it closed behind me as I step outside to greet Kay-teh and Nee-roh. "Hello," I say, focusing on the tone of my voice. Does it sound calm enough? I cannot appear as if I'm hiding anything.

"Hey, Bruv," Kay-teh replies. "So, word has it that Eleanor was last seen at the meal hall with you, loading up your plates before you were supposed to come back here and look at some security footage. That was yesterday."

I nod, not knowing what else I should say regarding how Elle-noor and I have spent the last day.

"I sincerely hope you didn't steal that woman from Bzzsil Chi just so you could murder her here on Oluura and eat her fingernails."

Now she has confused me. Does she truly believe I would harm Elle-noor? Or is it merely her strange way with humor? It is often hard to tell. "I do not understand, Kay-teh."

"Where is Eleanor?" Nee-roh demands, impatiently. "I have not even met this human yet."

As if summoned, Elle-noor appears from behind me as she quickly steps outside. "Hey, Kate!" she says enthusiastically. "And you must be the dragon. So nice to meet you, Niro."

"Draxilio," Nee-roh corrects with a proud grin. "Yes, I am."

"You're alive!" Kay-teh exclaims. "What a relief. The girls and Varrek will be so pleased."

"Indeed, she is alive," I repeat. "Now that you have confirmation, you may go."

Kay-teh chuckles, giving me a knowing grin. "See, that's the Bruv I know. Impatient and unpleasant." Then she shifts her gaze to Elle-noor. "You sure you're okay here? Blink twice if you need help."

Elle-noor laughs. "I'm fine, I promise. Going through the security footage is a long, tedious task, but an important one."

It is a believable story. For now, at least.

We wave to Kay-teh and Nee-roh as they leave, and then hustle back inside and up the stairs to find the pup fast asleep in the middle of my bed.

"Look at how cute he is!" Elle-noor whispers with a slight hop.

Cute. There is nothing cute about this wee beast, or what he has left on my floor.

CHAPTER 10

ELEANOR

"This is where you will place the dishes when they are clean," Waldric tells me as he points to the nearest table covered in a big beige towel. "The rags over here are used for drying."

I survey my little station with one deep gray bucket filled with dirty bowls, mugs, and food scraps stuck in between, and the other bucket with hot, soapy water that Waldric has prepped for me before I arrived. Letting out a sigh, I grab my first dirty dish and begin to scrub. All that time I spent studying animal medicine…and here I am washing dishes. My parents would be so disappointed.

However, I don't have to pay bills, or rent, or buy food. Everyone contributes to the clan in some way, and this is mine. Well, along with studying the tr'gorys, that is.

Waldric continues chatting, mostly about how the wet season is coming to an end, but I tune in and out of his small talk as I scrub the bowls. I want to be polite to my new boss, but I can't stop thinking about the tr'gory puppy. The twenty-pound ball of fluff that's currently in Bruvix's house. He's big for being just a day old, but I know by the time he's full-grown, he'll be massive, so it makes sense.

He needs a name.

Hmm. Does he, though? Because if I name him, I'll most certainly get attached to that furry little nugget.

Eh, fuck it. I'm already attached. That is a given.

Part of me feels I should honor my heritage and by giving the puppy my dad or grandfather's name. But a bigger part of me is compelled to continue my tradition of giving dogs very human-sounding names because it's funnier. Before Frank, there was Walter, and before Walter, there were Harriet and Bernard. Hollering "Frank!" or "Walter!" when your dog has just eaten something he shouldn't adds some comedy to an otherwise infuriating situation. And it's impossible to scold a dog named Harriet while keeping a straight face.

I search my mind for an old-timey name that would keep me smiling on the inside even in the most dire of circumstances, and within moments, it comes to me.

Stanley.

My sick little tr'gory puppy will now be called Stanley, and I'm going to feed him all the nutrients his body needs to grow into a big, strong, monstrous tr'gory. I mean, I don't want him to act like a monster, but he'll certainly look like the massive, intimidating beasts that make up the rest of his pack.

And once he's well, I'll return him to Nanay, where he belongs.

"Nalba, yo-you are looking well today," Waldric stutters, breaking me from my thoughts. "Healthy."

Speaking of puppy love…

Healthy? I suppose that could be considered a compliment, but that's something you only want to hear your doctor say. It's a word my mother used when I came home from college on holiday breaks, though she used it as a coded suggestion to drop a few pounds. To which I would immediately rebel and shove cookies into my mouth in front of her.

Poor Waldric.

"Um, I thank you, Waldric," Nalba replies, her tone dry and confused. "I will need a second plate of this today. Cloh-ee and the child inside her stomach are quite hungry."

"Of course!" he says, eagerly filling her second plate with the same bread, berries, some kind of rice cake, and meat that he put on the first. "I should include extra bread for her, yes?"

"I do not know what she likes," Nalba says, biting the pad of her thumb. "You see, it is usually Cloh-ee that brings me food. But she moves so slowly now." She shakes her head as if stunned and mildly disgusted by what pregnancy does to the body. "I cannot wait a whole afternoon for her to bring me my meal, so I must do it instead! And I was quite close to completing my work on the new additions to the laser guns for the crew." She huffs a breath, tapping her foot impatiently. "I suppose it will all have to wait, however, because my tiny human helper must eat."

Waldric, never getting a clear answer on the bread, adds three more slices on the side of the second plate. "You are kind to care for her during her physically demanding time."

Kind? Is that what he heard? Because all I heard was a complaint about how a very pregnant woman needs to eat more, and how inconvenient that is for Nalba. But the girls did warn me that she's an "eccentric genius" who can sometimes get on people's nerves. I guess that proves how completely smitten Waldric is with her if he can extract a kind gesture from all that whining.

"It is kind. You are right," Nalba replies. And I have to hold back my laughter as I scrape dried viiki spread off the bottom of a bowl.

Waldric clears his throat, lowering his voice, and says, "Your mind is like an untouched ball of dough, and I long to knead and caress it."

Oh, dear god. I bite the inside of my cheek, cringing at the terrible pickup line. I can't imagine Nalba will respond positively to it, and I really do not want to see sweet Waldric's heart broken on my first day of dish duty.

"I do not know what that means," she replies flatly. "But if you are saying I am brilliant, I know this." Then she nods, presumably in thanks for the second plate, and saunters off toward her shop.

Then I pour all my focus into scrubbing the bowl in my hands, even though it's already clean. I just cannot make eye contact with Waldric right now. I'm sure he knows I overheard the entire thing, but I have no idea what to say.

"It is fine, Elle-noor," Waldric says after a long moment of silence. "This is how Nalba responds to my words." He wipes his hands on a rag draped over his shoulder and dips his chin. "I do not know how to communicate my feelings to her."

Rinsing the bowl, I place it next to the other clean ones on the table. "Well," I begin, coming to stand next to him behind the fire pits, "have you ever considered not complimenting her on her intelligence?"

He scrunches his nose, baffled by my suggestions. "Why would I?"

"Nalba's a genius, right? The whole clan knows it. She knows it too." I tell him. "It's a compliment she receives all the time. There's nothing special about it at this point."

He scratches the neatly trimmed hair of his beard. "You are suggesting I tell her that she is not knowledgeable?"

I chuckle at the concept of alien males attempting to "neg" a female they have a crush on. The absolute dumbest flirting technique ever created—by human men, of course—and I accidentally just gave Waldric a lesson in it. I need to quash this right now. "No, no. That's not what I'm saying. I'm suggesting that you should compliment Nalba in other ways."

He taps his finger against his bottom lip as his eyes wander around the meal hall.

"What other things do you like about her?" I ask. "Her smile? Her hair? Her ass?"

"Yes, yes," he replies quickly. "All these things."

I pat his arm. "There you go, bud. Explore that." Then I return to my dish buckets.

"I shall," he finally replies. "Thank you, Elle-noor. I shall think on this."

By the time all the bowls, plates, and mugs are clean and dry, the sun is high in the sky. Waldric is busy prepping the fire pits for lunch, and knowing that he is too distracted to pay close attention, I make my way to the back wall where the fresh ingredients are kept. "Hey, Waldric, may I take a few items home with me?"

He lifts a large portion of raw kuhnypa meat onto the middle pit, and replies, "Certainly, Elle-noor. Take what you need."

For Stanley's sustenance, I take a large mug of tibbi, a sealed bowl of vegetable root mash, and finding no clear or easily liquefiable source of protein, I grab a handful of jerky and stuff everything into my pack as I sling it over my shoulder. I don't know if I can turn these items into a formula for him, but since this is all I've got, it'll have to do.

"Thanks, Waldric!" I call out. "I'll be back tonight to wash the dishes from lunch before the dinner crowd arrives."

"Enjoy your day, Elle-noor!" he calls back. I let out a relieved sigh as I walk toward Bruvix's house. He must be so tired of puppy duty right about now. I hope Stanley isn't giving him too much trouble.

Before I reach the front door, I hear Bruvix say, "That is good, yes. Your waste goes here, and not where we sleep."

Softly stepping along the side of the house and weaving through the rows of tall bushes that keep Bruvix's house mostly hidden from the rest of the village, I peek around the corner to find Stanley wiping his feet in the dirt, kicking up leaves and moss to cover the poop behind him. "Hello, boys!"

Stanley trots over with a wagging tail and his tongue hanging out the side of his mouth. "Hi, baby," I coo as I bend down to fluff the fur between his tall, pointed ears. Did he grow another five pounds since this morning? He looks bigger somehow, even though we've only been apart a few hours. "How'd it go?" I ask Bruvix as he makes his way over to me. "Any disasters?"

"No," he replies, scrubbing a hand down his face. He looks exhausted or stressed. It's probably both. "I am teaching the tr'gory where to leave his droppings."

"Stanley," I add. "His name is Stanley now."

He jerks back slightly. "You named him?"

"Of course. I'm not just gonna keep on calling him 'the tr'gory' or 'puppy.' Our boy needed a name, so I gave him a fun one."

"Stahn-lee?" Bruvix slowly repeats, adding the same pause in the middle that he does with my name. It's so cute I could throw up. Or maybe the drug berries aren't sitting well in my stomach. I should eat something.

"And I brought home some supplies to make him a formula," I say, then I stop. "Well, it won't be a traditional formula, but hopefully it'll get some nutrients into his system while settling his stomach."

We go inside and I pour the tibbi and root mash into a mug. Then I tear off tiny pieces of the jerky and mix the three together with a wooden spoon. Once the texture is thick and soupy, I remove the spoon and crouch down to Stanley's level, holding the mug out in front of me. "Come on, Stanley. Lunchtime, little nugget!"

He takes a few hesitant steps toward me, keeping a watchful eye on the mug. His little nostrils flare as he approaches, but he's clearly not sure what the mug is or if he should trust it. I hold it closer to him, now with one hand, and he paws at it gently. Then he smacks the mug out of my hands entirely and plops his butt down on the floor beside Bruvix's feet.

"We should probably be using a bottle or something to feed him. Do you have anything like that?" I ask.

"A bottle? Yes, I have many," he says, reaching into the wooden crate beside the basin with his casks of ale and pulls out a few glass bottles.

"No, not like that. Like, a baby bottle," I correct. "Something pliable that we can tip upside down and feed him."

"Oh, to simulate a teat?" he asks, scratching the side of his head.

"Yes!" I exclaim. "So, like a rubber top that we can cut a hole in and attach it to a soft bottle. Maybe one of Kaiva's fluid bags would work?"

Bruvix grunts in response. "How will we get one?"

"Excellent question," I say because I have no idea. I can't exactly ask to borrow one without an excuse as to what I need it for. "I'll just hand-feed him for now." Scooping the contents of the mug into my bare hand, I cup both palms together and hold them out toward Stanley. He's definitely more interested than he was before, now that the mug is out of the picture. Trotting over, he sniffs at my fingertips and gently licks the outside of my hands. "That's okay, Stanley. Take your time."

He does, at first, but as soon as he gets a taste of the formula, he starts snuffling and snorting as he shoves his snout into my hands, mouth wide open. I'm glad the root mash is so starchy and thick, otherwise, the tibbi would make the formula too messy to hold in my hands.

I spoke too soon.

The moment Stanley finishes eating, he sneezes, and it shakes his entire body, causing droplets and chunks of the formula that were on his face to fly all over me. "Well, shit," I mutter under my breath as I look around and find this portion of the entryway splattered with his sneeze as well. "I'm sorry," I quickly tell Bruvix. He's a bit of a neat freak and I'm sure he regrets letting me and Stanley crash with him. "I'll clean all of this up. And I-I'll come up with a better way to feed him."

He growls, the sound low, and not exactly angry, but definitely not pleased. Then he crosses his arms over his chest and says, "I must leave for the midday training session. I shall return later." The door slams shut behind him, and I'm worried he's going to tell Varrek about Stanley. And not only will Varrek be furious, but he'll also probably have me return Stanley to the forest, which he's certainly not ready for, health-wise. He needs more time to heal, and I need more time with him. I won't abandon him. That's not what I do.

I keep Stanley in my sights as I change into a clean tunic and leggings then wipe the pup's lunch off the shelves and the cask basin.

Within an hour of leaving in a huff, Bruvix storms in just as I finish cleaning, and I immediately notice the bandage covering his left shoulder. "What happened? Are you okay?" I ask as I rush over to him.

"I am fine," he replies with a tilt of his head as if surprised by my concern. "Here," he says, handing me three empty fluid bags with rubber caps on the ends. He must've gotten them from Kaiva.

But how?

"Oh my god! How did you get these?"

"I let Ahlvo nick me with his sword at training," he says with a mischievous grin. "Varrek sent me to Kaiva's, and I grabbed these from her stock when she left the room."

"You...stole these?" I ask, my voice breaking at the end. "For me?" Here I thought he was hatching a plan to get me out of his hair. But no, he was deliberately getting injured so he could help me care for Stanley. He wants me to stay.

"Well, yes. Feeding Stahn-lee by hand clearly does not work, and I–"

Before I can overthink it, I pounce on Bruvix, throwing my arms around his neck and smashing my lips into his. I'm sick of waiting for him to make a move, and I want him to know how much I appreciate what he's done. How much I want to feel his hard body pressed against mine.

When he groans against my lips and his cock hardens against my belly, I'm certain he has no doubt.

CHAPTER 11

BRUVIX

Her lips are softer than I remember. Of course, I had the berry drug coursing through my blood at the time, so perhaps my recollection is not accurate. It does not matter, though. Nothing matters apart from the fact that Elle-noor is kissing me. She moans as I part my lips, letting her tongue glide against mine, then tracing my bottom lip before giving it a bite that sends a jolt straight to the head of my cock. It thickens as she presses her body against me, wrapping her legs around my middle and crossing her feet behind my back. I hold her tighter, one hand getting lost in her soft mane, the need to feel all of her at once setting my skin ablaze.

She pulls back, breaking contact, and whispers, "Have you never been kissed before?"

Clearing my throat, I silently curse myself for not being more skilled at this. "I have," I begin, "but not often."

She tilts her head as her eyes dart between mine, searching. "How is that possible?"

I shrug. "People do not like looking at me. You assume the few who do, sought to kiss me? They are mostly warriors who like only females."

"I don't get it," she replies. "I'm looking at you right now, Bruvix. There's no part of you I don't want to kiss."

Does that… Does she wish to…

Before I can obsess over her possible meaning, she presses her mouth to mine again. This time, her lips are greedy, eager, and her taste is exquisitely sweet, just like her scent.

Needing more of her, I walk forward with Elle-noor in my arms until we reach the front door. I push her back against it, grateful for the leverage it gives me. My hands drift down to her face, and I hold it in my hands, stroking my fingertips along her cheeks and jaw, reveling in her smoothness.

Our tongues tangle once I am able to match her rhythm, and she moans into my mouth the moment I do. Knowing I am improving and making her feel good makes pride surge in my chest.

"Mm, much better," she mutters. "Fast learner."

I chuckle. "I am."

I want nothing more than to make Elle-noor cry out in pleasure as her soft, supple body writhes beneath me. If it is the only thing I accomplish in this life, I will consider my time well spent.

Her hand slides between our bodies and her hand covers my cock, my pants the only thing keeping her skin from mine. A growl rumbles low in my throat at the contact, and I nod at Elle-noor, so she knows it is a good sound. A sound of approval. A sound I make only for her. My lips leave hers, so I can kiss her cheek, her chin, then her neck, licking and sucking at the skin as I go. She is sweet all over, my human, and I am eager to dip my tongue between her thighs to confirm this.

Elle-noor strokes her hand up my cock, tracing the head, and then moves back down. I grit my teeth as she continues because it feels good. Too good. My hips buck in response to her strokes, but I must hold back. I cannot spill my seed in my pants, or I will look like a fool.

But I do not even get that chance because Stahn-lee nips at my pant leg, taking some of my skin between his fangs, and I howl in pain against Elle-noor's neck.

Elle-noor freezes in my arms. "What the——"

"Stahn-lee!" I shout. When I look down, he sits, wagging his bushy tail, beaming at me as if merely saying hello.

Elle-noor laughs when I groan in annoyance. "What a cockblocker."

"A… what?" I reply, confused.

"He ruined our sexy vibes, essentially blocking your cock from getting its needs met."

Ah, I understand now. Human terms are often strange and nonsensical, but this one is surprisingly accurate. I look down at the pup again. "You *are* a cock-block-er, Stahn-lee."

Then I lift my gaze to Elle-noor. Her skin is flushed, and her mane is messy. She is radiant like this. I could look at her for the rest of time. I should tell her how lovely she is. That is something females enjoy hearing, yes?

My heartbeat quickens as I search my mind for the right words. A statement truly worthy of describing Elle-noor's beauty. I feel my palms become slick with sweat as ideas pop into my head and I push them away, deeming them not good enough.

Swallowing the lump in my throat, I finally utter, "Your untidy appearance does things to my cock. Good things."

The moment the words fill the air, I wish to tear the tongue from my mouth. That statement did not match the thoughts in my head, and it certainly does not seem a worthy depiction of Elle-noor's beauty.

"Um, thank you" is all she says with a narrowed, perplexed gaze.

She does not seem offended or angry by my words. I suppose that is something. But I know the "sexy vibes" have been effectively ruined when she steps around me to pet Stahn-lee. "I should take him outside," she says.

"Very well," I reply, trying to look busy by gathering the empty fluid bags Elle-noor dropped on the floor and placing them on the shelf with my ale ingredients.

She returns a few moments later with a bright smile as she whispers "Good boy" repeatedly to Stahn-lee as he wiggles in her grasp. She sets him on his feet and sidles up to me. "So, I hear your ale is terrible."

The clan has been feeding her lies about my ale. Why am I not surprised? It seems to be a running joke among them, to mock the taste of my ale as they guzzle it down in large quantities, but I have yet to discover another clan member trying to make a better batch. I am about to explain this to Elle-noor when she says, "But I bet it's fucking delicious." And I am taken. My heart is no longer mine. It belongs to her. Wholly and completely.

"I must make a new batch soon," I tell her, eyeing the casks in the basin. "Would you like to assist me?"

Her eyes widen and she bounces lightly on the balls of her feet. "I'd love to!"

"Truly?"

"Yeah," she says, furrowing her brow. "Why do you sound so surprised?"

I shrug. "I did not expect you to be interested."

"It's something you enjoy, right?" she asks.

"Yes. Very much."

"Then, of course, I'm interested."

Such a simple response, yet such a powerful one. How? How do the correct words come so easily to Elle-noor? She speaks and warmth blooms inside my chest. I am envious. This is a skill I must practice because Elle-noor deserves to feel this chest warmth from *my* words as well. I should speak with Varrek and Ahlvo about this. They must have some wisdom to offer on the subject.

I pull the tools from the crate next to the cask basin and begin setting them up on the shelf above in the order we will use them. Once everything is in place, I start a fire in the pit and place a metal bin filled with water on the grate above it. Then I drag the cold box from the corner and place it next to the fire pit. "Once the water boils, we will add in the rihbah extracts, and the flavors we wish to include. The moment that is done, we must place the bin into the cold box."

"Rihbah, flavor, hot to cold. Got it," Elle-noor repeats with an eager nod. "Can I pick out the flavors we add?"

"Certainly," I reply. "This will be your ale, Elle-noor."

She laughs and claps her hands together. "Oh my god! Then we *have* to call it 'ale-noor.'"

"Ale-noor?" I repeat with a chuckle of my own. It is an interesting choice, but I am quickly learning that everything about Elle-noor is fascinating.

"Yes! Ooh, we should put those trippy berries in there!"

"No," I say immediately. "That is a very bad idea."

"I know, I know. I'm just kidding," she says, waving a dismissive hand. "I do want it to be sweet, though. Kind of like those berries, just without the hallucinogenic haze that follows."

"Ah," I say, rising to my feet in a flash. I know what she will like. I grab the glass jugs filled with yellow tuunnahi leaves, and the one with fresh buufcasi berries, and hand both to her. "Drop in a few of each as I stir in the rihbah extract. That should provide the sweetness you desire."

I catch her staring at my mouth, her dark brown eyes swirling with heat and her cheeks as pink as her lips. "Th-thank you," she finally replies, rubbing her forehead with her free hand. "Um, three each, you said?" Her voice is higher than normal, and she suddenly seems flustered.

I step closer to her, not wanting this moment to end, but her eyes drop behind me and fill with panic. "The water!" she shouts.

Finding it boiling to the point of flowing over the side of the bin, I wave my arm over it, settling the bubbles on top. Using heat-protective tongs, I grab the handles on either side of the bin and pull it off the fire pit. I set it on the floor and begin stirring in the rihbah extracts with the wooden spoon. "You may add your sweetness, now," I tell Elle-noor.

She stands next to me, and I feel the heat from her body as she presses her side into mine. "Happy to," she says, the tone a husky rasp.

I am tempted to knock the bin on its side, rip the clothes off Elle-noor's body, and fuck her so hard against the cold box that everything inside it melts into a puddle. But I do not know if that behavior would be welcome, and I have already made one blunder already this day with that untidy comment. I do not wish to make another.

She drops in her berries, then the tuunnahi leaves as I continue stirring the rihbah extract into the mixture. Once it is the color of the busay leaves before the rainy season, I toss the spoon to the side and place the bin inside the cold box. Elle-noor returns the glass bottles to the shelf and rinses the spoon beneath the spigot.

After sitting in the cold box long enough for the outside of the bin to cool, I pour the contents into a large mixing container and add more water. "Please retrieve the fungi additive from the crate," I ask Elle-noor as I shake the vessel, aerating it.

"What's that for?" she asks when I pour a few drops of da'koi sap into the mixture.

"I have found that it accelerates the organic decomposition process," I reply, placing the small can of syrup on the floor next to the bin.

"You mean the fermentation process that beer goes through." She nods with a knowing look. I nod also, having no understanding of fer-ment-aye-shun. "I've been through a couple brewery tours back on earth," she says. I simply nod again.

I let Elle-noor pour in the dry fungi additive, then I fasten the vessel closed. She helps me load it into the container of darkness, where it will remain for the next two days as the plants and flavoring mix.

"Container of darkness? That's what it's called?" she asks, her tone incredulous and slightly amused.

"Why, yes," I tell her. "Exposure to light would change the flavor, and most likely ruin the batch. So, it must be kept in here until it is ready to be consumed."

Elle-noor nods, satisfied with my answer. "I just love that name. I feel like that's what Kate and Niro should call their cave palace."

A burst of laughter escapes me at the comment. "That is true. They should."

I pour chilled water onto the fire, putting it out, and when I turn, I notice Stahn-lee fast asleep on the floor in the corner of the room next to the washroom. "I forgot he was here."

Elle-noor laughs. "Shit, I did too. Are we terrible parents?"

I push a lock of her mane behind her ear, and gently run my fingers through the smooth, silky ends. "I do not know how I fare as a tr'gory parent, but you," I pause, my gaze finding those mystifying brown dots next to her eye. Her *beauty mark* as she calls it. "You are spectacular, as you are in everything you do."

Her small pink tongue darts out, running along the length of her bottom lip, and I stifle a groan. My cock throbs against my thigh, almost painfully.

I cannot take this anymore.

I am not patient enough to wait for the right words to find me. Elle-noor's scent, her nearness, her beautiful eyes—they are driving me to madness. My hands ball into fists as I practically shout, "I must check something upstairs!" before racing up to my bedroom.

Whipping the door closed behind me, I tug my pants down to my knees and take my cock in hand. I give it a stroke, up and down slowly, as I picture that smooth pink tongue of hers peeking out between her soft lips. I imagine it swirling around the head of my cock as her eyes meet mine, and her name falls from my lips in a reverent vow, as if it is the only name I wish to say for the rest of my days. Gripping my length, I stroke it harder as I envision that tongue tracing the veins up the side, and my sac tightens against my body.

The creak of the door has me spinning around to find Elle-noor inside the room, pushing the door shut behind her. "Sorry. I didn't mean to interrupt. I just..." she sucks in a breath at the sight of my cock in my hand, "didn't want you to have all the fun without me."

She steps away from the door, and moves against the wall opposite me, leaning her back against it. "May I watch?"

My chest heaves as I reply, "You wish...to w-watch me? No! No, that does not seem–"

Elle-noor does not wait for me to finish speaking. Instead, she pulls her tunic over her head, tosses it to the floor, and cups her breasts. "It's okay," she breathes, her voice a husky rasp, "You can watch me too."

CHAPTER 12

ELEANOR

*W*ell, this took an unexpected turn. Not that I mind, though, because the sexual tension downstairs while we made ale was enough to make my pussy gush like a garden hose. I'm just sad Bruvix didn't invite me to the party he's having up here.

It's clear he's inexperienced sexually, and it would not surprise me at all to learn he's a virgin. So if this will help him take the edge off while getting a visual lesson in human anatomy, I'm happy to oblige. Not that I would consider myself anything remotely close to a "sexpert," but after the hand I've been dealt since being taken, I refuse to spend another second denying myself pleasure. This is the only life I've got, and I want to enjoy it.

Although, my fierce alien warrior still hasn't given me the green light to proceed. "Uh, Bruvix?" I say, resting my hands on the waist of my leggings. "I'm going to need verbal confirmation you're okay with this."

"Huh? Uhm, y-yes," he groans, his hand still wrapped around his impressively large dick. He felt big when I cupped him through his pants, but...wow. "Touch yourself for me, Elle-noor."

"My pleasure," I reply, holding back a chuckle at the wordplay. I push my leggings down and step out of them, then I'm completely naked in front of Bruvix. His mouth hangs open as I sit in the chair in the corner of the room and spread my legs wide. "What would you like me to do next?" I ask, placing one hand across my stomach and the other on my hip.

His hand starts to move again, stroking his long golden dick up and down as he stares at me, his eyes heavy-lidded and swirling with heat. "Play with your nipples."

I do as he commands, cupping my left breast and skating my fingers across the hardened tip. He wets his lips with his tongue, and his eyes darken as they roam my body. I feel myself getting wetter under his perusal.

"Spread your folds for me," he rasps, stroking himself harder now. "Let me see your pretty c-cunt."

With my other hand, I spread my pussy lips so my swollen, aching clit is on full display. Bruvix growls at the sight of it. "So wet. Y-you are so wet already," he mutters with a gulp, the flick of his wrist catching my eye as he focuses his grip on the crown. His chest heaves as he continues to watch me with rapt attention.

My hand drops away from my breast and lightly rubs my clit from side to side. I'm aching to show him how much he means to me. "For you, Bruvix. It's all for you."

His growl deepens, and I watch his hips buck as he pumps into his hand. "Mine," he grunts in agreement. "You are mine."

"Yours," I whisper as my breathing turns ragged. I trace circles around the engorged bundle of nerves as my heart thumps. If he's into possessive dirty talk, I'm game. I've never found it all that appealing before, but with Bruvix, it's different. Better. Hotter.

"Elle-noor," he pants as his face scrunches into anguished need, his nostrils flaring as his lower abs contract, accentuating each beautifully sculpted muscle around his middle. Yet people find him hard to look at?

Morons.

With his tunic still on, the scars on his chest and shoulders are covered. I would love to see them, if only to make it clear that they don't bother me at all, but this way, I imagine Bruvix more comfortable than he would with his shirt off. And getting him more comfortable with himself, with me, is the whole point of this anyway.

I let out a scream the moment I insert two fingers inside my core. I don't wait for him to give me further instruction. I'm getting too close. "Ah-ah!" I cry, rubbing my clit harder, faster.

A muscle in Bruvix's jaw ticks as he pinches his eyes shut. "No," I call out. "Keep your eyes on me." I want him to be in this moment with me, even though we aren't touching.

"I-I am close, Elle-noor," he grunts.

"Yesss," I hiss back. I am, too, and I want us coming together. Our gazes lock, our furious movements united though we're feet apart. When my orgasm rips through me moments later, my mouth falls open in a silent cry as my hips buck into my hands.

"Elle-noor!" Bruvix roars immediately after me as glittery, silver come spurts from his dick all over his stomach and runs down his thick thighs and all over his hand, still pumping.

When I finally come down, I feel boneless, but not tired. "Come here. I need you inside me. Please," I beg, holding out my hand for him to take. He takes a step toward me.

Before our fingers touch, we hear a big commotion coming from downstairs, followed by glass shattering.

"Stanley!" I yell, jumping up from the chair. Bruvix quickly pulls his pants up and wipes his hands on his tunic, then tosses it to me. I do the same and follow him downstairs in a panic. I bump into his back as he stops on the last step, and we see Stanley's head submerged in the bottom half of a large jug of ale, the top broken off and in shards next to him. "Stanley, no!" I scold as he ignores me and continues to lap at the booze like it's his last sip of water.

"Stay where you are," he mutters to me, holding up a hand to block me from the entryway. He looks over his shoulder at me and his gaze drops to my chest. It's then that I realize I'm still naked. Oh well. "I do not want the glass cutting your delicate skin."

"Okay, you grab Stanley and bring him to me. I'll take him upstairs while you get rid of the glass," I reply, offering a compromise. I have no idea what alcohol does to a tr'gory puppy's system, but with it already weakened with sickness, and the fact that the jug was mostly empty by the time we discovered him with it, I'm guessing wherever Stanley goes, a mess will follow.

Bruvix nods and steps carefully toward the pup. "Come here, Stahn-lee. No more ale for you," he coos, and I find the entire scene so ridiculously cute that I can't help but smile. A bare-chested Bruvix, his stomach still glistening with his silver come, trying to reason with a drunk tr'gory puppy.

How is this real life?

Stanley stops drinking to look at Bruvix and lightly wags his tail before returning to his adult beverage. Just as Bruvix gets within reach, Stanley leaps over the broken glass and speeds past me up the stairs.

"I've got him!" I shout as I chase him past the security room on the second floor—where the door is shut, thank god—and into the bedroom on the third floor. Stanley jumps onto the bed and lowers his chest onto the blanket with his front legs outstretched. He sticks his butt into the air and his tail swishes back and forth as he watches me in the doorway with those bright red eyes. "Stanley…" I say, warning in my tone, "Get down, little nugget."

His tail wags faster as he slaps his front paws on the bed, a clear invitation to play. But the last thing I want to do right now is chase this drunk beast through the house while I'm still naked.

I hear Bruvix downstairs sweeping up the broken glass, so as long as I can keep Stanley in here with me until he's done, we won't have to worry about his paws getting all torn up. "Get down, Stanley," I repeat, pointing to the floor. His eyes follow my finger, and he starts panting as he zeroes in on a pattern in the wood. "You okay, bud?"

He sits his butt down, then slides off the bed. And even though he lands on all four paws, he somehow stumbles and flops onto his chest on the floor with a grunt.

I hold my hands up in surrender. "Okay, you stay there. Stay." I keep my eyes trained on him as I reach for my tunic that's in a rumpled ball near the chair in the corner. As I'm pulling it over my head, I hear Stanley let out a baby bark and he whooshes past me out the door. "Shit, shit, shit!" I curse, pulling the hem of my tunic down to cover my ass as I follow him back down the steps. "He's coming!" I yell, hopefully giving Bruvix enough of a warning.

"O fahh," I hear Bruvix shout just as something heavy crashes to the ground.

I arrive just in time to see the cold box on its side and Stanley lapping at the water spilling out of it and onto the floor. The glass is cleaned up, thankfully, but it's still quite a mess down here.

"Thank you for handling the glass," I say with a sigh. "That was a close call."

"Yes," Bruvix agrees, lifting the cold box and putting it right side up again. "We were lucky."

Once Stanley finishes lapping up the water, he comes to sit at Bruvix's side, happily looking up at him with his tongue hanging out of his mouth. What a sight that is. My big, strapping alien with the puppy he still refuses to admit he cares for seated at his feet.

I hear a rumbling sound coming from Stanley's rounded belly, and just as Bruvix looks down with a confused expression, Stanley vomits water and ale and bile all over Bruvix's bare feet.

CHAPTER 13

BRUVIX

Despite the chaos that the tr'gory pup brings with his ongoing presence inside my home, I woke happier than I have ever been. That is because of Elle-noor. The tether between us is thickening, but that is to be expected. I also simply enjoy having her around. The way she touched herself last eve, her pink folds slick and glistening, and her fingers disappearing inside her body will remain burned in my memory until my last breath.

I wanted to continue things. I wanted to watch her face as I made her come, my cock pumping deep inside her. But Stahn-lee had to cock-block us, as Elle-noor says. And his cock-blocking did not stop there. After Elle-noor and I cleaned up his pile of vomit, and the vomit he left inside the washroom, she remembered she was needed for dish duty and left in a hurry. I stayed with Stahn-lee, watching over him as he got sick thrice more.

When she returned, we placed a sleepy Stahn-lee across the room in his bed made of towels and furs I do not often use and climbed into bed together. She wore only her tunic and pressed her back against my chest. I wrapped my arm around her middle, and in response, she wiggled her ass against my cock, still hard from our voyeuristic activities earlier in the day. Then she took my hand and guided my fingers through the triangular patch of fur on her pussy, and below, into her wet folds, pressing them down into her clit. I nibbled at the shell of her ear as she showed me how just she likes to be touched, and she let out a keening cry the moment I dipped inside her tight, hot channel.

That is when Stahn-lee howled in distress and jumped on the bed, wiggling down until he was lodged between our legs.

Cock-blocker.

I try not to be angry with him. He, most likely, does not realize what he is doing; ruining these precious moments between me and Elle-noor—moments I have never had with another.

I need to find another room he can slumber in because I refuse to be interrupted again and leave my female aching and unsatisfied. It is cruel.

Keeping the image of her lush pink lips in my head, I make my way from the morning training session to the meal hall. I grab two of everything that I can fit onto these plates and hurry toward my home. To my mate.

Balancing two heaping dishes in one hand as I open the front door, I am immediately hit with a foul odor the moment I am inside, and almost drop Elle-noor's food. Placing the plates on the shelf by the spigot, I remove my boots and trot up the stairs to my bedroom. I find Elle-noor fast asleep with her mouth hanging open and drool soaking my pillow. She is sprawled on her back with her face turned toward me while one leg dangles off the side, almost touching the floor, the other is extended across the width of the bed.

The pup is on the floor, wide awake and gnawing away on a pair of my pants. He wags his bushy tail when he sees me, and then immediately returns to his chew. I notice that his horns are starting to come in. Currently, they are nothing more than short white nubs that meet the length of his black fur.

Next to his empty bed is a pile of his stool, which is the obvious source of the odor. I was certain anger would be the most dominant emotion I would feel upon discovering this, but all I feel is relief, and a bit of pride, because his stool is no longer a watery puddle. It is more solid and dry. He is healing.

Quietly, I pull a dirty rag from my pocket and use that to dispose of his waste outside. When I return, I lift the pup in my arms and carry him into the washroom on the first floor. I wipe his bottom with a clean rag and grab a makeshift bottle from the shelf as I pass by it. We return to my bedroom, and I take a seat in the chair by the window. I shift the pup so he is lying on his back in my arms, and I hold the bottle above his mouth, just like I have seen Elle-noor do.

At first, he jerks his head away from the bottle. "I know it is not the same as a teat but this is all we have, Stahn-lee," I whisper to him. "There you go," I encourage as he begins slurping at the bottle, trying to pull the liquid from it faster. I gently pat his rounded belly as he eats and lean back against the wall as the light breeze tickles my neck through the open window.

At some point, the pup's bright red eyes meet mine as he feeds, and my heart skips in response. This tiny creature was so helpless. Still is, in fact. He is strong enough to walk on his own, but his feet are much bigger than the rest of him, and a slow trot around the outside of my dwelling often turns into a clumsy gallop with him landing face-first into a puddle.

How he finds the deepest puddle to fall into every single time, I will never know.

"Wow," I hear a sleepy Elle-noor mumble from across the room. She still lies in bed, but on her side, watching us with warmth in her eyes. "I want this image tattooed in my brain."

"What image?" I ask, feigning ignorance as I sit up taller and flex my arms around the pup.

She giggles, the sound light and full of joy. "Oh, you know exactly how beautiful you are right now, sir."

I can understand the objective appeal of a large creature caring for a small one, but beautiful? Me? That word has never been used to describe me. Not once. "You did not eat another vakopurri berry while I was gone, did you?"

"You think I'd have to be high to find you attractive?" she asks with a chuckle. "Have you never looked in a mirror before?"

I tip the bottle up slightly, so the pup can finish the rest of the contents, and I wait for the humorous ending of the joke. But she says nothing. She merely sits up on the bed with her lips pursed, waiting for my response. "I am quite aware of how I look," I finally reply.

Is she saying she finds my face and body appealing? Because that would make me feel like I was granted immortality. But I am not sure if that is what she is trying to communicate.

"The desire to look different? I get it," she says as she flops onto her back, staring at the ceiling. "I was constantly pressured to lose weight as a kid. And far into adulthood. Or to lighten my skin, so I looked more like my mom than my dad. Body: too fat, skin: too dark, butt: too big, blah, blah, blah."

I jerk my head back at her words because they do not make sense to me. She is not "too" anything. She is exactly as she is supposed to be. Perfect, from her head to her toes.

"Eventually, I learned to tune it out," she says, turning her head to look at me. "The words still play in my mind, but I regret the time I wasted trying to make other people happy."

I nod, a deep, visceral understanding passing between us.

She yawns and stretches as she rises from bed and comes to me with her arms outstretched. "I can take him," she offers.

I do not hand him over, though. "I do not mind, Elle-noor," I tell her. "Your morning meal is downstairs. Go eat."

"You sure?" she asks, putting her hands on her hips, clearly suspicious of me.

"I am sure," I vow, using the rag draped on my shoulder to wipe dribbled formula from his chin.

"My hero," she croons as she runs a hand through my hair, fluffing it on the top. I bite back a groan that threatens to escape at the feel of her fingers caressing my scalp. Every touch from Elle-noor makes me greedy and desperate for the next.

I listen as she skips down the steps and the sound of clinking dishes fills the air. Once the bottle is empty, I take it and the pup downstairs with me as I rinse the fluid bag and the inside of the bottle top. By the sound of it, Elle-noor is in the washroom using the wash box, and while she continues to ready for herself for the day, I take the pup outside to relieve himself.

He stays close to my legs, tripping over my feet a few times before letting his nose guide him a short distance away. Sniffing plant after plant, he finally finds a dying yiopix bush to mark with his urine.

When I bring him back inside, Elle-noor is standing by the spigot with my plate of food in hand. "Don't forget about your breakfast, mister!" she scolds playfully. Her mane is wet and shiny as it brushes the tops of her shoulders. I clench my fist behind my back, resisting the urge to run my fingers through it. Taking the plate from her hand, I distract myself by shoveling bread and berries into my mouth at an almost undignified pace.

"So, I'm running a bit late today," she says as she shoves her feet into her boots while securing her mane with a tie at the back of her neck, "but I'll be home as soon as I'm done with dish duty."

Home.

This is the first time she has referred to my home as hers. I wonder if she realizes that. I will certainly never forget it.

"That is fine. I can skip the next training session. Varrek will not mind," I lie. He is starting to wonder why I must leave early from each session. I tell him it is to help Elle-noor review tr'gory recordings, but I am not sure how much longer that excuse will work.

She bends down and gives the pup a kiss between the white stumps that will eventually become his horns. "Okay, Stanley. Be a good boy for Bruvix!" she says before closing the door behind her.

"Well, Stahn-lee," I say as I finish my last bite of bread, "onward with this day." He trots on my heels as we go upstairs to the security room. He lies at my feet while I check the views for the previous eve but see no tr'gory mother and pups. There is the pack of five fully grown tr'gorys that passes through the village, but the mother has not been seen.

I find this concerning. Where could she be? Her cries while giving birth were clearly the sounds that woke the clan, but she could not have strayed that far from the village, surely. Especially after leaving an ailing pup behind.

Stahn-lee is quite lucky Elle-noor has such a kind heart. If she had not rescued him from the woods, he might be dead right now. The thought sends a chill across my skin as I look down at the fluffy boy playfully swatting at the zip on my boot.

Frustrated by the lack of information we still have on the mother, I sweep Stahn-lee into my arms and carry him to my bedroom. I straighten the furs on the bed and rearrange the towels and furs of his bed until they are enticingly puffy. He leaps into the center of his bed, instantly flattening them, and I laugh as I kick off my boots and lie on top of the freshly made bed Elle-noor and I share.

A loud crash jolts me awake, and I do not know how long I have been asleep. When I look around my room, it is empty. Elle-noor is clearly not back yet. But where is Stahn-lee?

Oh no.

I race down the steps into my security room to find him tugging the cord from where my main server plugs into the socket. One chair is on its side while the other is pushed against the far wall. The table is upturned, and screen pads, monitors, keyboards, and docking stations are scattered all over the floor. Some screens are shattered, but most appear to be intact, though all of them are lit up with the red and black crinkly feed of a severed connection.

"Stahn-lee!" I shout. When the pup cowers at the volume of my voice, my rage dissipates, mostly. He does not know how valuable these items are to me. He merely sees them as toys he has yet to sink his fangs into. I take another moment to breathe in and out as I survey the damage.

Then I pull the screen pad from my pocket and send a comm to Nee-roh.

"Yes, scarred one?" he answers.

"I need your assistance. It is urgent."

He studies my face for a long moment and then replies, "I shall be there shortly."

I keep him at the front door when he arrives. "You must vow that you will keep what you are about to see to yourself. You may tell Kay-teh, because I assume you would keep nothing from her, but this cannot be shared with anyone else."

He crosses his arms over his chest. "I will not help you hide Elle-noor's body. That seems wrong."

I growl in response. He is starting to sound like Kay-teh and these twisted jokes are not what I need right now. "Elle-noor is fine! She is not here."

"Then what has got you so frazzled?" he asks as I step to the side and let him in.

I close the door just as Stahn-lee gallops down the steps with unburdened glee. He stops at Nee-roh's feet and vomits a bile-soaked cable onto the draxilio's boots, along with a bottle's worth of formula I fed him this morn.

Nee-roh's jaw hangs open, his upper lip curled in disgust, as he lifts his foot and examines the mess that is now all over it. "The favors you shall owe me outnumber the years you have left in this life, my friend."

CHAPTER 14

ELEANOR

Pushing the high-backed chair beneath Bruvix's desk, I take a step back to look around. "Not bad, huh?" I say to Bruvix as he plugs the server cord back in. His security room certainly doesn't look as organized and tidy as it did before Stanley rolled through here like a tiny tr'gory tornado, but it's pretty close to the original state, minus a few monitors that we haven't been able to replace yet. Niro is working on it, but it will probably take a few days to get it back to where it was.

Luckily, he promised to keep Stanley a secret for us before he left a few hours ago. I'm not sure if I trust him yet, but I do trust Kate. She won't let this get out.

Bruvix stands and puts his hands on his narrow waist. "Not bad. That is how I would describe this, yes. Not good. Not good at all, but also not...bad."

"I'm so sorry this happened. Really," I tell him with pleading eyes. I should've skipped dish duty entirely this morning and stayed home with them. I certainly didn't want to leave. Being here with them is the best part of my day. It's all I want to do now. And Bruvix has been such a good sport about this whole thing, especially considering how much of a mess Stanley has made.

Nursing him back to health has also helped me feel more comfortable here. The Frank-sized hole in my heart is slowly starting to close, and I've been able to put my skills to good use. I'm starting to feel like myself again.

"I am not mad, Elle-noor," he says as he gently rubs my arms. I take advantage of the opening and wrap my arms around his middle, pressing my head against his chest.

"You sure?" I mutter into his shirt. He stills but eventually places his large hands on the small of my back, and it becomes the most satisfying hug of my life.

"I promise," he whispers as he presses his nose into my hair, inhaling deeply. "I am concerned about the clan's safety without the ability to monitor the perimeter, but Nee-roh has assured me his cameras cover the outer border of the village, so that will be enough for now."

I pull back just far enough to look up at him and nod. "Makes sense."

"But it brings me pain to say," he begins, and I know exactly what's about to follow, "it is time to return Stahn-lee to his pack."

Yup. That's what I was afraid of because he's right. Stanley still eats from a bottle, but he probably doesn't need to. I just like feeding him with it. He doesn't seem to have any lingering respiratory issues, and his stools are much more solid than they were in the beginning.

Besides, with his need to chew on everything while simultaneously knocking it over, clearly, he's strong enough to hang with his tr'gory brothers and sisters. I had hoped by now we would've caught some glimpse of Nanay, but no such luck. I don't know where she's been with her babies, but I'm going to assume it's not far.

"Yeah, I know," I finally reply. "Just let me have one more night with him?"

His eyes dart between mine before dropping to my lips. Because I can't help myself, I stick my bottom lip out in a toddler-esque pout.

He chuckles at that, and I'm left breathless by that crooked smile of his. "One more," he agrees. "Then you will return him to the bush?"

"What? No," I reply quickly. I'm not just going to toss my baby boy outside on his own. "I'm going back to the falls to reunite him with Nanay."

He abruptly steps out of my embrace and scratches his head. "I cannot allow that. It is not safe."

"I mean, do I really need your permission?"

His brows lift as he scoffs at me. "What is your plan, then? To carry a heavy tr'gory pup through the village and hope no one sees you? That Varrek does not discover the secret we've been keeping from him?"

I suppose I didn't think this one through. I also didn't expect him to be so opposed to the idea of going back to the falls. "I wasn't planning to go alone. You'll come with me, right?"

He drops his chin and stares at the floor for what feels like several minutes. "No, Elle-noor. I cannot do that."

"Why not?" I ask. "You did it before."

Bruvix looks around the room as he absently runs a finger of the scar that cuts through his mouth, clearly at war with himself over this decision. "Fine. We leave just before the sun starts to rise. We will leave Stahn-lee near the den we found, and we should be able to make it back before the clan awakens."

I grit my teeth, holding back tears at the thought of leaving him out there and just walking away. "Okay," I say through trembling lips. "But I'm going to bed now so I can snuggle with him as long as possible."

He puts a finger beneath my chin and tilts my head up until my eyes meet his. "I would expect nothing less, zala kovvari," he says with a slight grin.

The phrase is translated to "tender heart" via my translator chip, and I melt where I stand.

We dispose of the last remaining bits of broken glass and frayed wires in the security room before we head up to the bedroom and climb under the furs. I don't even bother putting Stanley on his bed since he never stays on it long anyway. And this way, he can be my little spoon as I fall asleep. Stanley is the littlest spoon, and Bruvix is the biggest, with a very content me sandwiched in the middle.

* * *

I hate mornings, and this one is particularly rotten. Stanley keeps wiggling in my arms as we make our way on light feet through the village and toward the falls. I can barely see where I'm going since it's still dark out, and Stanley's grown to about thirty-five pounds of feet and fluff, which makes him hard to hold onto. He's growing quickly—shockingly quickly—it's like I blink and he transforms. I love him so much, I want to scream. And today's the day I let him go.

So yeah, this morning sucks.

Bruvix looks back and sees the strands of hair pushed in front of my eyes and Stanley's squirmy body and quickly takes him from my arms.

"Want me to take the sword?" I offer, knowing how vulnerable he must feel with his weapons sheathed as we enter the woods in the dark.

"It is quite heavy, but here," he says, turning and gesturing at the dagger hanging from his other hip. "Take that."

It *is* heavy, so heavy that I'm pretty sure I wouldn't have been able to lift the sword.

"Let me go ahead of you," I whisper. He's the one that's worried about this excursion, and he's the one without a weapon handy.

He says nothing, but he also doesn't let me pass him. We stay like this on the narrow trail toward the falls until it starts to open up at the end. I drop four douku orbs as soon as I have room to stand beside Bruvix, but the area where we found the blood and the den is clear. We figured this might be a possibility, so Bruvix sets Stanley down as I set up a cozy nest for him near the entrance of the den. I lay down his favorite fur blanket, and Bruvix's tunic that he loves to chew on—so he'll have the comfort of a familiar scent.

"Come, Elle-noor," Bruvix says as I remain crouched and rubbing Stanley's belly as he sprawls himself on the fur. "We must turn back."

He gently gnaws on my fist, just enough to brush the tips of his fangs against my skin, but not hard enough to make me bleed, and suddenly I'm not sure if I can leave him. My feet are planted in the dirt and everything inside me is screaming for me to stay. Or to grab him and run back home.

"Elle-noor," he repeats, clear warning in his tone this time.

Bruvix is right. Stanley is not some domesticated puppy I can train to play fetch. He's a wild animal that will soon be too big for me to carry, and eventually, he'll grow to be the size of an elephant. He belongs out here. Not with me.

He's not Frank, and I can't force him to be my pet simply because I miss having a furry sidekick constantly running around my legs.

Sighing heavily, I stand. "Be a good boy, Stanley," I tell him.

"Elle-noor," Bruvix says again. He's growing impatient. I get it, but I deserve to say good-bye, don't I?

"Stay safe out here, little gu–"

The words die in my throat when a steady growl emanates from behind the falls. I stumble backward until Bruvix grabs my arm and we watch as the blood-red eyes and large black body of Nanay come into view.

Bruvix tries to pull me behind him, but I rip my arm out of his grasp. "Wait!" I tell him. I need to see this. I need to know that Stanley will be okay. I also sense...something from the mother I wasn't expecting. Her head is bowed low, and she continues to growl, but her gaze is locked on Bruvix, not me.

Does she perceive both of us as a threat and is planning to attack him first? Or is she only afraid of him? I decide to test this theory, by dropping the dagger at my feet, and reaching into my pack for the raw meat we were planning to leave with Stanley.

"Do not," Bruvix warns as he tries to reach for me. The movement catches her eye, and she snaps her jaws at Bruvix.

"It's okay, Bruvix," I tell him. I hear his breathing pick up as I take a careful step in her direction. I hate that this is causing him so much anxiety, but I know I can do this.

Her lip curls and she exposes her fangs as I pull my hand from my pack, so I lift both in surrender with raw kuhnypa meat hanging from my left hand. Her gaze lands on it, and I watch the tip of her snout scrunch up as her nostrils flare.

"Okay, Nanay," I whisper softly. "I'm not gonna hurt you," she tilts her head to the side as I speak, still showing off her fangs. "Just returning your boy and leaving you a snack. That's all." I drop the meat to the ground and take three steps back.

Stanley's red eyes light up the moment the meat hits the dirt, and he scampers over as if his biological mom and adoptive mom aren't in a tense standoff right now.

She makes a sound low in her throat, not a growl, exactly, but more of a grunt that makes Stanley stop in his tracks. Her gait is graceful, lethal. Her large paws hit the ground heavily and with purpose as she approaches the meat.

But then she stops and assesses the smaller tr'gory. She sniffs at Stanley's head, around his ears, and gives him a single lick on the snout. He lifts a paw as if to playfully bat her away but then flops onto his side, exposing his belly.

She continues checking him over, cleaning random spots with her tongue, and he basks in her attention. I feel a tear roll down my cheek as I watch the two of them. The pup she abandoned, assumed dead, now alive and well right in front of her.

Nanay lifts her large head, and her eyes meet mine. I know I should look away as she could see my steady gaze as a challenge, but I can't. It feels like she's trying to tell me something. Obviously, I have no idea what that is, but I can feel it in the way she holds herself, less rigid and afraid than when she first saw us. Maybe it's bullshit wishful thinking on my part, but it feels real.

She drops her nose to the meat and then picks it up between her fangs. She uses her paw to tear off a chunk and drops it in front of Stanley. He sniffs it, then licks it a few times before he starts to chew. Nanay does the same, ripping off a bigger chunk for herself.

"Elle-noor," I hear Bruvix whisper. I quickly turn my head to find him now several feet behind me. He's been backing away this whole time. "We must go," he says, gesturing me to follow.

I nod, and I know he's right. I should leave them be. We came here to release Stanley with the hope that his mother would find him. She did. We accomplished our goal.

So why does it feel impossible for me to leave?

"Elle-noor," he says again. I quickly reach into the pack and pull out a few strips of jerky. I toss them toward Nanay and Stanley, and they land a few feet in front of them.

"Until we meet again, I suppose," I mumble quietly. I know they can't understand me, but it didn't feel right to leave without saying anything at all.

I walk backward with my hands raised in front of me until I bump into Bruvix. As Nanay and Stanley are happily munching away on their snacks, Bruvix takes my hand, and we get back onto the narrow trail that'll lead us to the village. Once the tr'gorys are completely out of sight, we run the rest of the way, and we don't stop until we reach Bruvix's front door.

Slamming it closed behind us, we lean back against it as our chests heave from exertion. Wiping the sweat from my brow, I smile up at the ceiling. "We did it," I say with a triumphant chuckle.

"We are lucky," he replies, his gaze still wild and full of worry. "That was too close."

"Yeah, it was risky," I admit. It could've gone very, very wrong… but it didn't. Because I know what I'm doing. And I haven't even begun to scratch the surface on learning about these creatures. "Next time, it'll be much smoother."

"Next time?" he asks, jerking his head back. "There will not be a next time. We returned Stahn-lee. That is it. We move on."

"No," I reply in a forceful tone. "The more I learn about them, the less of a threat they'll be to all of us. We just need to understand them a bit more. I'll get there."

"Elle-noor, we could have died this eve."

"But we didn't!"

He sighs, his shoulders dropping. He rubs his eye with the heel of his palm. "Can we discuss this another time? Perhaps after the sun has risen?"

I take his hand in mine as I lead him up the stairs. "Sure thing," I say. But hours, days, weeks—it won't matter when we revisit this, my answer will remain the same. This is something I know I can do. This is how I'll contribute to the clan. With or without Bruvix's approval.

CHAPTER 15

BRUVIX

"That should do it," Nee-roh grunts as he slides out from under the table in my security room. He has gifted me three of his own monitors and five new cables to replace the ones that Stahn-lee destroyed.

I flip the server on, and the screens light up as they come to life. Within moments, I am seeing the feeds from each of our security cameras placed around the village, and a sigh of relief rushes out of me. "I am grateful to you. It appears they are running again."

He rises to his full height and wipes the dust from his hands. "How grateful, exactly?"

My lips form a grim line. I am already indebted to the draxilio for keeping Stahn-lee a secret. How much more will I end up owing him? "Three casks of ale's worth?" I offer.

"Mmm, that is enticing," he says, rubbing his chin. "For now, I shall take two casks, and a vow to assist me in building a cradle for my child."

"Done," I reply quickly. That is an easy trade. I have assisted him in building the entire home he shares with Kay-teh in the village. A cradle will take no time at all. "So we are even?"

"Ha!" he barks out. "Not even close. But I shall let you know when your debts are cleared." He gives me a hard pat on the arm before he leaves.

I plunk down in my chair and go through the logged recordings from the past moon cycles and find that the day the system was not working properly is lost entirely. The cameras were operational, but the view was not sent with the server disconnected. I groan as I place my head in my hands.

We are fortunate nothing tragic occurred during that time. I would have no way of explaining why the recording is missing. I hope Varrek does not wish to see it. He probably will not, but I do not like keeping secrets from him.

Now that Stahn-lee is back with Nah-naye, we do not have to worry about that, but Elle-noor has expressed desire in observing the tr'gorys up close, and I fear she will want to keep that from Varrek as well since he would never allow it. I am torn. I understand the information she gleans from watching them will be beneficial to our clan, but the risk she is putting herself in is too great. I will not let her approach them during the night by herself, but I also do not wish to be anywhere near a tr'gory.

If she asks me to accompany her, I will not be able to refuse. Elle-noor must be aware of this by now—I will give her anything she desires. Seeing her face light up with joy is worth whatever sacrifice I must make to win her smiles.

"Hello, hello! I'm home!" she calls out from downstairs.

As with every time I see her face, my heart leaps into my throat, and I feel my palms become slick with sweat. The tether grows stronger each day we do not solidify our mate bond, and I am desperate to taste her cunt. It is on my mind more than it is not.

She runs into my open arms and presses her face against my chest as I hold her against me. "Greetings, zala kovvari," I mumble into her hair as I breathe it in. "How was dish duty?"

"Oh, fine," she says with a dismissive wave of her hand. "The usual. Waldric went on and on about Nalba's snack saver tincture and how brilliant she is. Then when she stopped by to grab a bowl of buufcasi berries, he got all frazzled and wouldn't stop talking to her about the rain."

I shake my head as a chuckle escapes my lips. "Poor fellow," I mutter. He does not like clan members knowing how fast his heart beats when he is with Nalba, but it is common knowledge among us at this point. He does not hide it well. The only person not aware is Nalba as she is far too focused on her inventions.

Elle-noor kicks off her boots by the door and pulls back her mane into a messy knot atop her head. "It's like, just tell her she looks pretty, or something. Make the move!"

"But he will not," I tell her. "He does not think a mind like hers would ever find value in a male who cooks."

She crosses her arms over her chest and scrunches her nose, incredulous. "That's insane! Where I'm from, a man who cooks is the ultimate prize. When my dad started learning how to cook, my mom was thrilled. It made her life easier, and the Filipino dishes he made were delicious."

Hmm. I did not realize cooking is such an important aspect of human mating rituals. Ahlvo and Varrek did not say they prepared meals for Aye-vah and Cloh-ee when they were courting them. Perhaps I should ask Nee-roh about this.

"Shall we have final meal at the hall tonight?" I ask her. It will be a good opportunity to dine with the others, if only to prove to Kay-teh and Nee-roh that Elle-noor is alive, and I have not killed her.

"Sure thing," she exclaims, cheerfully. "Let me just take a shower really quick." She heads toward the stairs but stops before ascending. "Oh! Was Niro able to fix the feeds?"

"Yes, we do not have views from when Stahn-lee had his little outburst, but the feeds are recording, so all from today forward, we will capture."

She smiles warmly at the mention of the tr'gory pup. "Right," she says, nodding, before going upstairs to get a change of clothes. Elle-noor did not ask if she could continue staying here after we returned Stahn-lee to the falls—she just stayed. And I would not have it any other way, because I want this to be her home, perhaps even more than she does.

Hearing her walk through the door each day… it is like I am being given a gift I am not certain I deserve. Elle-noor could stay anywhere in the village, but she has chosen to stay here, with me. Her mind could change. But I am determined to keep her because she is mine.

* * *

"What on Earth are you wearing?" Elle-noor asks as I straighten the poncho Kay-teh made for me.

"We are not on Earth, Elle-noor," I remind her. What a strange thing to forget. She must be tired. "It is to protect me from the rain. See?" I turn around so she can get a full view of the filmy sack Kay-teh worked so hard on, and then pull the hood over my head.

"Kate makes clothes for you?" she asks, her expression turning stony.

"Yes," I reply, somewhat confused by the change in her mood. "Does this bother you? Jealousy, is that what this is?"

"Of course, I'm jealous!" she hollers. "I want new clothes too!"

Ah. I see. Why did I assume Elle-noor would be bothered by my closeness with Kay-teh? She is not bothered by any matter, it seems. She has yet to claim me as hers, or acknowledge our tether, so I should not assume she feels what I do. "I am sure she would make you garments if you asked," I tell her, trying to mask my disappointment by continuing to fiddle with my hood.

"You think she could make me a jumpsuit? I had this pink one back home that was so comfortable. I wore it everywhere," she continues. She describes her pink jumpsuit, and the other jumpsuits in various colors she misses wearing, in great detail, as we walk to the meal hall.

When we arrive, Kay-teh, Nee-roh, Ahlvo, Aye-vah, Cloh-ee, and Varrek are all seated together and chatting away as they eat their final meals. Elle-noor and I quickly fill our plates and join them at the long table in the center of the hall, most of it shielded from the rain.

"Hey, guys!" Kay-teh beams as we sit at the end of the table across from her and Nee-roh.

"Mmm, I'm so glad Waldric made stew tonight," Elle-noor mumbles as she shovels a heaping spoonful into her mouth. "It's perfect in this weather."

"Oh my god. I know, right?" Cloh-ee adds. She turns to Varrek and is just about to show him her empty bowl when he leaps to his feet, grabs it from her hand, and strides over to Waldric for another helping. "Don't mind me," she chuckles when everyone notices Varrek's quick response to her silent request. "I'm in the vacuum stage of my pregnancy."

"Vahk-yoom?" I repeat, slowly. The translation in my chip indicates some kind of cleaning mechanism.

She nods and points to her heavy, rounded tummy. "Yeah, I'm inhaling everything in front of me. Doesn't matter what it is. Give me seconds and thirds."

The chatter dies down as we focus on our meals, but the quiet is comfortable. Warm. I am surprised to find socializing in this context is enjoyable. It is pleasing to see Varrek tend to his very pregnant mate, and to see Ahlvo smile as Aye-vah fusses with his hair. I worried he would not escape the dark place in his mind after being injured. And, of course, there is Kay-teh and Nee-roh, a pairing I repeatedly attempted to sabotage not long ago, but seeing them now, laughing together over a joke only they know, I am glad I did not succeed.

I look over at Elle-noor and realize she has been watching me. She gives me a knowing grin as she takes my hand beneath the table, lacing her short, delicate fingers with mine. She gives my hand a single squeeze, and my worries from before, about her lack of jealousy, all but evaporate.

So what if she does not get jealous? It is clear she cares for me, and that is all I want. I will take her love however she gives it.

After we finish our meals, we remain at the table, digesting our food and conversing about everything and nothing. At some point, I am not sure how, but the tr'gorys are mentioned, and my jaw ticks in response. Nee-roh gives me a cautious look as if to remind me to stay quiet. As if I needed a reminder.

"How is your research going, Elle-noor?" Varrek asks.

Elle-noor clears her throat and straightens her spine. "Um, really well. Yeah. I-I'm starting to understand the way they care for their young. It's a lot like wolves from Earth."

Why did she have to bring up the dynamics between mother and pup? That is precisely what we are trying to hide from Varrek.

"Wow, that's interesting!" Cloh-ee exclaims, leaning forward on her elbows. "I know this is going to sound bonkers, but when Varrek was attacked, it really felt like I was looking into the eyes of a giant dog."

"What makes you say that?" Elle-noor asks, curiosity swirling in her gaze.

"Before it saw Varrek on the branch above me," she continues, and then pauses. "I don't know… It wagged its tail, and then did that head tilt thing dogs do, and oh! It dropped onto its chest in the dirt with its legs spread in front of it. Like that play pose dogs do. The thing was legit behaving like a dog."

"Then what happened?" Elle-noor asks with a soft smile. She wants so badly for these feral creatures to be like her Earth pets. Why can she not take an interest in plants, as I have? They are living things she can care for that do not wish her harm.

"Then it saw me hiding on the branch and lunged at Cloh-ee," Varrek adds. "I jumped down to intervene, and it sunk its fangs into my shoulder. There is nothing sweet or innocent about them."

"I know they're wild animals, but there's something truly fascinating about them," Elle-noor replies wistfully. "I'm excited to learn all I can."

"Do not expect Bruvix here to protect you if you come face-to-face with one," Ahlvo says with a snicker. "He would freeze and then run away. He cannot afford to lose any more of his face." He is howling with laughter by the time he gets the words out. Then turns to me. "Right, Bruvix?"

He is only joking, so I do not mind. This is a joke the entire clan cannot seem to get enough of. Ahlvo is not saying it to be cruel, he is mere–

"What a fucked-up thing to say, Ahlvo," Elle-noor pipes in. I see the tension in her shoulders, and her eyes hold nothing but fury. "Is that supposed to be funny? Because of his scars?"

Ahlvo's mouth is agape, and he clearly does not know how to respond.

"What, you find his scars ugly?" Elle-noor raises her voice at Ahlvo, slowly rising to her feet. "Because, actually, they're physical proof that he survived something he probably wasn't supposed to. He couldn't be taken down. I happen to find that extremely fucking sexy."

Her eyes are swirling with heat as she pulls my hand to her chest. "Come on, let's go home."

I quickly get to my feet and follow her out of the hall and into the rain. I do not care what Ahlvo is feeling right now, or what anyone thinks. All I care about is that Elle-noor referred to me as "sexy." She did it in front of everyone I care about.

She is not disgusted by my scars.

When she breaks into a run, I follow her lead. We jog side by side until we reach my dwelling. She slams the door shut behind her once we are inside, then grabs the front of my shirt and pulls me down until she can press her lips to mine.

I move my mouth against hers, soft at first, but then demanding, just how she likes. When I feel her lips part, I slide my tongue between them, stroking her round pink tongue as she moans into my mouth.

Suddenly, she pulls away, but only to rip off her cloak, toe off her boots, and pull her shirt over her head.

My mouth waters at the sight of her light brown nipples on display, her heavy breasts bouncing as she drops her arms to her sides. I lean down to close my lips around her left nipple, but she pushes me back to my full height, and I am worried I have done something wrong.

"Get this off. Need you naked," she hisses as her hands wrap around the lower hem of my poncho. I help her, pulling off my tunic with my poncho in one swift motion. What Elle-noor wants, I am eager to give her.

Desperate to feel her bare chest against mine, I pull her into my arms, one hand gripping her ass and the other tangled in her mane. Her mouth is on mine instantly, and her tongue slides against my longer, rougher one in a way that sends the blood rushing to my cock. She wraps her legs around my middle and digs her heels into my lower back as I stumble around the first floor of my dwelling, searching for a flat surface to put her on.

The window ledge. The moment I remember its existence, I extract my fingers from Elle-noor's soft mane and wave it behind her back, knocking over everything that stands in the way of me sinking deep within her cunt.

When I finally find it, I reach my hand for the side of the frame, but I miss and shove the jugs filled with flower petals to the ground in a shattering heap. That is a problem for tomorrow, however. Because Elle-noor's mouth is on my throat, her hands tug at my mane, Stahn-lee is not here to interrupt us, and I will do nothing else before I take my mate.

CHAPTER 16

ELEANOR

’m fuming over Ahlvo's insensitive little "joke" about
Bruvix's scars, but it's hard to stay mad when a growling
Bruvix is tearing my pants off my legs with the primal vigor of a lion
seizing its prey.

Once I'm completely naked, he takes a step back and looks me up
and down.

"Are you okay?" I ask when he continues to stare at me.

"Y-yes," he replies, his voice low and husky. "I forgot how to
breathe for a moment."

I let him look his fill, letting the heat of his gaze warm me, but after
a few moments, I miss the feel of his skin against mine. He can look at
me another time. Right now, I want him stretching my insides with that
humongous cock of his. "Get over here," I say, spreading my knees
wide as I tug him toward me by the hand.

His mouth is hot on my chest as he presses kisses along my collar-
bone, and then down between my breasts. His dark blue eyes sparkle in
the soft light of the douku orbs in the corner, and he holds my gaze as
he runs the tip of his tongue in a circle around my nipple. Letting out a
moan, I arch my back, feeding more of my breast into his greedy

mouth. And he takes it all, licking and sucking and lightly biting until my entire body is trembling with need.

Reaching behind me, I shove the thick curtain aside and wrap the end around my forearm, so I can feel the night breeze against my back. It's still raining, but now it's a soft drizzle, and the infrequent droplets splashing on my skin is a welcome contrast to the sheen of sweat starting to cover my body.

Bruvix growls as he moves farther down my body, kissing across my stomach and along the stretch marks that cover my hips. "Your scent," he says in a low, breathy rumble. Then he shoves his nose into my pubic hair and groans as his eyes roll back in his head. "My body craves it."

"Mmm," I moan as his tongue traces a line from my entrance up to my clit. "Fuck that's good." When I shove my hand in his silver hair and pull, he takes it as a note to suck harder, and my back comes off the ledge as I scream.

His growl intensifies as my legs start to shake, and it's as if just giving me pleasure is getting him off too. The more he growls against my clit, the slight vibration of it creating a delicious rhythmic friction, the closer I get to falling over the edge.

"Come, Elle-noor. Come on my face," he commands, and my body obeys. My thighs clench around his head as I rock against his tongue erratically, riding out my release. I can't scream. I can't breathe. I can't do anything but sink deeper into the explosion that's lighting me up from the inside.

As I slowly come down, he stands and kisses me, stroking deeply into my mouth, and I taste myself on his tongue. Reaching between us, I untie the laces at the top of his pants and tug them down as far as I can. He chuckles against my mouth when I can't reach them anymore, and he finishes the job.

Then his cock springs free, and I'm eager to trace it with my tongue. He's huge, and the sheer size of his dick is either going to kill me or destroy my pussy for any future lovers. I'm too enticed by the latter to worry about the former.

I wrap my fingers around his hard length and stroke him as my other hand cups and massages his heavy balls. He moans into my mouth as I use the pre-come pooling at his tip to lubricate him before stroking again.

Guiding him toward my entrance, I feel him freeze, and immediately I let go. "What is it?" I ask, suddenly worried.

"I… This…I have not done this before," he says quietly. Avoiding my eyes, he starts to pull away, but I stop him immediately. "I wish I were skilled…in this. For you."

"Hey, that's okay," I tell him, placing my hands on either side of his face. "Thank you for telling me. Don't worry," I reassure him, pressing his tip to my core once again. Then I rest my hands on his back and push, making him surge inside me as I whisper, "I'm a *very* good teacher," against his lips.

A groan rumbles deep in his chest, and even though we've just begun, I feel a sense of pride hearing him make that sound just for me. Then he thrusts deep, and I'm the one left breathless. He pulls back, almost all the way out, before surging back in. "Tight. S-so tight," he growls, and after two strokes, he comes, roaring into my neck.

That was…quick. But it was his first time, so of course, it was.

"How soon can I make you come again?" he asks through ragged breaths as he kisses along my throat.

"You're ready to go again? This soon?" I ask. He can't have recovered that quickly. That seems physically impossible. But I can feel him growing and thickening inside me. That's when I realize alien dicks don't play by the rules.

"I am," he rasps into my ear, just as he pulls back and slams into me. Then he's unhinged, fucking me hard as I scratch my nails down his back, as if that first time was an awkward fluke and he was determined to get it out of the way so he could really show off.

"Like that!" I cry out, sucking air through my teeth. It burns a little, to be stretched this much, but more than anything, the fullness of him, how he's touching places deep inside me that I didn't know existed—I don't ever want him to stop. "Keep going."

I lift my legs higher, crossing my feet behind his back so I can meet his thrusts as I brace my hands against the window frame.

"You steal my breath," he whispers, stroking my jawline and pushing my hair behind my ear. "Beautiful."

I nip at his thumb, grazing the pad with my teeth before wrapping my lips around it and running my tongue over his claw.

When he starts to vibrate inside me, I almost pass out.

Fuck, he feels so good.

I pull his hand down between us and press his index finger against my clit. "Rub here," I pant. "Circles."

He does, and he follows the pitch of my moans until he finds the speed and pressure that cause my thighs to quake around him. Each time my pussy contracts and squeezes his cock, I'm rewarded with a deep, rumbling growl and his grip on my ass tightening so much that his claws bite into my skin.

I realize, as I stare at this scarred warrior buried deep inside me, that I'm the one getting to see him truly let go for the first time. I'm lucky enough to witness him in this vulnerable state, feeling the most pleasure he's ever been on the receiving end of.

It's hard to believe, honestly, that no other male or female ever found his rugged, hard exterior appealing enough to pursue.

Their loss is my gain. I show him how much I adore his body as I kiss along the scar on his jaw, then down the silver lines that crisscross along his neck, and at the top of his chest. This magnificent beast and his exceptionally large cock are mine. All mine.

"Come with me," I say as I nip at his earlobe, my body wound tight like a bowstring about to snap.

Two more hard thrusts and I'm gone, bursts of light war with darkness at the edge of my vision as I scream into his chest. He follows close behind, bellowing his release through the open window, into the cold rainy night.

When our breathing returns to normal, he gathers me in his arms and carries me up the stairs to his bedroom. Well, our room, actually. He doesn't seem to mind that I've parked myself here since we returned Stanley, and I have no plans to leave.

He pulls back the covers on the bed and gently places me on my side. Climbing in next to me, he covers us with furs and pulls my back against his front, letting out a contented sigh when I kiss each of his knuckles.

Stanley was certainly fun to spoon, but he's no Bruvix.

CHAPTER 17

ELEANOR

"Time to wake, *zala kovvari*," Bruvix purrs into my ear.

I groan at first, refusing him, and snuggling deeper into the thick, warm blankets. But when he says, "I have a pile of junasii bread for you," my stomach growls and I decide this is the perfect time to start the day.

"Mmm, okay," I mumble as I pull Bruvix down for a quick kiss. "Breakfast in bed?" I ask, opening my mouth as he holds up the plate.

"You wish for me to feed you?" he asks, looking puzzled.

"You would refuse the woman who punched your V card?" I ask in mock surprise.

His brow furrows even more, and I'm pretty sure I've lost him. "What is this vee card?"

I sit up and take the plate from his hands and shove a big piece of warm junasii bread into my mouth with a moan. "It means I took your virginity," I tell him after I swallow. He hands me a mug of gu'tuu tea, and I take a long sip. "By the way," I begin, remembering the thing I've been meaning to tell him ever since our friendship went from platonic to sexually beneficial, "I'm bisexual, just so you know."

He says nothing. Just blinks his dark blue eyes, waiting for me to elaborate.

"It means I'm attracted to men and women," I tell him. "Is that… going to be an issue?" *Please don't let it be an issue*, I silently pray.

He tilts his head to the side. "Why would this bother me?"

"I don't know," I reply. "Sometimes it bothers people."

He clasps his hands in his lap. "I did not know there was a name for such a thing. On Trovilia, my home planet, people chose pleasure mates among all genders. It was not discussed in such a way."

"Wow," I reply, envious that he grew up in such an open-minded environment. "So people loved whomever they loved?"

"Fucked whomever they fucked," he adds as his mouth quirks up on one side. He takes a piece of bread off the plate and holds it against my lips until I open for him. "You are just as you should be."

I bite into it and let out an "mmm" that's partially for the food, but mainly for the most lovely response he just gave.

"I must tell you something," he says next, his chin dropping to his chest.

"Okay…" I reply, nerves twisting my insides.

He clears his throat, and whispers, "You are my mate, Elle-noor. My inara."

Oh.

Oh wow.

I'm not exactly sure what "inara" means, but given the context, I'm guessing it's similar to mate, and that's a big fucking deal. I… don't know how to respond. I mean, I know how I feel. I love being with him, and the sex is the best I've ever had, but am I ready to like, get married to this guy and promise him forever?

The girls all seem deliriously happy with their alien mates, and I know those courtships did not last a long time before they officially became mates. I just don't know if I'm ready for that.

Before I can respond, Bruvix presses a finger against my lips and says, "It is all right if you do not return my feelings. I understand this."

"You…do?"

He nods, dropping his hands in his lap. "Humans do not feel the tether in the way we do. Cloh-ee had no idea she was Varrek's inara. He had to tell her."

Interesting. I nod, my mouth still agape as I mumble, "Oh. Okay…"

"That is why I am prepared to wait. I do not care how long it takes, Elle-noor." The corner of his mouth quirks up, forming that crooked smile I can't get enough of. "I shall spend the rest of my days trying to capture your heart the way you have captured mine, if I must."

Stunned. I'm stunned. I've never been on the receiving end of such a romantic statement before. "I don't know what to say," I finally reply. I want to return the sentiment, but this soon, I wouldn't be telling the truth. I don't know for sure that Bruvix is my mate; the one I want to spend the rest of my days with. Things are going well between us, but the beginning of a relationship is always thrilling. What happens when the thrill is gone?

"You need not say anything at all, Elle-noor," he says. Then he continues to feed me breakfast, occasionally mushing the viiki spread used for dipping on the corner of my mouth and then promptly licking it off. When there's no more food to play with, I reluctantly get up and change into a tunic and leggings and pull my hair into a loose ponytail.

Bruvix says good-bye with a long, toe-curling kiss that has me tempted to call in sick for dish duty, then gives me a slap on the ass before I head out the door.

I find myself skipping, actually skipping, to the meal hall.

"Morivikka, Elle-noor," Waldric says with a big toothy grin when I arrive.

"Mornin', Waldric! How goes it?" I reply, filling one of the dish buckets with soap.

"It goes…well," he says after a look of confusion flashes across his face. "You seem quite jovial today, Elle-noor. More so than usual. Why is this?"

"I'm alive, I have a roof over my head, and food on the table. What's not to be happy about?" I reply, repeating a phrase my mother would often say when I was a kid. She always tried to get me to see the good in everything, no matter what was going on in our lives.

"I see… That was true yesterday, and the day before, however," Waldric points out, "what is different about this day that puts the twinkle in your eye?"

Well, isn't he observant? It's not that I'm trying to keep my relationship a secret from the clan. They've seen me with Bruvix several times, and I'm sure most, if not all, are aware that I'm staying at his house. "I guess I'm finally feeling settled here," I tell him, letting Bruvix's words settle into my mind. "This place is better than I expected it to be."

He nods, his expression warm as he reaches for the mashing tool and starts mixing a pot of boiled root vegetables together. "I understand this. It is a good life."

I want to scream that his life would be better with the clan's stunning inventor by his side, and that he should make a move already, but I focus on scrubbing the crumpled, drying tea leaves from the mugs instead. It's not really any of my business.

By the time my dish shift ends, and the last bowl is placed on the drying rack, I notice Krahn, one of the hunters and the backup cook when Waldric needs a break, coming to begin the lunch shift.

Score!

While the two of them discuss the meal selections for lunch and dinner, I sneak over to the compact freezer that sits beneath the storage shelves along the back wall of the meal hall, my pack in hand. It's right next to the dirty rag box, so I fold a few on top, pretending to look busy. Then, after I check to make sure they aren't looking this way, I pull out a thick slab of raw kuhnypa meat and shove it in my pack. Then I fiddle with the rags for a couple extra minutes for show.

I drape the strap of my pack over my shoulder and shoot Waldric and Krahn a quick wave. "Bye, guys!"

"Oh, Elle-noor! Before you depart..." Waldric trails off as he jogs over to me.

Shit, shit, shit.

"You forgot this," he whispers as he holds out a strip of fabric that looks like a padded compression sleeve.

"What is it?" I ask because it's definitely not mine.

"You will need it to preserve the raw kuhnypa meat you took."

He saw me? I really thought I nailed that little food caper. I go to reach for it, but he pulls back. "You must make a promise to me."

"Okay," I reply timidly. Does he know I've been observing the tr'gorys up close? He can't know. No, there's no way.

"Whatever it is that you are doing, keep yourself safe," he says, his eyes swirling with concern like a big brother. I love him for it. "You do that, and I will not tell a soul about the items that have disappeared from the hall as of late."

I nod as he hands me the cold pack. "I promise."

He gives me a sly grin before turning back to rejoin Krahn at the grills, and I head home with a tasty snack for Nanay and her babies, that definitely won't go bad now.

I shout Bruvix's name once I get inside, but he's clearly not home. Probably still at a training session. So, I take a leisurely shower and spend the next few hours reviewing the overnight footage from the security cameras.

By the time Bruvix gets home, I'm frustrated. Nanay, Stanley, and the rest of the litter are nowhere to be found on the feeds. The all-adult pack is captured as they do their nightly stroll through the village, but Nanay and the babies aren't with them.

"I am going to work in the garden, Elle-noor," he says, leaning down to kiss my forehead as I check the different perimeter cams from other angles, slowing it down to see if I can catch a glimpse of a tail or a flash of red eyes.

"Mmm-hmm," I mumble, not looking up from the screen. I don't understand why she doesn't want to be seen. Or how she's even able to avoid the cameras when they're set up all over the damn village. Does she take a super long back way to come up from behind the falls? Is she doing it intentionally? We really need to set up another camera out there.

When I've looked through the feeds twice more and find nothing, I throw in the towel. Hopefully, I'll be able to see her tonight and figure out how she remains so elusive.

A heavy knock at the door pulls my attention, and I jog downstairs to answer it. Swinging the door open, I find Ava and Ahlvo wearing matching apologetic smiles.

"Hey, Eleanor," Ava greets with a small wave.

"Elle-noor," Ahlvo says, his tone grave. "I wish to apologize for my comments about Bruvix's face...and his scars. I apologized to him at the training session, earlier, but I wanted to tell you as well that it was not my intention to offend. It was merely a joke. A terrible one that was not humorous at all."

"Thank you," I reply, pleasantly surprised once again by the kind hearts of this clan. "I appreciate you saying that."

"Yeah, it's a joke the guys have been throwing around for years," Ava adds. "I don't think they realized how cruel it was until you pointed it out."

"I get it," I reply with a nod, remembering the times I've repeated an insensitive joke because I knew the group I was with would laugh. Sometimes you need an outsider to call you out in order to see that your behavior is toxic. "We're good," I say to Ahlvo before we exchange good-byes.

"Elle-noor!" Bruvix hollers from upstairs, just inside the door to the roof garden. "I wish to show you something."

He's leaning against the door with his arms crossed, a lazy smile lifting the corners of his lips when I meet him on the top floor. His hair is mussed and a layer of dirt and sweat glistens on his face and bare chest.

"You've got a surprise for me?" I ask, leaning up on my toes to press my lips to his.

"I do," he mutters into my mouth as he swings the door open.

My breath hitches at the sight in front of me. Dusk has just darkened the sky to a deep, eggplant purple, and dozens of douku orbs line the wall enclosing the garden. The flowers dance in the slight breeze, and the newly bloomed pilois, some tall, some short, and in various shades of pink, provide a warm, romantic contrast to the cool greens and yellows of the rest of the plants.

But the best part is the pile of furs situated between the beds of growing piloi flowers. They're growing so tall, and there's a subtle droop to their thick, velvety petals, indicating they will fall soon. For now, though, they lean over the blankets like a protective canopy shielding us from the night sky and the rest of the universe.

I'm about to tell Bruvix just how lucky he's about to get, but I'm pretty sure I'm the lucky one here.

CHAPTER 18

BRUVIX

The glow of the douku orbs pales in comparison to the breathtaking sight of Elle-noor's smile as she takes in the romantic setting I created for her. She has been so focused on the well-being of Stahn-lee and the tr'gorys ever since she arrived, and I realized when I was deep inside her wet heat that I have not done enough to prioritize her. I want so many more of her smiles. I am greedy for them.

She takes my hand and leads me toward the stack of furs I assembled and pulls me down with her until we are seated side by side. "This is...wow," she mutters, looking around with wide eyes. "You did all this for me?"

Of course, it is for her. "I did not do it for myself," I reply. Handing her a mug filled with amber liquid, a thick layer of white foam hovering at the top.

"Is this…" she asks.

I nod, reaching for my own full mug. "It is. Ale-noor, ready to taste."

She lets out an excited giggle, then tips her head back as she takes a big sip. I watch, studying her reaction, hoping with every cell in my body that she likes it. "Mmm," she mutters, smacking her lips together as she looks down at the remaining contents of her mug. "It's the perfect amount of sweet! I honestly did not expect it to taste good at all." Her eyes widen as she takes another sip. "I'm not much of a beer person. Never have been, but this is delish!"

I had a feeling she would enjoy it. I tasted it the moment I removed it from the container of darkness, and while it is sweeter than I usually prefer my ales to taste, I knew Elle-noor would deem it perfect. "I am glad your ale is to your liking."

She laughs, and the way it causes her breasts to jiggle makes my cock stir.

"Tell me about Earth," I say, after taking a pull of ale-noor. "Do you miss the life you had?" The more time I spend with her, the more I realize how little I know of her life before she came here. I wish to remedy that this eve, because when it comes to Elle-noor, I want to know everything there is to know.

"Well," she begins, tilting her head back to stare at the sky above, "Frank was the center of my universe before I was taken, but you already knew that."

This is true. She has told me many tales about her dog-goh, as she refers to him, and how his humorous antics would make her laugh.

Sadness flashes across her face as she takes another sip. "I just..." she stops, sucking in a breath. Clearing her throat, she starts again. "I found Frank at an abandoned house down the street from me. His owners moved and just...left him there, in the front yard." A tear slips down her cheek. "My neighbors told me about it, actually. They said he was super aggressive and wouldn't let anyone get close. But when I went through the gate," she wipes the drip from her nose and smiles, "I crouched down at the edge of the property and waited.

"And within ten minutes, he came to me. Just...trotted over with a nervous, but hopeful wag of his tail. At that moment, he became mine. I took him home and we were inseparable." Elle-noor stares off into the distance and puts her mug down. Then her forehead creases and a sob racks her body. "I know Olivia will treat him well, I just..." The tears are coming in steady streams, and the muscles in my chest clench at the sight. "I don't want him to think that I-I left him t-too," she mutters through deep sniffles. "He deserves better th-than that."

I am desperate to take her pain away. But I do not know how, and it is breaking my insides. "What can I do, Elle-noor?" I plead. "Is there someone I can destroy? Would that ease the pain in your heart? Give me a name and I shall bring you their head."

"No," she chuckles, wiping her sleeve across her cheek. "But you can hold me. That will make it better."

Before I take my next breath, I lift her into my arms and drape her sideways across my lap. She drops her head against my chest and sighs.

"Mmm, thank you," she whispers. After a few moments of quiet, she says, "I had a good childhood."

"Oh?" I ask. "Tell me."

"My parents worked hard. We didn't have much," she says with a nod. "We had all the basics to keep us comfortable, though." She is no longer crying, and that puts me at ease. I feel her smile against my chest. "Once a month, my mom would take me with her to the Korean grocery store in the next town, and she'd let me pick out candy or a treat. Whatever I wanted. I remember running through the aisles and grabbing the biggest treat I could fit in my hands."

"These tiny hands?" I say, flattening her palm against mine. "I do not imagine you were able to hold much."

She laughs, the sound warm and sweet. "Usually, it was just tea cookies or rice cakes."

"Your mother sounds kind."

"She is," Elle-noor replies. "She was tough on me sometimes, mostly about my weight, but I know she loved me, even if she didn't always show it. Whenever I had a friend stay over, she always had a new pair of slippers for them to wear. And her kimchi!" She lets out a squeal. "It was the best."

I press my lips against her mane, breathing in her scent.

"What about you?" she asks, lifting her chin to meet my gaze. "Tell me about your parents."

"Well," I start, "my mother's soul took its final rest after contracting the virus that ravaged our people. It took Varrek's mother as well. My mother went not long after Varrek's mother. They were sisters, you see," I explain.

"I'm so sorry, Bruvix," she says, squeezing my hand.

I squeeze back, silently thanking her for the contact. "My father, he is a good male, but stubborn…aloof."

"Hmm, who does that sound like?" she asks, her tone teasing.

"I pleaded with him to leave Trovilia with us. To come here and begin anew."

"He didn't want to?"

"No," I reply, huffing a breath at the memory. "He refused to spend his remaining days away from my mother's resting place. He said he could never be happy if he could not visit with her each morning."

Her eyes widen. "Wow, that's incredibly romantic, and also heart-breaking."

I nod in agreement. "It is. I hope her nearness continues to give him the comfort he requires."

"I'm sure it does," Elle-noor says. "Do you miss him?"

"I do," I tell her. "Knowing he is where he wishes to be makes it easier, however."

She smiles, and it makes me forget my own name. "Okay, enough about the past. Did you have a good day?"

"Yes, it was wonderful," I reply.

"Really?" she asks, bending her knee and placing her pointy chin in her palm. "What was so wonderful about it?"

"Well, most of the day was fine. Adequate. But when I came home to you, it turned wonderful. That is always the case," I tell her.

Her long eyelashes flutter closed as her cheeks turn pink.

I look down at her wide brown eyes, always shining with curiosity and love. "Kay-teh asked me about you today. I saw her after her witch lesson, and she asked how my heart feels about you."

"Oh yeah? And what'd you tell her?"

I tap my claws on the outside of the mug, enjoying the memory of the conversation. "I told her that you are…the one I never expected to find."

"You scare me, you know?" Elle-noor replies. Then visibly gulps. "Because you feel like everything."

I run a finger along her cheek and down the slope of her tiny nose. "I do not want you to fear me, Elle-noor. There is nothing I would not do to keep you safe."

"No, not like that," she says, her gaze dropping to the ale. "I just wasn't expecting to fall so hard so fast."

"This is… a bad thing?" I ask, worried about her answer.

"Not bad. Not at all. Just a surprise."

A comfortable silence stretches on, but eventually, Elle-noor breaks it. "Um, I was thinking of going to feed Nanay and Stanley tonight. Will you come with me?"

This does not come as a surprise to me. I have seen her body deflate slightly when she watches the tr'gorys on the feed. It is interesting to her but is not the same as seeing them close. We still have not been able to track the mother on any of the cameras. She finds this as puzzling as I do, and while my solution is to merely leave the mother alone and forget about her and her litter, Elle-noor wishes to get close to them and observe them with nothing to protect her from a sudden attack.

"I do not like it," I tell her honestly. "You are in great danger each time you face them. Especially a mother with her pups. You do not know of what they are capable."

"Yes, I do!" she exclaims. "I don't take any of this lightly. I can do this in a way that's safe. I promise." When I do not immediately respond, she says, "I understand why this is hard for you. I'm sure it triggers all kinds of memories of your friend who was killed."

"That is not it," I tell her. Those memories are certainly not good ones, but that is not what rattles my bones each time we approach the falls, knowing a tr'gory will probably show its face. I suppose it is time to tell her the real reason. If I am going to woo her, if she is to become my inara someday, she should know how I got these scars she is so fond of.

"I was in training. My warrior training. Still a very young male. I was dropped in the wilds on the planet of Xelai where we were to make camp on our own and traverse the mountainside in search of our individual targets," I explain. "My target was a bot, tied up and wearing a bright yellow shirt with the matching symbol we were each given at the start of the mission. We were required to capture our target and take them to the designated location."

Elle-noor does not ask questions. She does not interrupt. She merely watches me with rapt attention as I continue my violent, tragic tale.

"The warrior who completed the mission the fastest would get a full day's head start on the next mission. We never knew what that mission would be, but time was currency, and that amount of time could mean the difference between life and death, in some cases," I say, running a hand through my hair as I dive deeper into this memory.

"It was the second eve after the mission began. I was exhausted, cold, and not sure of my direction in this section of the forest. I spent so much time retracing my steps that I was unable to acquire a safe place to sleep that eve. So, I wandered and continued until I heard something behind me. Following me." I swallow the lump forming in my throat, making it feel as if it is shrinking.

"I pulled my dagger from its sheath, but by the time I turned, it was too late. The beast was on top of me. The mit'xcruul," I say, a shudder racking my body as I picture the creature. "It clawed and slashed and dug at my flesh as if it were looking for something deep inside my chest cavity. I suppose that thing was meat." I bark out a sardonic laugh. "I tried to fight. I stabbed it several times in the side, and in the gut, but when it went for my face, I–I don't know what happened," I say, feeling Elle-noor's hand curling into a fist as I speak. "I remember feeling my skin hanging off my cheek."

Elle-noor lets out a gasp.

"And feeling the wetness of the blood as it ran down onto my chest. And...and the sharpness of my bone. I felt it. My brow bone," I say, mimicking the motion from that eve. "I woke up with a bandage covering half my face, and several around my chest and shoulders."

"My god, Bruvix," Elle-noor says in a choked whisper. "You're so lucky to be alive."

"I am," I agree. "I do not know what made the mit'xcruul halt its attack, or who found me and transported me to the healers, but by all accounts, I should not have survived."

"But you did," she points out. "Look, I understand why you don't want to be anywhere near a tr'gory."

"It is less about me being near one and possibly attacked," I realize, this very moment, "and more about seeing one attack you, and being unable to stop them."

She nods as a tear slides down her cheek. "I get that," she says, huffing out a breath. "If it helps, I can go alone."

Did she not just hear me? "That does nothing to ease my concerns, Elle-noor. I do not want you going. It is you I worry about," I repeat.

"I know, but ignorance is bliss, right?" she says with a casual shrug. "If you're not watching me feed them, you won't experience the same amount of distress as you would if you were right next to me."

"No," I reply. "I will go with you."

"Bruvix," she begins, "I don't want you to put yourself in that situation. I don't want you reliving that trauma. I can ask someone else to go with me. One of the hunters," she says. "I'm sure they'd be willing to keep it hush, hush."

I do not care if every hunter in our clan gleefully volunteered to accompany Elle-noor to observe the tr'gorys and vowed to keep it secret. I am the one who will go with her. "It will be me."

"Why?" she asks. "Why would you put yourself through that?"

I tell her the truth. "Because the others are not as willing to die for you as I am. Which means they are incapable of protecting you the way I can."

She sighs, rolling her eyes. "Fine."

I smile at her and watch as her eyes brighten the moment I agree to accompany her on this quest. There is nothing I would not do for those smiles. They breathe life into my bones.

Leaving our home, I keep her smiles in the forefront of my mind as I lead the way toward the falls once the village grows quiet and the clan is asleep. Her smile is what I see when I hear a branch snap nearby, when Elle-noor lets out a gasp, thinking she saw something when it was merely a shadow. Her smile is what keeps my feet moving forward once the narrow path widens, once Elle-noor steps around me, exposing her small, vulnerable body to Nanay and her pups once they emerge.

The way her entire face lights up the dark forest when Stahn-lee eats a strip of jerky the moment she drops it in front of him. The way her lips quirk up as she scribbles notes onto her screen pad as the tr'gorys consume the meat she brought for them.

One of them could pounce on my chest right now, and if it made Elle-noor smile the way she is now, I would let them rip me apart. I would endure it, for her.

CHAPTER 19

ELEANOR

"No longer seems to be nursing."

"All pups seem to be eating solid foods."

"Pups are now the size of adult golden retrievers. Continuing to grow at rapid pace."

"Nanay makes sure all pups feed before taking her portion."

I continue making notes on my screen pad about last night's feed before I forget. Getting to watch the tr'gorys interact up close was a breathtaking experience. I'm learning so much about the dynamics between mother and baby that I'm starting to feel less afraid each time I meet them at the falls.

I wish I could say the same for Bruvix. He's clearly still shaky when we get close to them, or specifically, when *I* get close to them, but he's handling it like a champ. He knows how important this is for me, and he wants to be part of it. And that makes me fall even harder for him.

At tonight's feed, I'm going to try to hand-feed Nanay and, if she'll let me, the pups too. I feel like I'm starting to gain her trust, so it's likely that she will. All I do is show up and offer food without trying to take anything from her. She's realizing I'm no longer a threat to her and her four babies, and that makes me feel like a million bucks.

There's no greater gift than earning an animal's trust.

"Will remain in seated position about four feet away with meat in open hand," I write down as part of my action plan for tonight. I want to get there early, right when the sun goes down. After his final training session of the day, which is in a few hours, Bruvix is planning to meet me by the gray tree that's always dropping meatball-sized acorns at the start of the narrow path. The clan will still be awake, and most will be at dinner, so it's a risk, but I'm trying to gauge whether they're actually nocturnal animals, or if they stay away from the village during daylight hours because of us.

I finish with my notes and hop in the shower for a quick rinse. Once I'm clean and my wet hair is tied in a ballerina bun, I head up to the roof to water Bruvix's flowers. We're about to enter the cold season, so the rainy days are about to get few and far between.

A jittery chirping sounds from behind me as I prune the dead leaves from the vakopurri plant, and I turn to find a small brown bird with a white beak and green and white speckles covering its wings. "Hiya, birdie," I say, crouching into a squat.

It continues chirping as it hops around in a half circle, then it stops when it comes across a crumb on the floor from the bread I was eating earlier. "Ah, looking for a snack, huh?" I rise, lightly stepping over the bird and toward the ledge where I left my crust wrapped in a napkin. I return to the bird's side and drop a few more crumbs in front of it.

Within moments, three more of the bird's friends arrive, and I turn into "the bird lady," one landing on my head, and another landing on my shoulder as they lightly peck at the crumbs that I drop for them. Once the breadcrumbs are gone, I wonder if my unique animal connection is really that unique, or if animals have always sought me out because I frequently had food in my pocket.

Will the birds stay now that the food is gone? Or will they fly off and only return when they want more bread?

The one on my shoulder flies off immediately. Then the original bird, the one with the brown spot on the tip of its beak, starts hopping around on the floor with a light flap to its wings. "What are you trying to tell me?" I ask.

When it turns and starts hopping away, I instinctually follow. If the bird wanted to leave, it would just fly away, wouldn't it? The bird from atop my head flutters down and lands on my wrist as I continue trotting behind the one with the spotted beak.

"Okay, this is a thing that's happening," I mutter to myself, wondering how silly I look. "I'm following a bird around a garden."

When it leads me to the expansive huutra vines, I hear a louder, angrier chirping coming from above. I look up and spot a nest made of brown reeds and blades of grass tucked into the top right corner of the doorway leading into Bruvix's house. Another of these birds sits in the nest, cawing and chirping at a frantic pitch.

Now I'm confused. Why did this bird want to show me its nest?

Is there an injured bird somewhere around here? Spotted Beak hops around the outer huutra vines, doing its little dance around my feet.

Hmm.

The bird perched on my wrist flies back to the nest as I bend down and slowly pull back the vines, one by one. Spotted Beak hops closer to me, and its chirps grow louder, and that's when I see it: a brown egg. Smaller than a standard chicken egg, this one is about two-thirds the size, and slightly wider.

Carefully, I pick up the egg and place it in my palm. I step onto the wooden chest next to the door and lift my fragile cargo toward the nest. "Is this okay? You gonna let me do this?" I ask the birds as they squawk and hop on the edge of the nest, seemingly saying, "Yes! That's it! You found it!"

"Here you go, little bird family," I whisper as the two birds guarding the nest hop aside, so I can place the egg in the center, surrounded by three other eggs. "Okay," I mutter once my job is done. "See you later."

Spotted Beak flies toward my face and I flinch. But when I open my eyes, I find the bird with its claws wrapped around the neck of my tunic. It brushes its beak against the tip of my nose, just once, before flying away.

My lips form an unwavering smile as I continue checking on Bruvix's plant babies, reveling in the fact that for whatever reason, animals do feel safe with me. It just adds to my confidence that I can keep observing the tr'gorys up close in a way that's safe for all involved. I carefully transfer the alien caterpillars to the other side of the roof from the qam shrub, according to Bruvix's very specific instructions, and I grab my pack on my way out to meet my man.

Several minutes pass after I reach the acorn tree, but there's no sign of Bruvix. It's okay. His training session is probably running long. It's fine. He'll be here. He wouldn't forget about me.

I fiddle with my grandmother's ring to pass the time. I pull it off, then tug it back into place, again and again, as the minutes tick past, wondering where the hell he is.

Eventually, he'll come. I know he will, but how long will I have to wait here? And what if someone sees me? It's risky enough being out here when the clan is still awake. It's not like I'm loitering on the main path for all to see, but I'm not completely hidden, either.

When I check the time on my screen pad, it tells me that Bruvix is officially forty minutes late. Maybe he decided against coming with me? Maybe this much face-to-face interaction with the tr'gorys has proven too triggering for him?

If I step onto the main path and go back for him, at this time of day, someone will see me for sure and they'll wonder what I'm doing on the path toward the falls. It's safer if I wait it out.

But what if he never shows up? What if I'm leaning against this stupid meatball acorn tree until the sun rises?

Ugh, fuck it.

I'm going alone. Bruvix knows exactly where I am, and he can meet me whenever he's done. Even if he doesn't, I've shown him that I can handle myself, haven't I? I mean, he explicitly told me he didn't want me going alone, but that was before last night's feed. He saw how smoothly that went. I'm sure he trusts me enough to let me do this without him.

I step lightly down the narrow path until I reach the clearing. Nanay and her babies aren't here yet, but that gives me time to get situated. I set a towel down in the dirt and kneel on it, placing my open pack at my side, so I can easily reach in for tr'gory snacks.

After about half an hour, I hear a branch snap from beyond the falls, and Nanay slowly steps out into the moonlight, her pups on her heels.

I smile, mouth closed, just in case she interprets exposed teeth as a sign of aggression and remain still. One of the pups begins to gallop toward me, but Nanay ducks her snout down just as he's about to pass her, blocking him from coming any closer. I think it's Stanley, but they're all getting so big, it's hard to tell.

I let Nanay get comfortable, plopping her butt down on the ground as the pups roll and crawl and lie down next to her. Then I reach inside my pack and pull out a slab of raw kuhnypa meat. For this one, I toss it toward the tr'gorys. I want to reaffirm the trust we've been building before I make the move to hand-feed them.

Just like the last two feedings, Nanay tears the meat into chunks using her fangs and claws, dropping them one by one in front of her pups. Once they're fed, she devours the rest of it.

Carefully, I pull out my screen pad to jot down some notes about her body language and the order in which the pups are fed to see if I discover any patterns. Then it's time for me to do what I came here to do. I pull out a smaller slab of meat and leave it in my open palm. Nanay looks down at my hand, then her gaze lifts to mine, then back down at the meat. We play this game for a while, then, ultimately, she stands and lumbers over to me, always keeping her eyes on mine. She's not looking at the meat as she approaches. She's waiting for a trap.

But I surprise her by remaining perfectly still, shoulders relaxed and spine straight. I mean her no harm, and I want her to fully understand that. Almost in slow motion, her lips curl back, exposing her fangs, as she reaches for the slab. Without touching my hand, she sinks her front fangs into the slab and pulls as she retreats. When she's back to her original position, about three feet away, she visibly relaxes and begins the process of sharing the meat with her pups.

I'm down to my third and final slab, and I have big plans for this one. Knowing she shares with the pups, I took this slab home and chopped it into even chunks, so I could hopefully feed each of them myself.

This is all about timing, though. Since I'll be feeding them and not Nanay, I need to make sure they each get their portions simultaneously, so there's no roughhousing or competing for their share. I reach into my pack with both hands and grab the chunks from the frozen sleeve. I pull them out in tight grips, turning my palms over so they can't just pounce on me. Moving my hands in front of them, and after they each sniff and lick at my knuckles, I drop a chunk in front of the closest pup. This forces them to be gentle, in a way, because they don't get rewarded if they bite their way to the treat. They need to wait until I'm ready to release it.

Stanley's tongue hangs out the side of his mouth, almost as if he's smiling at me, as I hand him his piece. I make sure to give his chest a quick rub as he eats, so he knows I remember him.

I keep the biggest piece in the center of my left palm, and turn my palm over as I present Nanay with her treat. She takes it gingerly, much like last time, but with slightly less hesitation.

I'm buzzing with excitement that this worked, and I can't wait to tell Bruvix. As I go to lean forward and wipe my hands on the towel, my screen pad falls from my lap, landing with a soft thud at Stanley's feet. Just as dropping my phone back on Earth would send me leaping into traffic to protect my screen from shattering, my hand shoots out instinctively, reaching for it before I can truly comprehend what I'm doing.

Nanay must perceive this as an act of aggression, or at the very least, an unexpected action that must be stopped, just in case it brings harm to her or her babies. Her black lips curl back, as a bark mixed with a growl shoots out of her.

She sinks her fangs into my forearm, and I'm so shocked by it that I don't even realize what's happened until I look down at the dirty screen pad in my hand and the furious tr'gory attached to my arm.

A scream dies in my throat as I yank my arm, attempting to pull myself free. But that just makes her angrier, and she deepens her bite until I can feel her fangs hit bone. A sob bubbles up in my chest, and I wonder if this is how I die—doing something I love. Something I'm supposed to be good at. Something I've been told not to do on my own.

"Please," I beg as tears stream down my cheeks.

At some point, Nanay must sense my distress, or maybe she decides a sad human makes for a mediocre meal, I don't know, but she lets go. I scramble to my feet, dropping my screen pad once again, this time leaving it behind. Covering the open wound with my other hand, I run. I refuse to look down at it because I don't want to see the damage. Frankly, I'm not sure I can stomach it.

Wetness drips from my fingertips as I apply pressure, and I can only imagine how much blood I'm losing right now.

I cry out as I continue to push forward.

Just make it to the main path.

Help is on the main path.

I repeat this in my head until I break through the trees, tripping over a raised stump, and spill onto the dirt and moss on my knees. "Help! Help me, please!" I bellow, looking for someone, anyone, because I'm not sure I can make it to Kaiva's on my own.

At that same moment, Bruvix and Varrek step into view, and when Bruvix's stormy blue eyes meet mine, fear paralyzes me.

Bruvix charges toward me, and my last thought before everything goes black isn't if I'll survive this, but whether Bruvix will ever be able to forgive me.

CHAPTER 20

BRUVIX

"Now we finish with a round of bow sprints!" Varrek calls out to the crew. Happiness ripples through the normally stoic group of warriors because this drill is a favorite.

Normally, I would be just as excited, but today is not that day. Time draws near for me to meet Elle-noor by the ayy-corn tree, as she calls it, to accompany her to another tr'gory feeding. If I am late, she will worry.

As we line up, bows in hand, Varrek signals for the next warrior to take off in a full charge. He waits to the count of ten, then signals the one after. When it is my turn, I run as fast as my legs will allow, doing a full lap around the clearing that makes up our training grounds. Reaching the end of the circle, I raise my bow with my left arm extended, arrow nocked in place. Pulling the string back to line up with the edge of my mouth, I let out an exhale, and release. My arrow whirs through the air, making a slight curve at the end of its journey, landing in the center target with a quiet *thunk*.

After all ten of us hit the center circle, knocking each other's arrows from the target block, we tidy up the space by putting our bows and arrows in the weapon shed.

I feel a sense of relief that the drill went so quickly as I jog out of the clearing, but when Varrek calls my name, my heart drops into my gut.

"Come to my dwelling for a moment. We must discuss a strategy to handle Bzzsil Chi," he says when he reaches me. I want to give him an excuse as to why I cannot, but he says, "Queen Ekoya will be calling shortly, hopefully to assist us with this."

I let out a sigh. "Very well," I tell him.

"You do not have other pressing matters to attend to, correct?" he asks.

Yes, I must meet my mate, who has not indicated she is interested in becoming my mate, to feed a tr'gory and her pups that you still have no knowledge of. "No, certainly not."

"Come," Varrek exclaims as he clasps my shoulder. We meet Ahlvo in Varrek's training room and strategize possible ways Bzzsil Chi could attempt to retaliate. If he shows up, I will be alerted via the perimeter scanners.

"We shall usher all non-hunters and non-warriors into the top level of Kaiva's home," Varrek says, running through the plan we decided on. "Apart from the few who have designated roles in the attack."

Ahlvo nods, adding, "That is the most secure area in the village as it can lock from the inside. The rest of us will hide in our specified locations and attack from above once they enter the village."

It is only after Varrek clears his throat, sending me a questioning gaze, that I realize my foot taps against the chair. "Are you well, Bruvix? Do you not think this plan will work?"

"It is fine," I bark out, the tone harsher than intended. "I do not like envisioning Bzzsil Chi's presence here."

They seem to believe my story, nodding in agreement. "He is an utter waste of functioning organs," Ahlvo says. "But we will make it through whatever he unleashes upon us. I am not worried."

I am not either. Bzzsil fails as a formidable opponent. In hand-to-hand combat, I would best him with my eyes covered and my hands tied to a tree. The question remains who he will bring with him, and how much experience they have in committing senseless acts of violence. Because of the way Bzzsil works, he will want no witnesses, and he will gladly walk away from a bloodbath if it protects his empire.

Whatever occurs, Elle-noor lives. I will not have it any other way. I hope she is still by the ayy-corn tree. She would not go on her own, would she? Surely not after I asked her never to do so.

Just as her bright smile enters my thoughts, Varrek's screen pad buzzes, and Queen Ekoya's face appears in front of us.

"Ah, my friends," she says in greeting.

"Queen Ekoya, it is an honor to speak with you," Varrek says with his head bowed in respect. "Thank you for taking the ti–"

"Enough of this, Varrek," she interrupts. "Do not address me as if we did not spend our childhood together using rags and furs to build fortresses in this very castle."

The three of us chuckle at that, and I marvel at the sight of her—wearing a crown when, by all accounts, she should be dead. It still amazes me.

"I have been briefed by Nalba on the current situation," she continues, and to that, Varrek scoffs.

"I realize she is your kin, but she should not be providing details on security concerns. That is my duty as leader of this clan," he mutters, crossing his arms over his chest.

Ekoya shrugs. "It is what she does. If you wish to change her, be my guest."

He scoffs again, this time with a half-chuckle. "That is a pointless quest that would only end in misery."

She laughs. "Yes, I concur. Now, I have a contact at the Nu'Piix Enbalo tavern who says they can keep watch Bzzsil Chi's movements over the coming days."

"How did you manage to establish this contact?" Ahlvo asks with a grin, clearly impressed.

"I have many contacts all over the galaxy, Ahlvo. I am a queen, after all."

"This is true," he adds with a chuckle.

"They will track shipments in and out of port and can secure access to the travel logs if any of his ships leave," she tells us.

"There are many reasons I am acquiring ways to monitor the comings and goings of Bzzsil Chi. Assisting you is a delightful bonus."

Varrek nods, seemingly pleased with this information. "If he sends someone this way, or decides to travel here himself, we will have two days to prepare for his arrival."

"Correct," Ekoya replies. "I shall alert you immediately with any updates."

"Thank you for your help, My Queen," I say, though it comes out as an impatient growl.

"Pleasure as always to see your scowl, Bruvix," she replies, then disconnects the call.

The three of us look at each other, silently agreeing this is the best possible outcome for a potential attack on our village. If Bzzsil is foolish enough to attempt this, we will be prepared. He will not live to see another day.

"Right," I say. "I am leaving now." Varrek says he will join me on my walk toward the meal hall as Ahlvo departs, heading back to his home. "I am not hungry," I tell Varrek. "I must see to other tasks."

Varrek stops me just before we reach the main path and clasps a hand on my shoulder. "I do not see you at the hall very much lately, cousin. Is all well?"

No. All is not well. I am extremely late to meet my female at the falls so she can feed a dangerous predator raw meat from her hand. "Yes" is what I reply, however, because I cannot reveal the truth.

He stares at me for a long moment, his lips pursing as he searches my face. Finally, he shrugs, accepting my words. Just as we step out onto the soft blue moss that covers the main path, a familiar voice cries out for help in a frightened and anguished tone. My heart stops beating in my chest completely at the sound.

It is Elle-noor.

We spot her a long way ahead of us, clutching at her forearm as blood spills from beneath her hand, running down to her elbow and onto her clothes. My body reacts in an instant—adrenaline pumping hard through my blood as my feet race to reach her. She collapses onto the ground before I can catch her, and I see the whites of her eyes as her lashes flutter closed.

I hear Varrek shout something at my side, but I do not know if it is directed at me, Elle-noor, or someone else, and I do not care. All I care about is Elle-noor.

I gather her carefully in my arms and lift her, looking for any other visible wounds on her fragile body. Finding none brings me no peace, however, because of the large gash on her arm. Her skin is turning a shade of pale I have not yet seen. Her lips are dry, and the normal rich pink of them has been replaced by a faded, dull blush.

"I-I'm okay," Elle-noor mumbles in a hoarse whisper as she awakens.

"You are not," I reply, my tone harsh and angry as I turn and run toward Kaiva's. She went to feed the tr'gorys alone. She left without me at her side. What was she thinking? "That tr'gory could have killed you."

I feel the growl in my chest as I press Elle-noor tighter against me. It was a tr'gory that did this to my female. Which tr'gory, it matters not. Playful little Stahn-lee could have done this, and I would feel the same level of fury rattling my bones. They *dare* harm my mate? The one who has summoned the courage to approach them in order to offer them food? The one who saved the unwanted pup of a tr'gory mother and nourished him until he was strong enough to return to his pack? The one who prioritizes their needs above her own? They think they will successfully get away with this treachery?

I would tip my head back and laugh into the night sky if I were not so worried about Elle-noor's condition.

"It's just a small bite," she reasons, her teeth chattering together.

I look down at her wide, brown eyes, shining with tears that continue to tumble down her cheeks. Her nose is red and puffy from crying, and I am confused by the conflicting urges to yell at her for her soft heart and hold her in my arms for the rest of our days, acting as her eternal shield.

"You are a fool" is what I settle on because it is the most prominent thought in my mind. "Those beasts could have killed you," I tell her through gritted teeth. "Sliced you into ribbons and left you to die in the dirt."

"Bruvix," she says, her bottom lip wobbling as she continues to put pressure on her forearm.

But her sadness cannot sway me. Not now. I could have lost her this eve. The possibility of that sends a shudder down my spine. "Do not."

"Here," Kaiva instructs me as I burst through the front door to her med room. "Put her here."

I do as she says, placing Elle-noor on the middle bed. Kaiva runs around, turning on overhead lights and gathering supplies she tosses onto the metal tray next to Elle-noor's bed.

"Got your comm!" Aye-vah shouts as she rushes into the room. She quickly scrubs her hands in the basin behind the section of beds, then organizes the tools and salves on the tray in the order in which Kaiva will use them. "It's okay, Eleanor," she says, confidently, almost convincingly, as she offers my mate a warm smile. "You're going to be just fine."

I want to believe that Aye-vah speaks the truth, but part of me is sure it is merely to calm the nerves of her patient, who is looking at me with panicked eyes as she reluctantly lets go of her arm so that Kaiva can inspect the wound.

I wince as Kaiva shines the overhead light onto Elle-noor's arm. The flesh is torn in such a violent way, as if she had to rip it from the beast's mouth, no matter what would be left of it in the end.

"Don't look at it, okay?" Aye-vah asks of Elle-noor as they press clean wraps into her skin, trying to stop the bleeding. "This is for the pain," she says just before sticking a needle into Elle-noor's bicep.

"And this will prevent infection," Kaiva adds, releasing three drops of a yellowish liquid onto Elle-noor's tongue.

"Are you mad at me?" Elle-noor asks me between loud sniffles.

I do not respond. I am too focused on watching Kaiva and Aye-vah as they work. They are fast, careful, and skilled at their craft. I am grateful to have both of them among our small clan. "We shall not discuss this now," I bark out as I am too angry to have this conversation in front of an audience.

Elle-noor pinches her eyes closed as more tears fall, and she drops her head against the thin pillow, looking defeated. "It was an accident. I promise," she says.

"I do not understand," Varrek says at my side. "How did this tr'gory attack you? Where were you when it happened?" I forgot he was here. And now we will have to reveal the secrets we've kept. What a spectacular debacle.

My fists ball at my sides. When I look down, I realize they are covered in Elle-noor's blood. I rip a large chunk from the bottom hem of my tunic and furiously wipe the redness from my palms. The blood is starting to dry, though, and is proving difficult to remove. Frustrated, at myself, at Elle-noor, and… everything, I toss it into the waste bucket with a guttural scream.

"Both of you, out!" Kaiva yells, gesturing toward the door. She does not look up from Elle-noor's wound, but it is clear she is speaking to Varrek and me.

My cousin follows me outside, close on my heels. I feel the wetness pool in my eyes as I run my claws roughly through my mane, not caring when I scratch the skin of my scalp. Bending at the waist, I grab a rock the size of my fist and hurl it across the width of the main path, into the forest. Then, because I cannot do anything else about the predicament I have found myself in, I pace. And pace, and pace, as Varrek stands with his arms crossed over his chest, watching me.

"Why do you stare as you do!" I shout at him. I do not want his judgment. I do not want his pity. But mostly, I do not wish to reveal how I've betrayed him.

He lets out a sigh, then drops his arms to his sides. "You will have to tell me at some point, but I can see how upset you are, and I will not force you to do it now."

"It is fine," I reply, flatly. If nothing else, telling him the truth will give me something to do until Kaiva allows me to return to my mate's side.

I tell him of all that has come about. From the accidental consumption of the vakopurri berries that led to us finding Stahn-lee, to taking him in and Elle-noor nursing him back to health, to the day he destroyed my security server, causing us to lose a day of perimeter footage. I fill him in on what it was like seeing Elle-noor return Stahn-lee to his mother, and how playful the pups are when they are young. And last eve, when Elle-noor and I snuck out to feed them under the cover of night.

He says nothing until I finish speaking. Just nodding and following me with his rich, green eyes as I pace back and forth. He scrubs a hand down his face and clears his throat. "I should be angry with you, cousin. I should. And there is a part of my heart that is crushed that you chose to lie. You deceived me."

I do not breathe. I remain perfectly still as Varrek readies to deliver a disciplinary strike that will surely leave me banished from the clan forever.

Then his lips quirk up on one side, forming a slight grin. A look I was truly not expecting. "If you had done this for anyone else, I would send you back to Trovilia, never to return. These choices you made could have put yourself and your clan in great danger. But," he continues, "all of this was for Elle-noor. A human female. Your inara, yes?"

"I-I…" I stammer out a sigh. "Yes. She is."

Varrek strides toward me and stops until we are facing each other, about an arm's width apart. "It is all right. Discovering that you have an inara is an incomparable experience. It makes every drop of sanity, intelligence, and rationale leave your head."

He is right. I have not been myself since Elle-noor's arrival. "Yes," I reply again.

Varrek nods once then turns toward the med room. "Come. Let us check on your female."

We enter to find Elle-noor sitting up inside the med tube in the corner of the room.

"She's all stitched up!" Aye-vah exclaims with a bright smile.

Kaiva helps her out of the tube and leads her back to the middle bed. "Yes, Elle-noor will be just fine. The bite was quite deep, but we were able to clean it properly, and now that it is sewn up, she shall heal nicely over the next several days."

Then Kaiva looks at me. "You will keep watch on it for me, yes? And bring her back if her skin starts to look worrisome?"

I nod because I cannot currently form words. I am feeling too many things.

Kaiva and Aye-vah clean up the bloody wraps and used tools around the middle bed silently as I pull a stool over to the other side of Elle-noor. I whisper, "He knows."

"It wasn't Bruvix's fault," Elle-noor blurts to Varrek. "The whole thing was my idea. He wanted nothing to do with it. He just didn't want me to go alone. But I… I forced him." She continues to yammer on nervously. "I blackmailed him. I said if he didn't help me with this, I'd…" she pauses, clearly trying to figure out this tale as she tells it, "I'd destroy his entire garden. Rip out every flower and plant by the root!"

Varrek turns to me. "Garden?"

I shake my head as I let out another sigh, not interested in addressing *that* right now.

"Elle-noor, slow yourself," Varrek says, soothingly. "Bruvix has told me everything. I am not punishing him. But you are forbidden from continuing these close-up observations. You are lucky your heart still beats in your chest."

She bites her lip as her cheeks pinken once again, and she is clearly on the verge of tears. "Okay, that's fair...but don't you think if they wanted me dead, I'd be dead right now?"

"What are you asking?" Varrek replies.

She takes a breath, pushing back the tears, and says, "You know how vicious they can be. If they wanted to kill me, a human all alone in the woods, they could've done that. Easily. With a single swat of a paw. They didn't want to kill me. This whole thing was a misunderstanding. A mistake on my part."

"Are you saying you wish to continue these feedings?" Varrek asks, and my stomach drops as I wait for her response. Partially because I know what she is about to say, and I do not wish to hear it.

She does not speak the words, but the nod of her head says it all. "The other feedings went well. This time, the mother thought I was reaching for her pup, to take him from her, or something, but I wasn't. I dropped my screen pad. That's what I was grabbing."

Varrek scoffs as if he cannot believe Elle-noor's idiocy, or bravery. I'm not sure which. Then he walks in a slow circle before returning to the foot of her bed. "If you wish to resume these feedings once your arm is fully healed, I will not stand in your way."

"Varrek—" I shout, incredulous. How can he allow her this? Especially knowing what she is to me. "You cannot let this happen."

"Bruvix, I have learned many a lesson when dealing with human females, and one is to step out of their path when they want something badly," Varrek replies. "Denying them will only create chaos. And the clan needs none of that."

I am ready to continue my protest, but Varrek turns to face Elle-noor with a somber expression. "Do what you wish with these tr'go-rys, Elle-noor. But I urge you to consider the impact of you risking your life has on others," he says, gesturing to me. "If this kind of mishap were to happen again, and you were not able to recover, think what that would mean. More importantly, who that would hurt."

Elle-noor's gaze finds mine as Varrek leaves behind Aye-vah, Kaiva making her way up the stairs to her home, and we sit there, looking at each other with heavy lids weighed down by stress of every kind. She takes my hand in hers and traces my knuckles. I let her as the contact settles me. She begins to cry, and I wrap my arm around her shaking shoulders, offering her the only comfort I can. I do not know where we go from here.

I should remain quiet instead of letting my feelings out into the air. But I cannot help myself. I am angry and scared of losing her. "Why do you do this? Why would you ruin us like this?"

"What are you talking about? How is this ruining us?"

Pulling my hand from her grasp, I stand. Then I run my claws over my scalp again as the thought of Elle-noor possibly dying tonight plays in my mind. "You put your life in danger, to-to bond with a creature that cannot speak to you? That could easily kill you? What is the purpose of that?"

Her mouth falls open, but no words come out. So I continue airing my grievances.

"Do I not make you happy? Am I not enough for you?" I whirl around to face her. "Because you are more than enough for me, Ellenoor. You are my mate. My inara. I have known it from the very first moment I saw you and breathed in your scent."

Her chin dips in shame.

Throwing my hands up, I shout, "Have I not shown you time and again I would do anything, risk everything, to keep you safe? What more do you wish me to give? Tell me and I will give it."

"Bruvix, please," she begs softly.

But I am in no mood for calm discussion. "Would you like a piece of my heart? Say the word and I will carve it from my chest for you."

"Stop yelling at me," she grits as tears continue to stain her cheeks. "I know this doesn't make sense to you, but this is the only thing I've ever been good at. I planned to spend the rest of my life helping animals. I was at the beginning of my career doing just that when I was taken and thrust into this life." Her voice lowers, almost to a whisper. "I'm doing the best I can. I just...I just want to find my place here."

I let out a heavy sigh, coming to sit at her side once again.

"I get that the mit'xcruul attack has changed your view of wild animals," she continues. "I understand why you wouldn't trust them, or any animal, to not treat you as prey. But I've had thousands of interactions with animals throughout my life, some wild, most domesticated, but all required the same amount of care, caution, and optimism. And I've only been hurt twice."

"Twice?"

She clears her throat. "Yeah, tonight, and the time I tried making friends with a snake that was hanging out in my bathroom in Australia. That was an ill-advised, drunken endeavor, so I don't really count it, but... you know."

The message she is trying to communicate becomes clear, and I understand it, but I still do not like it. "So, because you have had more pleasant encounters than aggressive, you choose to believe these tr'gorys are worth caring for, and do not want you dead?"

"Yes."

I nod because I have no more words to speak on this subject. It is clear Elle-noor stands firm in her desire to continue caring for the tr'gorys, no matter the cost. She wants me to trust her. She thinks trust is required to keep her safe.

She is wrong. It is not that I do not trust *her*. I do not trust her life with a bloodthirsty, wild creature. A creature that killed a member of my clan. How can she expect me to support her in this?

I cannot say if Elle-noor will someday become mine. Is there nothing more important to her than caring for these tr'gorys? I cannot watch her continue to hurt herself in this quest for a bond that does not exist. Tr'gorys are not meant to stand beside us. They are predators, and we are their prey, nothing more.

Elle-noor is the center of my world. She is my light, my reason. But if I am none of these things to her, I fear we are doomed.

CHAPTER 21

ELEANOR

"**F**uck!" I shout under my breath as I drop another bowl into the soapy tub of dirty dishes. My wound is covered by a waterproof sleeve with several layers of wraps and healing gel beneath. It's protected from the dishwater, so that's not a concern, and Kaiva cleared me to resume my normal activities (sans tr'gory feedings) immediately, but a single twist of the wrist or twitch of the elbow can leave me doubled over in pain.

It wouldn't have hurt to take a day off from dish duty, considering I was attacked by a tr'gory less than twelve hours ago, but the emotional pain of lying in bed, envisioning the devastated look in Bruvix's eyes would've hurt a lot worse than this.

Picking up the bowl, I try again, keeping my bad arm as still as possible and using the muscles in my good arm to handle the scrubbing.

I can do this I tell myself silently. I can clean the dishes three times a day, and I can find some other tasks to fill my free time. The tr'gorys will be fine on their own. That's how they've always existed anyway, right?

I mean, would it have been incredible to continue feeding them, observing them, and learning about them as a species? Sure. Would it have been rewarding to solidify that trust between us and them, making the clan safer and ultimately creating allies with another species on this strange alien planet? Of course.

Is that worth losing Bruvix? And possibly, my life?

No. And no.

Although, the risk to my life is not as great as the others make it seem. The bite was bad, of course, but that happened because I wasn't paying attention. I won't be that careless again. Also, is it any more dangerous than Bruvix training with deadly weapons each day? And what if Varrek decides that a battle with another clan or planet is necessary? Would Bruvix refuse to partake because it could be dangerous for him? Because if the answer is no, which I very much assume it would be, then this argument feels unfair. Borderline sexist, even.

Protecting the clan alongside Varrek and Ahlvo is his duty. His calling. No one here would ever expect him to give up that responsibility simply because it's dangerous.

Yet, somehow, the rules are different for me because I'm a human woman?

No, don't do this.

If I go down this road, it's only going to make me angry and resentful. Besides, life on Oluura is generally pretty great. Peaceful. Quiet. The clan supports each other and cares for one another in a way I've never seen before. I can get used to the quiet life. I can eve–

"Eleanor! Come, quick!" Kate shouts as she runs toward me, arm-in-arm with Jobaki, or "Jo" as Kate calls her, from the direction of the Hexrin house. "Chlo is in labor and it's all hands on deck!"

"Labor?" I ask, puzzled and in shock, because as far as I knew, Chloe still had a month or two to go before the baby came.

"Yes, the child is early," Jo says with a shrug.

"Come on!" Kate says as she takes the bowl from my hand and drops it into the soap bucket. "You're one of three people in the village with any kind of medical experience. Chlo needs you!"

I turn to look at Waldric and he shoots me a big smile as he shoos me away with his hands.

"Okay, then," I say, wiping my hands on the rag sticking out of my pocket. "Let's go meet that hybrid baby!"

* * *

The med room is buzzing with activity when the three of us arrive. Chloe is groaning loudly from the middle bed, the balls of her feet pressing against leather stirrups that keep her legs spread and elevated. Varrek has Chloe's hand in his, pressing kisses to her knuckles and palm as he whispers reassuring words into her ear. Kaiva and Ava move fluidly around the bed and each other in what looks like a choreographed routine as they gather supplies.

"Hey, Chlo! How we doing?" Kate asks.

Chloe's face turns red as her jaw clenches, and she grips Varrek's hand tightly. "This suuucks!" she yells.

And Nalba is here for some reason.

"Hey, Nalba," I say to her as I join her in the corner of the room, staying out of everyone's way. "Here to witness the miracle of childbirth?"

She's nibbling on her knuckle as she watches Chloe pant and scream as a contraction rips through her body. "I... I do not know, to be truthful." She pauses and then looks down at me with a furrowed brow. "I wish to help Cloh-ee, but I do not know how."

"Right," I reply, unsure of how to comfort her.

Nalba shakes her head, then taps a finger on her chin. "I know nothing about delivering babies into the world. It seems... quite messy."

I laugh at the sheer look of disgust on her face.

"I understand this feeling, Nalba," Jo says. Then she turns to Kate. "I am not sure why I am here either."

Kate crosses her arms over her chest and scoffs in protest. "Excuse me? Do *not* spew that negativity in my presence, got it?" she demands, looking between Jo and Nalba. She puts a hand on Jo's shoulder. "Jo, you're the most powerful creature I've ever known." Then she whips her head back around to face Nalba. "And Nalba, you're the smartest.

Women have been giving birth for eons surrounded by mediocre chumps. I'm pretty sure, between the seven of us, we can safely deliver Chlo's baby."

She's right. We can totally do this. Besides, we have Kaiva and Ava leading us, so as long as we follow their lead, Chloe will be fine. I approach Ava by the washbasin. "How can we help? We've got several eager hands without any medical experience, so simple tasks, please."

She looks over her shoulder and beams at me. She surveys those of us standing in the corner. "Fantastic! Nalba!" Ava calls the inventor over and starts giving her instructions. "Stand behind Chloe and keep a cool wet cloth on her forehead at all times. When the towel starts to dry, swap it out with one from the cold box. We have more prepped and ready to go." Nalba nods enthusiastically and scurries off toward Chloe with the cold cloth in her hand.

Kate steps up next. "And for me, Doc?"

"Not a doctor," Ava quickly replies with a snicker. "The gals from the sewing circle are on standby to wash used towels, so once that tub gets full," she says, pointing to the large cylindrical bucket next to Kaiva at the foot of the bed, "take it outside to Zohma for me. We have a substantial stack by the washroom with clean ones, but if we start to run low, Zohma will provide more as she washes and dries the ones we give her."

"Okey doke, my precious plum," Kate says as she pinches Ava's cheek.

Then Jo takes a step forward into the spot Kate just left. "Jo, I know this isn't a typical scenario for you, but…" Ava trails off.

"You would like for me to provide meditative support for Chloe to keep her mental health strong during this time, yes?" Jo asks, leaving Ava stunned to silence.

After a brief pause, Ava says, "I-I mean, yes. How did yo–"

"It is what I do," Jo replies with a wink. Then goes to stand on Chloe's other side and gets to work immediately by holding her hand and having her take deep breaths in and out.

"And Eleanor," Ava says as I'm the last in the group, "if you could report Chloe's vitals to Kaiva as we go through this, it would be super helpful." She hands me a screen pad that's already open to a screen with colorful squiggly lines all over it, and numbers beneath each one. She shows me which ones track Chloe's heart rate, blood pressure, respiratory rate, and oxygen saturation, and which ones are currently tracking the baby's. "If any of those numbers change, you shout it out."

"Got it," I tell her. "Oh, what's this?" I ask when I accidentally swipe to a different screen, which shows a blob growing and then shrinking.

"That's just a visual of the baby inside the womb. We'll be able to see if any complications arise before she delivers," she replies, then swipes it back to the vitals.

Just then, Ahlvo pops his head in the front door. "Need any help, little noodle?"

"No, no," Ava says warmly. "We've got it. Thanks, my love."

"It is time!" Kaiva hollers, tossing a blood- and fluid-soaked towel into the bin beside her.

"Kayyt," Jo calls out before Kate approaches the bin, "do your chants as I have shown you."

Kate nods and mumbles something under her breath as she pinches her eyes shut. I don't hear it clearly, but I pick up, "blood is white" and "not red" and I remember that Kate gets a little squeamish around blood. This must be her way of altering what she sees so she can get through it.

We get into position, surrounding Chloe on all sides as she lies back on the bed and breathes with Jo.

"You will push when I tell you to do so, o-kay, Cloh-ee?" Kaiva says.

Chloe nods, and her knuckles turn white as she squeezes Varrek's fingers. "You can do this, inara. You are stronger than you realize." He kisses her sweat-covered forehead with reverence, then rubs the tip of his nose against hers.

"O-kay, Cloh-ee. Push now. Push until the count of ten," Kaiva instructs, and as much as I want to watch this little alien's progress as he or she enters the world, I keep my eyes on the screen pad in my hands, checking the numbers.

Chloe grunts as she bears down, pushing her feet against the stirrups. Ava is doing the counting as she hands Kaiva the tools she needs, and she's at number five. Chloe screams as Ava gets to seven. "Aaahhhrrrghhh! Fuuuck! Fuck, fuck!" she shouts.

"And stop!" Kaiva yells as soon as Ava reaches ten. "Now, breathe."

"Can you not give her something for the pain?" Varrek asks, his face twisted in anguish.

"We can, but we're unsure of how the dosage will affect the baby," Ava says. "Since it's half-human and half-Trovilian, we don't know if the medication we have will be too much or too little. She's gonna have to do this the natural way, I'm afraid."

"Heart rate and blood pressure are up," I tell them. "Heart rate is one hundred forty. Blood pressure is ninety-six over one hundred thirty-two."

Kaiva nods then pats Chloe's foot. "Again, Cloh-ee. Push to ten."

Varrek strokes the side of Chloe's face. "Push, my sweet Cloh-ee. You can do this."

And she does. She goes through this routine several more times—pushing, breathing, pushing, then breathing. Jo keeps pulling Chloe's attention when the pain becomes too much and presses the back of Chloe's hand against her forehead as she chants quietly.

At one point, Varrek rises to his full height and yells, "Stop this now! My mate is suffering!"

To which Ava calmly responds, "Varrek, we talked about this. Childbirth is painful and Chloe will experience pain. But she needs you to be her rock. Steady. Unwavering."

He nods, but unhappily, with his mouth forming a childlike pout.

"Because if you can't, I'mma kick your ass outta here. Mmkay?" Ava adds.

"Yes," he replies, then plops back down onto the stool at Chloe's side.

By the time she pushes again, Chloe lets out another bellow, and I hear Kaiva say, "It is coming."

Ava keeps counting, but at that news, she lets out an excited shriek.

I look up from the screen pad in my hands to see Jo whispering something into Chloe's ear. Then, Chloe's pupils dilate, and her face turns as beet red as she pushes harder.

"Ten!" Ava yells.

"Breathe, now," Kaiva tells her.

Chloe cries out in relief as she flops back onto her pillow. She only takes a single deep breath before Kaiva tells her to push again. "The child is coming. You will need to push until it is out."

"Hard as you can, Chlo. Come on!" Ava cheers.

"You've got this, Chlo!" Kate adds. "Squirt that little weirdo out!"

I peek over Kaiva's shoulder just in time to see a small golden head emerge from Chloe's vaginal canal. "Oh my god," I mutter to myself.

Then come the shoulders, and the little arms and hands, with four fingers instead of five.

"Chloe, it's coming! It has gold skin like Varrek, but a tuft of dark hair like yours," Ava says as tears fill her eyes.

Next, I see the round squishy belly, followed by–

"It is a female!" Kaiva yells, pulling the rest of the baby girl out, followed by the umbilical cord wrapped around the baby's chubby ankle.

She and Ava wipe the child clean and suck out any fluids or mucus from her mouth before wrapping her in a towel and placing her on Chloe's chest.

The baby lets out a long, angry wail, and Chloe just laughs as tears stream down her face. "Hi, sweetheart," she coos.

Varrek gently caresses his daughter's misshapen newborn baby head as Chloe kisses her cheek. "She is here," he says, his eyes wide with awe and glistening. Then he looks down at his mate with fierce admiration. "You did it."

"I did," Chloe replies with a wide grin.

Ava hands a pair of surgical scissors to Varrek and he cuts the cord.

My gaze travels from the baby to my screen, confirming that both of their vitals are normal, or at least haven't drastically changed.

Nalba tosses a face cloth aside before pressing a new, cold one to Chloe's forehead.

"Um," I hear Kaiva murmur.

"What is it?" Ava asks, nervously.

"Elle-noor, take the child and continue cleaning her," Kaiva commands, her tone wary, but firm. "Aye-vah, get me the binnup tongs, the cvilki tilfr, and a dose of the xiy for Cloh-ee."

"What is happening?" Varrek asks as he anxiously watches me take his daughter to the other side of the room.

"It is fine, my son," Kaiva replies calmly. "Cloh-ee is still losing blood. But we will stop it."

Chloe looks between the baby in my arms and Kaiva. "What, wha—"

Ava hustles over with the items Kaiva requested, and they get to work. I sneak peeks between wiping the wiggly newborn with a damp cloth. Ava adds something to Chloe's fluid bag, I'm guessing a drug, as Kaiva snips and ties and puts pressure on the area to stop the flow of blood.

"Am I going to be okay?" Chloe asks as she lets out a loud sob.

Varrek's face turns a pale shade of yellow, and I worry he's about to faint.

Ava hands Kaiva another tool, and it looks like she's pulling something out of Chloe. Then I see it. Her placenta. "Of course, you are," Ava tells her confidently. And whether she's telling the truth or not, I believe her.

The bucket of dirty towels is now full, so Kate quickly swaps it with an empty one and runs the dirty towel bucket outside to Zohma.

Through her tears, I see Chloe's eyes dart around the room and land on the tiny squealing baby in my arms. Her tears stop as the corners of her mouth turn up into a slight smile.

The baby continues to wiggle and cry as the vibe in the room remains frantic. It's scary, holding this child in my arms and trying to comfort it as I clean its pale, slightly golden skin, not knowing if Chloe is going to pull through this. She has to. This gorgeous bundle in my arms needs her guidance, her strength, her warmth. This world needs Chloe in it, as much as her child does.

Several minutes pass, and Jo continues to whisper into Chloe's ear as she keeps her gaze locked on her daughter. Whatever Jo is saying, coupled with the sight of her child, seems to be keeping her somewhat calm.

Once she has the placenta in her hands, Kaiva places the large, pinkish-gray blob onto a metal tray beside Chloe. Then she sews and cleans and snips and cleans until finally, she says, "There. The bleeding has ceased."

"Oh, thank fuck," Kate says with a loud sigh.

Varrek and Chloe look at each other and also let out deep breaths, and Varrek kisses her palm as he whispers, "My light. My everything."

Ava gives me a single nod, and I know that means I'm cleared to return Chloe's daughter to her. The baby continues to burble and squeal as I place her against her mother's chest, and Chloe goes back to crying, but this time, I'm certain they're tears of joy.

Kaiva removes the gloves from her hands and comes to stand at Chloe's side. "She is stunning. Truly. Just like her mother."

"Absolutely perfect," Varrek adds.

Ava leans in next to Kaiva and clears her throat. "Have we decided on a name yet?"

Chloe and Varrek exchange a look, then Chloe says, "Yes, Vahla. After his mother."

Kaiva sucks in a breath, her hand covering her heart. "Lovely. Just lovely."

And just like that, the first human-Trovilian baby has entered the world.

CHAPTER 22

BRUVIX

"She is too small," I tell my cousin as I look down at his daughter. "I should not be holding such a delicate thing. I will break her." I try handing her back to him, but he refuses.

"I trust you, Bruvix," he says with a warm grin. "You are doing a splendid job thus far."

I grunt in response. Sure, I have not dropped her...yet. Or scratched her light golden skin with my claws, but it seems only a matter of time. She is too fragile. Too...pure for a large, gangly oaf like me to hold.

Varrek shushes my grunt and points to the center of Kaiva's med room where Cloh-ee is fast asleep.

"How long must she recover here?" I ask.

Varrek scratches his chin. "Another day. Kaiva was worried Cloh-ee would tear her stitches if we left only a day after the birth. So she must rest here until tomorrow."

Little Vahla squirms in my arms as a bubble of spit forms between her lips and then pops as she begins to cry. "Oh no," I mutter under my breath. Then I rock her slowly from side to side as I hold her closer to my body. "Shh, little one," I tell her. "I am your family. Your clan."

"Ooh, is that my squishy little niece?" Aye-vah coos as she and Ahlvo quietly enter. She sticks her arms out and I place Vahla in them, relieved that I did not drop her. Then Aye-vah hands her over to Ahlvo, who twists his face into strange shapes and makes low-pitched, comical noises at her.

"How's Chlo doing this morning?" Aye-vah asks Varrek.

He looks at his sleeping mate, and his eyes gloss over with adoration. "She is quite tired this day. She has successfully gotten Vahla to latch, but only once."

"Latch?" I ask, confused by the term.

"Breastfeed," Aye-vah translates. "I'll wake her in a bit so she can try again," she says to Varrek.

Vahla begins to cry, and Cloh-ee wakes immediately. "Oh, hey, guys," she says through a yawn. Aye-vah hands Vahla to her mother, and she pulls down the neck of her tunic, pressing Vahla's mouth to her nipple.

It takes a few moments, and a slight adjustment of Cloh-ee's breast, but soon, Vahla is feeding and Cloh-ee and Varrek are beaming with pride as they look upon their daughter. I feel envy, thick and unyielding, pump through my veins at the sight. This... this is what I wish to have with Elle-noor. Not the child, necessarily, if the concept of motherhood does not interest her, but the level of intimacy and trust that no others can touch. The deep bond we feel down to our marrow that puts us in our own world, leaving others to watch us from the outside.

I believed we were building such, but that was before the tr'gory attack.

As several members of our clan come in and shower Varrek and Cloh-ee with gifts and well wishes, I quietly exit the med room and head toward the meal hall where I know my mate is busy cleaning dishes.

"Ikiihri, Bruvix!" clan members shout as they pass by, a phrase commonly used on holidays or special occasions where something grand has occurred. It is a way of acknowledging our many blessings and to express our gratitude to the goddess.

When I reach the meal hall, I find it empty, apart from Waldric and Krahn, squabbling in the back about the measure of a certain ingredient within a stew recipe. At the front of the hall is my Elle-noor, humming to herself as she dries a mug with a rag.

"Hello," I say as I reach her side.

She jumps, not having noticed me. "Ah!" she squeals. "You're too quiet! How'd you sneak up on me like that?"

"Perhaps because you were too busy singing to be aware of your surroundings. That is not wise, you know," I tease, resting my weight against the table nearest her and pick up a dry rag and a mug.

"You don't have to help me," she says with that dazzling smile of hers. I feel my tongue tying itself in knots at the sight.

"I am aware," I tell her honestly. I enjoy helping her—it does not matter with what. Besides, the less time it takes her to dry the dishes, the quicker she and I can return to our home.

"Did you go meet Vahla?" she asks.

I nod. "I did. Are human babies always so little?"

Elle-noor chuckles. "Vahla's twelve pounds! That's big for a newborn."

Placing the dry mug with the others, I grab another damp one. "Twelve pounds is still alarmingly small in my hands."

Her gaze lands on the mug in my grip, and it heats as her eyes travel along my fingers, ending at my claws, and then over my palms and wrists. "You do have big hands," she says, slightly breathless.

I shall never tire of that look. That look of longing and lust as she takes me in. It makes me feel different. As if I am someone different. Not me. Someone without the scars I bear. Without the anger I carry. Someone truly worthy of her.

As she finishes drying the final mug, she puts it in line with the others and takes my hand in hers. "Come," she says. "Let's go home."

I say nothing; I nod in response, allowing her to pull me along the main path. By the time we reach the front door, she is pulling my face down as she lifts onto her toes. She presses her lips to mine and sighs against my mouth as if she has waited centuries to feel my mouth on her.

I lift her into my arms, and she immediately wraps her legs around my waist, rubbing her core against my lower belly. Blood surges toward my cock, making it stand at attention between our bodies. She claws at my shirt, and I lift my arm one at a time as she pulls it over my head, so I do not drop her.

We have yet to address the attack again, and what Elle-noor will do now that Varrek has given his approval for her to continue observing them. The tether continues to draw me toward her, making my body respond to her every movement, her every breath, but I do not know if Elle-noor and I will complete the bond. What I do know is that she is in my arms, and her lips are pressed against my throat. That is all I need.

Once we are inside, my tongue is traveling from the base of her neck up to her ear, how she enjoys it. "What's that?" she asks, a slight nervous pitch to her voice.

"I hear nothing," I say. Then I hear it. A steady beep coming from my security room. Instantly, we separate and run up the stairs to the second floor.

I look over everything, the server, the feeds of each camera, the perimeter tracker, and I find the source of the unpleasant noise. It is the storage folder, angrily blinking at me from the main screen. When I open it, I discover several error messages from the previous eve, all the way into the morning. The cameras, every single one of them, cut out in the early hours of the morning. The footage from that time has been lost.

"What does that mean?" Elle-noor asks from behind me.

I sigh, confused, but mostly worried. "It means our cameras have been tampered with." I am certain it is not a fluke or an issue with the replacement parts Nee-roh generously provided. The cameras are of the highest quality, and there has never been a time when they have simultaneously stopped capturing footage. This is deliberate and strategic.

I pick up the nearest screen pad and send a comm to Ahlvo. He answers, and it is clear he is stepping outside the med room so as not to disturb the new parents. "A problem?" he asks.

"Very suspicious," I reply. "Get Varrek. He needs to hear this."

Ahlvo nods, and I am turned upside down as he heads inside and quietly extricates Varrek from the large group of people who have piled into the med room to meet baby Vahla.

"What is it?" he asks, looking exhausted and too distracted for anything other than talk of his newborn daughter.

I take a long breath before I begin. "Recordings from last eve into this morn have been dropped from all cameras. It seems a deliberate move to disable our security systems."

"You are certain?" he asks, his face hardening as he shifts back into his role as leader.

"Bzzsil Chi" is all I reply. I know it is him. I feel it deep in my blood.

"No," Varrek says quickly. "If he were here, we would have been notified by Ekoya. We have heard nothing."

"I do not think we should rely solely on this unknown spy Ekoya knows from the tavern," I tell them. "This is not simply a camera malfunction. There are backups in place for each camera, and they each have their own smaller servers that are linked to the main one."

"Simpler language, Bruvix, I beg you," Ahlvo replies with an exaggerated sigh.

"If one camera fails, whatever the reason, three other channels must fail for that individual camera to stop working. For all of them to fail at once?" I shout. "For several hours? It is unthinkable. This was deliberate."

Varrek and Ahlvo exchange a glance that indicates they think I am paranoid, and this is not worth pursuing. I ready my voice to roar with fury, but Varrek replies, "I will contact Ekoya to see if she has heard anything. The crew will also scan the perimeter of the village to ensure nothing is amiss."

I let my shoulders relax and unclench my jaw. Elle-noor places her hand on my arm, and I cover it with my own. I almost forgot she was in the room with me.

"Are the feeds back up now?" Ahlvo asks.

I nod. "Yes, all working as they should. They have been recording since first meal."

"Very well," Varrek says. "Keep your screen pad close. I shall alert you with updates."

The screen turns black, and I pull Elle-noor around to my front. She plops herself on my lap, leaning her head against mine. "What now?" she asks. "Are we in danger?"

My arms tighten around her. "No, Elle-noor. I will not let anything happen to you." Then I push a lock of her mane behind her ear. "We stay safe. We remain in the village. And, if needed, we fight."

CHAPTER 23

ELEANOR

Something weird is happening, and it's not just the drop in security footage from last night. It's the tr'gorys. After Bruvix and I sat in his security room for a while in loaded silence, he left, saying he wanted to discuss his Bzzsil Chi theory a bit more with Ahlvo.

I stayed put and reviewed the footage from before and after the cameras went out. The adult pack appeared not once, but several times. They ran multiple laps around and through the village, looking strangely restless. I also spotted Nanay and her pups for the first time on camera, and while the pups seemed their standard level of clumsy and adorable, she was anything but. Her head was dipped low, and her fur stood straight up as she passed by the camera at the falls. Like she was hunting something. Or someone.

But that's not the only eerie occurrence I've noticed in the last twenty-four hours. Since Vahla was born, I've felt eyes on me. Following me. Watching me. And not one set of eyes, but many. I heard the crunch of leaves deep in the woods, just out of view, when I walked along the main path. This morning, I swear I caught a peek of red eyes, surrounded by long black fur, looking back at me through the trees. I recognized those eyes.

Why are they watching me, though? Are they trying to tell me something?

I've followed the rules. I've stayed away. I've let them live their lives without intruding. Are they trying to tell me to come back? To resume the feedings? To bond with them a little more?

If only.

I shake my head and shoulders, letting the thought pass. I don't need to care for an animal to belong to this clan. It doesn't matter how much I enjoy it. It's too risky an endeavor to pursue.

Perhaps if animals on Oluura were tiny, kitten-sized balls of floof, but they're not. They're gigantic with sharp claws and terrifying fangs. Plus, Bruvix risked his life, and the safety of his clan to save me. The least I can do is not actively put myself in danger.

Guilt sits in my gut like a solid brick as I recall each time I asked him to come with me to the falls. Or when we found Stanley and I pressured Bruvix into keeping him at his house and nurse the little pup back to health. Or, worst of all, when I went to the falls alone, and Nanay bit a chunk out of my arm.

Waves of pain radiate from my elbow down to my fingertips as I rub the wound. It's healing quickly, but there's still a sting every time something brushes against it, and an uncomfortable pull when I push myself too hard on dish duty.

I know I've been sulking a bit lately, ever since the bite. I've been trying to hide it, but I tend to wear my heart on my sleeve. Bruvix can sense it. I know he can. He's attuned to me in ways I don't fully understand, and he's kept a watchful eye on me, even when he thinks I don't notice. And that just makes me feel like even more of an asshole. He's given me so much, and he's asked for nothing in return. He's also put himself in the same vicinity as tr'gorys, which triggered the very trauma he's been trying to forget for decades.

I should tell him how sorry I am. Not only for the carelessness that led to the bite, but for everything leading up to it. Just because I've been missing Frank doesn't mean I should've subjected Bruvix and the clan to close encounters with the tr'gorys. It was selfish of me to seek that human-animal bond on an alien planet.

Heading outside, I quickly shift from a walk to a slow jog in the direction of Ava and Ahlvo's house. Bruvix said he was meeting with Ahlvo, so that's where he should be.

I wave and smile to everyone I pass on the main path, a new level of appreciation for this community blooming inside my chest. When I reach Ava's, I knock three times, but no one answers. Maybe the guys aren't here, and Ava is still at Kaiva's, keeping a close watch on Chloe. I run over to the med room and practically burst through the front door. Not that anyone notices, because there are about twenty people in here visiting Chloe and Vahla, and it's shockingly loud for a venue with a newborn baby in it. No sign of Bruvix and Ahlvo, however. I give Ava a nod before I close the door behind me.

Maybe they're at the meal hall. I'm not sure where else they would go to discuss a possible sneak attack on the village. Varrek was still in the med room with Chloe, so they obviously wouldn't be at his house.

I'm out of breath by the time I make it to the meal hall, only to find a few of the elders lingering about, waiting to be the first in line for dinner. Bruvix and Ahlvo aren't here after all.

"The training grounds," I whisper. That's the only other possible place they could be.

As I cut across the path, I almost collide with Kate and Niro. "Shit! Sorry, you two," I tell them, wiping the sheen of sweat from my brow.

"Easy there, Speedy McGee," Kate says with a chuckle. "Where you headed?"

"Training grounds," I say with a huff as I catch my breath. "Looking for Bruvix."

"Ahh," Kate replies with a knowing grin. "A late afternoon snack, eh?"

"What?" I ask, shaking my head. I know what she's implying, and I'd have no trouble admitting it if it were true, but it's not. "Nah, I just need to talk to him."

She elbows Niro in the side. "Sure, sure."

"What in the world was that for?" Niro softly scolds, rubbing his rib cage.

"Oh, that didn't hurt. Don't pretend like it did," she tells him. Then she turns back to me. "We're heading back to the caves for a few days. I need to work on some baby clothes for Vahla. But we'll be back soon. Let Chlo know for me?"

"Okay, cool. Yeah, I'll tell her."

"Oh! By the way," Kate mumbles as she digs through the bag slung over her shoulder. "Here, I keep forgetting to give this to you." Then she hands me a thick, pink garment made from a cotton-like fabric folded into a neat square.

"What's this?" I ask, slowly unfolding it. A gasp escapes me when I hold it up. "A jumpsuit?" It has a peter pan collar, large tortoiseshell buttons from the neck to the waist, short sleeves, and cuffed bottoms that look like they'll hit just above my ankles. It's perfect.

"Yeah, Bruvix said you wanted one. I guessed your measurements, so let me know if it doesn't fit and I can fix it."

I'm stunned. Of course, Bruvix asked her to make this for me. He heard me talking about something I wanted, and he found a way to get it for me. "Wow" is all I can say as I clutch it tightly to my chest.

"What was your personal style on Earth?" Kate asks. "So, I can make you more pieces. Were you more preppy? Or, like, Sporty Spice? Or were you more into dresses?"

I think back to the many fashion phases I went through, and what all of them ultimately led to. "I guess I would describe it as, middle-aged dad on the top and hippie art teacher on the bottom. Does… that make sense?"

Kate's eyes lift to the sky for a moment, then she chuckles and says, "Does that mean, graphic tees and flannels paired with long skirts on the bottom?"

"Yes!" I shout. "That's exactly what that means."

She nods. "Awesome. And I'm glad you like the jumpsuit! I'll make you more outfits soon," she says, patting me on the arm. "Okay, catch ya later."

Niro smiles, his perfectly white, sharp teeth gleaming. "Farewell, Eleanor."

Tossing the jumpsuit over my shoulder, I jog the rest of the way toward the training grounds. Once I arrive, though, I find it empty. It's a wide patch of dirt the size of a soccer field, so if Bruvix and Ahlvo were here, I'd see them.

For the sake of efficiency, I make my way over to the weapon shed, looking for clues. A few feet before I reach it, a familiar furry face pops out from behind a bush and gallops toward me. "Stanley!" I squeal with my arms outstretched. He races into them and starts eagerly licking my face. He sniffs my cheeks, eyes, and then the jumpsuit still draped over my shoulder. Then he sinks his teeth into the soft fabric and tugs, and I scramble to hold onto the bottom cuffs of my new jumpsuit as he tries to rip it from my grasp. Eventually, he does, and I call his name as I chase after him.

How am I supposed to explain this? "Sorry, Kate. My tr'gory puppy ate that jumpsuit you made me. Can you whip up another one?" I need to get this one back before he destroys it.

Calling his name, I order him to turn back, which he ignores entirely. Once I follow him into the trees, he vanishes, running out of sight, and I stop. This is just asking for trouble, and I can't betray Bruvix's trust again. I won't. He deserves better.

A clicking sound breaks through my thoughts, and as I whirl around, I find a gun pointed at my forehead. "Don't move, female. You're worth a sack full of credits, but I'd also enjoy cutting you open and having a look at your insides."

I swallow, lifting my hands in surrender as the reality of my situation settles in. "Bzzsil Chi, I presume?" I ask, my voice cracking on the last word. He certainly matches the description I've been given by the girls. Oily yellow scales covering his wide, short body? Check. Bulbous brown knobs running down his back and tail? Check. Giant black eyes that bug out in opposite directions? Check. He's also barefoot and wearing a short-sleeved black shirt that looks like it's made from a blend of cheap felt and polyester, with matching black pants that brush the top of his clawed feet.

"Indeed, pretty one," he spits, droplets of his saliva landing across my cheek. "And these are my guards." He gestures behind him to a small army of males in drab yellow suits with bronze armor covering their chests.

This is bad.

Very, very bad.

Like, *asteroid heading toward us at a trillion miles an hour* bad. I am so fucked.

"Wh-what brings you here to Oluura?" I ask in a shaky voice.

Is the warrior crew about to arrive for a session? Or are those done for the day? Bruvix spends half his life right here on this dirt patch. Why did this oily lizard man have to catch me here the one time it's empty? Maybe if I stall long enough, they'll show up.

Keep him talking. Keep him talking.

He laughs, but it sounds more like the cackle of someone with a severe head cold. "You see, something was stolen from me. And I am here to get it back."

Keep him talking.

I already know the answer to this question, but I ask it anyway. "Oh yeah? And what's that?"

He takes a step closer, pressing the cold barrel of the gun right between my eyes. "You, pretty one. You."

CHAPTER 24

BRUVIX

"Has Elle-noor been by this eve?" I ask Cloh-ee and Varrek as I sway side to side with little Vahla in my arms. I feel much more comfortable holding her this time. Perhaps it is because her skin is brighter than it was before. She looks stronger, somehow, as if she is already growing into the formidable female she will one day become. Pride heats my cheeks as I smile down at her, this wrinkly little thing.

"No, haven't seen her," Cloh-ee sleepily replies. "But I fell asleep for a while there."

Varrek hands his mate a cup of water and kisses the side of her head. "I was awake during that time, and I did not see her."

"Hmm," I grunt. After I met with Ahlvo in Varrek's weapons room, we came here to see if he heard back from Ekoya, which he hasn't. I assumed Elle-noor would come by after dish duty following the final meal, but she has not. Although, it is just as likely that she returned home immediately after her shift. She seemed tired earlier this day.

Nalba leans over my shoulder and lightly pokes at Vahla's cheeks. "She is fascinating to look at, is she not?" she asks me, shaking her head in wonder.

"I never took you for having an interest in children, Nalba," I say.

She grumbles "o fah" under her breath and gives my arm a slight shove. "Nor I, you, Bruvix."

I suppose that is fair.

"It is my turn," Varrek declares, gently taking the sleeping bundle from my arms. "I have waited all day to see my brilliant daughter." He says it as if speaking directly to her in a soft, gleeful tone she would understand. Then he rocks her side to side, and his smile grows, stretching across his entire face.

"Hello!" Waldric hollers as he enters the med room, a heaping plate of food in one hand. "I brought this feast for the lovely Cloh-ee, whom I assume is famished after bringing a new life into the world."

"Waldric!" She squeals as quietly as she can so as not to wake Vahla, but in reality, not quietly at all. Then she holds out her hands as he presents her with a stack of junasii bread and marinated kuhnypa meat with berries and root vegetables in little piles around the bread. "You are a gem."

Waldric crosses his arms over his chest and grins, proud to watch Cloh-ee enjoy the food he prepared for her. Then he turns to me with a furrow on his brow. "I was surprised to miss Elle-noor at the final meal. If she is not feeling well, please tell her she does not need to clean the dishes for first meal in the morning, yes?"

"She…" I pause, scratching my chin, baffled by the words Waldric just spoke. "She was not at final meal?"

"No," he replies. "I have not seen her since middle meal."

It is not like Elle-noor to cast aside her duties. Even when we were nursing Stahn-lee back to health and not getting much sleep at all, Elle-noor made sure to fulfill her dish duties at each meal. A chill races down my spine at a thought that I refuse to entertain. No. No, she is fine. She is well. She is merely at home. She probably fell asleep and missed final meal completely. That is all.

"I must go," I choke out as I race out the door. Once I am on the main path, I push my legs as fast as they will take me. I ignore all who greet me as I pass because I must confirm Elle-noor is okay. That she is safe.

"Elle-noor!" I shout as I whip open my front door. "Elle-noor!" I continue to holler as I race up the stairs, pausing to check each room. I make it to the garden on the top floor and yell "Elle-noor!" as I stagger around the flower beds, hoping to find her curled in on herself, peacefully snoozing in a spot I would not expect to find her, in a place that is not easy to see, because the alternative… it is unfathomable.

Finally allowing the thought to take root in my head, I let my blood run hot with rage as I charge down the stairs and back out into the night. Racing toward the med room, I think of nothing but violence, vengeance—cold and satisfying.

"She is gone," I blurt as I throw open Kaiva's front door. All the eyes in the room are on me now, some frightened, some in denial, but most in anger.

"He is here," Varrek says through gritted teeth.

"Yes," I reply, my hand going to the dagger in my belt.

"Bzzsil Chi? You're sure?" Aye-vah asks, her breath coming out in short pants.

Then, Varrek's screen pad beeps with an incoming comm. "Ekoya," he says.

Ahlvo and I race to stand on either side of him just as he answers the comm. "Varrek. I just received word from my contact that Bzzsil Chi was supposed to collect a shipment at the port yesterday. He never appeared. Sent another in his place. That is not like him."

Varrek scrubs a hand down his face as he groans.

"There is something else," Ekoya says, her tone turning somber. "One of his ships left two days ago with tags removed from the exterior and no destination entered in the travel logs. You must be on the lookout."

"Why did your contact not alert you of this sooner?" Varrek barks out.

Ekoya straightens in her seat and lifts her chin. She says nothing, and Varrek squirms in place. "I apologize for my tone. The human we rescued from Bzzsil Chi's clutches is now missing, and we must now scramble to thwart an attack from an enemy who is clearly already here."

"Many apologies for the delay," she says calmly. "Bzzsil Chi keeps his travels secret from most at Nu'Piix. Several bribes were needed to get this information."

Varrek drops his head, running a hand through his already mussed mane. "I understand. Thank you for the information, Queen Ekoya."

She tilts her head slightly, then leans in close. "Destroy him, Varrek. I do not care how. Do not share the details with me, but get it done. This galaxy shall brighten the moment his heart stops beating."

"Indeed. We shall," he replies, then disconnects the comm.

My fists are balled at my sides, and my jaw is clenched so tightly, I am certain I will break a fang. I am ready for war.

Varrek sighs then twists his neck to one side, and then the other, letting the bones crack. "Now," he begins, "we must prepare the clan for battle." He turns to Aye-vah. "Aye-vah, contact Kay-teh and Nee-roh. Tell them they must return at once." Then he steps in front of me. "You have created a plan for this, cousin, have you not?"

My feet lift, and I bounce lightly on the balls of my feet. "I have."

"Then," he steps aside, gesturing with a sweep of his hand, "I shall let you lead us in this fight, Bruvix. We follow your command."

I feel my lips flatten and spread into a smile as adrenaline rips through my bones. "Then let us fight."

CHAPTER 25

ELEANOR

These jackasses are so annoying, I can't wait to watch them die. Three of them keep throwing pebbles and clumps of moss at each other like fucking children, while the rest, about fifteen of them, stand around looking bored. Then there's Bzzsil Chi, who keeps waddling in a circle as he mumbles something under his breath.

I think it's his plan of attack on the village because occasionally I'll pick up on words like "slaughter the leader" and "take the females" and each time, bile rises in my throat. He waves the gun around as he babbles on, dramatically gesturing with it every few minutes. God, I hate him.

I'd tell him that myself, but I'm certain he would respond by shooting me. Plus, my mouth is gagged, and I can't say anything at all. My arms and legs are also tied to a tree on the outskirts of the forest, rendering me helpless. I can no longer keep him talking, either. I guess I'll just have to wait to be rescued. But has anyone even noticed I'm missing?

Based on the dark blues and violet colors of the sky, it's nearing the end of dinner time, which means I've been out here for just under an hour.

Fuck, I'm so screwed.

"Enough of that, you fools!" Bzzsil Chi shouts at his bonehead guards. "We must ready ourselves. The night is about to awaken."

"Yes, sir," they reply in unison.

"Now, what must you do?" he asks them.

"Kill the Trovilians. Take the humans."

"Yes, yes," Bzzsil Chi says, his beady eyes gleaming with excitement. Sick fuck. "Use this one to negotiate with them," he says as he points the gun at me. "Get the other females. Then kill the rest. Leave no witnesses."

"What of the child?" The one with an axe in his hand asks.

Oh god, Vahla. They've been watching us closely for days, it seems.

He taps his wide, two-toed foot on the ground. "It is not human, correct? A hybrid?"

"Yes, sir. A hybrid," the guard with the spiky black hair replies.

"Kill it. A mixed creature like that is worth nothing."

And there goes my last remaining shred of composure. I kick against the bark of the tree as I let fly a string of obscenities that they can't even hear because the gag in my mouth muffles all of it. That just makes me even angrier, so I scream into the cloth gag until my throat burns.

The guard missing three of his front teeth and has swollen, gray gums gives me a hard kick to the shin, and I double over in pain, wailing into the gag. "Quiet, human whore."

The rest of them laugh at my pain. A tear falls from my eye, landing on the toe of my boot, and I focus on it as it slides from my boot onto the moss beneath. It's the only thing keeping the throbbing pain from my shin from swallowing me whole. So, I continue tracking my tears, even when Spiky Hair kicks my other shin.

And again, when Bzzsil's two-fingered hand curls into a fist and connects with my cheekbone. And again, when Gummy sends a punch straight into my gut, stealing the breath from my lungs. The tears splatter my boot like rain, drops of blood soon follow from the cut Bzzsil's claws left on my cheek. They fall. They splash. Then they roll to the ground.

This could be the last trace of me left on Oluura, I realize. Just tears and blood, far from the place I call home, far from the male I've fallen madly in love with. Far from everything and everyone that matters and tied against a random tree.

"If this is it, may my memories embrace those I love with the warmth I can no longer provide," I whisper into the gag. Then I close my eyes, letting images of Bruvix fill my mind. His captivating dark blue eyes, his bulky biceps, his large, rough hands—only tender when he's touching me. And his scars. The beautiful, unforgettable features that mark him as a survivor. A warrior. A powerful fucking beast. My beast.

"Come along, pretty one," Bzzsil croaks as two of his guards untie me from the tree. For a moment, I think I might have a chance to bust free of this rope and run, but one of them quickly uses the rope from around the tree and wraps it around my wrists while five others keep their pistols pointed towards my face.

Then I'm dragged through the woods by the rope—no assistance offered when I trip or stumble over a fallen branch, of course—back toward the main path. What will happen when we come face-to-face with the clan? Am I really about to watch my clan get murdered right before my eyes? Am I about to be sold into slavery alongside Ava, Kate, and Chloe?

No. No, no, no, no. This cannot be how it ends.

I spent months floating around space, yanked in and out of consciousness each time I was sold, and then returned. I can't go back to that life—waking up and wondering where the hell I am, who owns me, and what I'll have to endure.

Though, I'm fairly certain I'll be daydreaming about my weeks in stasis if Bzzsil Chi is my new owner. He might just sell us off to the highest bidder, but he could also keep us and have us work in that wretched brothel I've heard mentioned by Varrek and Bruvix. I can't decide which would be a worse fate.

"Hurry up, hideous slut," Gummy yells as he shoves the butt-end of his pistol into the base of my spine.

I yelp in pain, but he doesn't let me stop to take a breath before he's shoving me forward.

"You find her unpleasant to look at, G'rugivic?" Axe Hand asks from in front of me.

"All humans are," Gummy yells. "Too weak."

"So you would not take her cunt?" Axe Hand asks with a sickening laugh.

"Well, of course, I would," Gummy replies as if this should be obvious. "From behind, though, so I would not have to look at her."

Wow. As if the gaping hole in his mouth where teeth should be is a fucking work of art. I'd rip that pistol out of his hands and shoot myself in the temple before I'd let him touch me. All of them. Creepy shitbags.

I can't let them reach the village; I suddenly realize. If they do, it's certain death for everyone I care about. I can act as a distraction. Bother them. Taunt them. Infuriate them. That, I can do. At least for a little while.

Planting my feet in the dirt, I lean back on my heels, coming to a full stop. Gummy shoves me forward, but I don't fall. He does it again, and I land on my knees.

Good, good. Keep going.

I groan as if in pain, which I'm still in from the kicks and punches from earlier, but not this little tumble. But I act as if I can barely hold myself up, then collapse onto my side. Gummy calls for Axe Hand, and yells at me to get moving. I don't though. I curl in on myself, forming a tight ball. Because I know what's coming, and as much as I'd rather avoid getting beaten by these thugs, I'd much rather waste a few more minutes to protect the clan.

Axe Hand sends his boot into my shoulder, and several black spots fill my vision. Okay, this might've been a terrible idea. If I pass out from the pain, they're just going to carry me to the village. That'll take less time. I can't have that. I can't make this easy for them.

"Inbred fucking cowards!" I yell, but the gag makes it sound like gibberish. Gummy's yellow eyes go cold, and a shiver races down my spine. He stands there, fists balled at his sides as he tilts his head, trying to figure out what I said.

So, I do it again, this time in Tagalog, as memories of learning cuss words while visiting my cousins in the Philippines flood my mind. "Putang ina mo!" *Your mother is a whore!*

And again. "Wala kang kwenta!" *You're fucking useless!*

Clearly, yelling into the gag is the right way to go, because since they can't understand me, their imaginations fill in the blanks, and they assume I'm saying something much more offensive than I actually am.

"Gago, subukan mo lang!" I shout. *You fucking bastard, just try me!*

Then Axe Hand and Gummy decide they've had enough of my confusing insults, and both start kicking me. Hard. Gummy kicks my back as Axe Hand kicks my front. When Axe Hand kicks the spot where Nanay bit me and my entire body goes numb. When that subsides, the pain comes in a wave, crashing down on me to the point where I can't breathe.

"What is the hold up here!" Bzzsil Chi shouts as he waddles over to me. "Get her up! We've got to move!"

Gummy and Axe Hand lift me by the arms just high enough to keep my feet from dragging, and race to catch up with Spiky Hair and the rest of the guards. I can't feel my legs anymore, and I can barely keep my head up. The fight has left me.

"I'm sorry," I whisper into the gag as we reach the tree line. I taste the blood running from my nose, mixed with snot and tears I didn't realize had started to fall again. "I'm sorry I couldn't protect you," I say to the clan, knowing they can't hear me, but also knowing it might be my last opportunity to say anything at all to them.

Spiky Hair steps out onto the main path with Gummy and Axe Hand following closely behind as they lift me over a fallen tree. Bzzsil is behind us, surrounded by his army, demonstrating the opposite of how a fearless leader should act.

My vision has turned blurry, but immediately, I notice that the main path is empty. There's no one here.

Did...did they get away? *Please*, I silently beg. *Please have gotten away.*

"Where are they?" Spiky Hair asks as he turns to face me. He now has two heads, and I can't decide which one is uglier, the left or the right. As I stare at him, he gets in my face, yelling, "Well! Where are they?"

In the next second, a loud bang sounds from somewhere off to the left, and when I look down, Spiky Hair's head is separated from his now lifeless body.

Then all hell breaks loose.

CHAPTER 26

BRUVIX

When the male with the black, oddly pointed mane falls in a bloody heap with his head rolling into a puddle, I feel at ease. There are still many guards that remain with Bzzsil Chi, but we can defeat them. We can get Elle-noor safely away from these monsters and kill them. Slowly.

There is nothing I have ever wanted more.

I suppose I wish for Elle-noor's safety slightly more than I long to torture Bzzsil Chi and his henchmen, but it is a very close second. They have hurt my mate. I see the blood dripping from her nose and cheek and the bruises covering all exposed parts of her skin from where I stand on the second level of Nalba's home.

My claws extend at the sight of her head lolling to the side, and it is clear she is on the verge of losing consciousness. A growl starts low in my throat, and Ahlvo elbows me in the side instantly.

"Do not lose your focus!" he whispers. "Your mate needs you."

I nod, slowing my breaths, and willing the panicked, rapid beat of my heart to follow. Elle-noor needs me, and I will not let her down.

"You have the boot silencers Nalba made?" Ahlvo asks me.

"I do," I reply, lifting my foot to show him the thin layer of scratchy fabric that covers the bottom of my boot.

"Good," he says, showing me his as well. "Where do you need me?"

Right. I am leading this fight. I find it difficult to remember as my battle instincts are so conditioned to look to him or Varrek for guidance. But I have developed this carefully choreographed strategy, and I must remind my crew of what comes next. "Give Kaiva the signal to unleash the douku storm. Then leap down from the back and take her and Aye-vah through the trees back to her house. Do not leave until you see them safely reach the second floor. Then meet Jobaki and the Hexrins by the meal hall and have them begin the sound and memory enchantments."

"Got it," Ahlvo replies with a sinister grin.

I narrow my gaze at him. "What?"

He fiddles with one of his braids, twirling it around his claws. "I have missed this."

I grunt in response. "Let us not celebrate this bloodshed until our body count has risen significantly, yes?"

"Certainly. Certainly," he replies in an apologetic tone. He lifts the maroon poncho Kay-teh made for me and waves it back and forth over his head. Within two heartbeats, hundreds of douku orbs, from the size of a pebble to the size of the moon fall from the trees above. Bzzsil Chi fires off a few shots of his laser pistol at the soft orbs of light, zapping them into dust before realizing they are not meant to harm.

It gives Ahlvo just enough time to jump off the balcony of Nalba's second floor, landing silently onto the ground below. I do not understand the science of these boot silencers Nalba created, I just know that the fabric muffles and absorbs any sound made into it. And when placed on the bottom of boots, each step taken is as quiet as a leaf hitting soil.

The douku orbs continue to fall around Bzzsil and his men, bouncing once as they hit the ground, causing them to shout in anger when all they can do is stand there and wait for this distraction to cease. Mietrik and Rahsku take this opportunity to let their arrows fly from the trees, quickly taking out four of Bzzsil Chi's guards.

The distant flap of wings catches my ear and I smile. Nee-roh has arrived just in time. His draxilio form is too big to fight with us inside the village, but that is fine, because soon, he will destroy Bzzsil Chi's ship, leaving them with no means of escape.

"What is that?" Bzzsil Chi shouts in alarm as flames light up the night sky beyond the trees, and the crunch of metal components caving in on themselves fills the air. "My ship!"

Ah, there it is. Good work, Nee-roh.

Bzzsil Chi pulls Elle-noor in front of him by her hair. She winces in pain as he yanks her forward, using her body like a shield.

I will not sit here and watch as my mate is abused right before my eyes. Putting my foam sound blockers into my ear canals, I straighten and leap off the balcony. Once I land, I let out a whistle. Just one.

Simultaneously, Varrek, Grotahk, Drasko, Eduno, Nemyx, and I emerge from the tree line, surrounding Bzzsil Chi and his guards with our newly upgraded and fully charged laser pistols pointed at them.

"Surrender now, release the female, and we may let you live," I tell him flatly. I cannot hear his reply with the sound blockers in my ears, but his words do not matter anyway. He waves his pistol around angrily and continues to point it at Elle-noor. He is not surrendering. I knew he would not. "Very well."

The expressions on their pitiful faces quickly go from confident to tormented. They rush to cover their ears while Elle-noor does not react to the sound at all. The enchantment that Jobaki has released does not affect human ears, but the simulated high-pitched shriek of a bebbahtilo hawk during mating season certainly affects the rest of us. It is deafening and deeply unpleasant.

Instead, Elle-noor looks around, slightly confused at the reactions of the surrounding males, then sags against Bzzsil Chi, her energy completely drained. We must act fast, I told the crew as we planned our strategy, but do not shoot unless you are certain Elle-noor will not be harmed. If you are not certain, refrain. We have a much better chance of separating them, one by one, and killing them once they are away from Elle-noor, than trying to pick them off as they huddle close to her.

Until then, we manipulate, we confuse, we distract, and repeat that cycle until they become lazy or frightened and break off from the group.

This sound simulation does not seem to be enough of a distraction, though. Letting out another whistle, and another, I wait for Jobaki to catch my signal. When the guard wielding the sharp metal blade of a gohrun falls to his knees, dropping his weapon, I know she has heard me. I cannot hear it, but I know the order in which she was planning to torture these males, and if she is following her original plan, then they are witnessing the most traumatic moment of their lives play out in front of them, the volume of that event blaring in their ears.

Gohrun Hand rocks back and forth for a moment with his eyes pinched shut, and I raise my fist next to my head, letting the other warriors know to move in a few steps. We shall get closer and closer until we can pluck Elle-noor from their grasp and slash their throats wide open before they realize what is happening.

Bzzsil Chi's eyes dart around the sky, nervously, and the guard with the misshapen mouth flesh shakes his head back and forth in denial.

We move in another step.

Gohrun Hand leaps to his feet and charges Eduno, letting out a sharp bellow as he goes. He raises his weapon as he gets closer, and Eduno just stares back at him, blinking several times. As Gohrun Hand goes to release his blade, Eduno lifts his laser pistol and pulls the trigger. The gohrun falls from the guard's hand as he tries to cover the seared wound in his chest. Eduno shoots him again, this time in the stomach, and he topples over, landing on his back. Eduno approaches, his expression cold, and shoots him a final time in the head, burning through his eye and brain with the laser before shrugging and returning to his original spot.

The rest form a circle around Bzzsil and Elle-noor, firing their guns at us, forcing us to retreat behind the trees.

That is fine. We can handle this minor setback.

Drasko is hit in the leg before he can leap into the safety of the forest, and he bellows in pain as he lies on his side, clutching his leg. Eduno races behind the trees and pulls him to safety.

Varrek yells something to Grotahk as they creep backward toward the trees, taking turns firing shots at the five guards bearing down on them.

A bullet whirs past my ear and nicks the tree I am next to, and I return fire immediately, singeing the eye sockets of the guard edging toward me. Another one down.

I peek around the tree again to find three more with their guns trained on my location. I am stuck here.

"G'rugivic, now!" Bzzsil Chi shouts. It is the only warning we are given before Bzzsil dives to the ground, taking Elle-noor with him. Mouth Flesh reaches up to his chest and tugs on two red cords that sit on either side of his uniform. This releases a secret compartment within his armor where multiple automatic blaster grenades are hidden. He pulls two out and throws them toward Varrek and Grotahk. I see my brothers dive into the trees before the grenades hit, but I do not know if they safely escaped, as the ground explodes in a flurry of moss and dirt and flames.

I watch in horror as Varrek rises from behind a bush to fire off a shot from his pistol and is hit in the shoulder, falling to the ground with a groan.

An arrow soars down from above and lands into the side of a guard's neck with a wet *thwack.*

Then Nemyx is hit in the side, and he goes down, his hand covering a steady stream of blood exiting the wound beneath his ribs. I duck as a bullet whizzes over my head and scramble back to take cover behind a bush.

No. This is not how it is supposed to happen—

A flash of blue skin catches my eye, breaking through my thoughts. Nee-roh? But he cannot shift into his draxilio inside the village. It will not work. There will not be enough room.

It is only when I see the long, black mane flowing behind this creature that recognition hits. It is Alu, Nee-roh's sister. He must have called her to assist us. But how will she do that?

My gaze follows as she races along the tree line, and when she breaks through, she stands at the entrance of the training grounds not far from where Nemyx still lies. Mouth Flesh notices her and approaches with purposeful steps, a blaster grenade in hand. He tosses one in her direction, and she flips in midair to avoid it. It explodes behind her, lifting the ends of her mane, but not shaking her stride at all. This only infuriates Mouth Flesh even more, and he runs toward her at full speed. When he gets close, he pulls another grenade from his armor, and pulls his arm back, ready to release.

But it is too late to turn back because Alu has shifted into her draxilio, massive and terrifying, and occupying a large portion of the training grounds—the only open space in the village wide enough to fit this version of her. Her cerulean scales glimmer as she lumbers forward, opening her jaws to reveal hundreds of sharp white teeth. It is not a bite that Mouth Flesh must worry about, however. Alu sucks in a deep breath and rears back before unleashing her flames upon his body. They envelop him in an instant, destroying his uniform and melting the skin from his bones.

Alu shifts back and stands behind her fire, admiring her work as Mouth Flesh's eyes disappear, and his skull is slowly revealed.

Suddenly, a scuffle coming from the Hexrin house draws my attention. "Jobaki, you cannot!" Tibik shouts as he chases her onto the main path. She stops in the center, her chest heaving.

What are they doing? This is not part of the plan. We did not discuss the use of Jo's powers at this stage.

"I can!" she yells back. "I can end this!" Her gaze locks onto Bzzsil Chi and the few guards remaining at his side. She lifts her hands to her chest, her palms pressed together, and her eyes pinched shut. When she separates her small hands, a glowing orange orb appears between them.

Bzzsil Chi has not noticed her, however. His focus is locked on Elle-noor's limp frame as he struggles to haul her up.

Tibik shakes his head as he yanks her hands apart, making the orb sizzle and fade away. "You are not strong enough for this!"

I do not pay much mind to the Hexrins, but since Kay-teh has been honing her enchantment skills with Jo, I have heard that tensions between Jo and Tibik, the leader of the coven, are high.

Jobaki stumbles backward but doesn't fall. She looks frazzled, but only for a moment, because then her expression calms, and becomes something chilling. Calculating. "I do not answer to you, Tibik. You would do well to remember that."

She takes a breath, pats the front of her tunic down, and creates the orb again. It grows bigger as she expands the space between her hands, and when it is the size of a small boulder, she opens her eyes and smiles.

"I will not have it!" Tibik shouts, reaching for her hands again. The moment he grabs hold of her, Nalba races out from behind a nearby tree, ducking her shoulder into his rib cage and tackling him to the ground.

"Noooo!" I hear Jobaki shout as the three of them go down together, and I see her hands instinctively turn outward to protect her face. But the orb does not fade. This time, it shoots from her palms like a beam of light bouncing off the surface of the water and hits Nalba in the chest. Nalba screams as she's shot backward into the air, her body slamming into the wide trunk of a tree. She slides down, boneless, and her head smacks against a rock the moment she lands.

"Nalba!" Jobaki cries out as she crawls over Tibik and races to her side. "Oh goddess, no!" Tibik, along with several others, crowds around Nalba, and gently lift her body before carrying her out of sight.

I… may have just lost my friend. I have no time to let that sad thought take root, however, because Bzzsil Chi still has a pistol trained on my Elle-noor.

CHAPTER 27

ELEANOR

Standing slowly, Bruvix emerges from behind a bush, firing his pistol at the guards facing in the other direction. They go down, one after another, until three of them lie in a heap all around us. "Let her go, Bzzsil."

Bzzsil scrambles to his feet and pulls me in front of him, pressing his pistol against my cheek. I let out a pained moan as I feel the steel scraping the edge of the open wound. "I have lost nothing," he spits back. "Your clan is falling. You wish to save her, and yet, with a pull of my trigger, I can take her from you. I hold the power here."

"I know you do not wish to kill her," Bruvix says, dropping his pistol to the ground and lifting his hands in surrender. "She is worth too much alive."

"I am not opposed to bringing her back with some bruises," he says with a chuckle, tapping the barrel of the gun against the side of my head. I grit my teeth when he hits a bruise, trying to hide my pain from him as much as I can. When I unclench my jaw, the gag dips down beneath my bottom lip. It should be a victorious moment, but yelling isn't going to do me any good right now.

"Those will heal," he adds, then he pauses. "Though I suppose I should be wary of scarring. Wouldn't want a pretty thing like this to end up maimed and hideous like you."

Something inside me snaps, and I see nothing, and I feel nothing... nothing but the depth of my own rage as it rips through me. "He...is not...hideous!" I shout through ragged breaths before bringing the heel of my boot down hard on Bzzsil's bare toes. He yelps in pain, dropping the gun away from my head. I take the opportunity to shove my elbow into his throat, the spot where an Adam's apple should be, but on Bzzsil Chi it's just fleshy gray scales that are slick and greasy. Disgusting.

The gun falls from his hand and lands on the ground with a soft thud. I quickly kick it away and run. My wrists are still tied, but luckily, my feet are not, and I run faster than I ever have in my life toward Bruvix. My home. My future. Nothing else matters but him. I don't need anything as long as I have him by my side.

He opens his arms as I get closer. His expression full of longing, love, all the things we haven't said, along with all the things we should've before this very moment—it's all there in his navy-blue eyes, sparkling like the sea.

"It's okay," I try to tell him with my gaze. "Everything will be okay. We have time, and we won't waste it."

My fingers brush against his as soon as he's within reach, but something...changes. His eyes widen with horror and instead of pulling me into his arms, he presses his palm against my chest and shoves. I land on my back the same moment I hear the gun go off.

When I lift my head, I see Bruvix on his back, his legs twitching and his hand covering his chest. I scream as soon as I see the blood.

Crawling through the dirt, a near-constant sob escaping my lips, I place my hands on top of his and press down. "I-it's okay. We can stop the bleeding." I duck my nose into the crook of my arm to wipe the snot away while keeping my hands pressed firmly into his chest. "It's okay!" I tell him, not even sounding convincing to my own ears. "You're going to be okay."

His teeth are gritted, and his breath is shaky as he tries to hold on. His eyes meet mine, and he relaxes his jaw. Then his whole face relaxes, and his lips curl up into a smile. "Elle-noor," he says in a hoarse whisper. He coughs, and I can feel my heart sink as his skin begins to turn a pale shade of gold.

"It's okay, Bruvix. Don't talk," I tell him. I have no idea what else to say. There's so much I wanted to tell him. So much I was finally ready to say. Our life together was just beginning.

His eyes roll back in his head, and I worry he's passed out. "Bruvix!" I shout, moving my hand off his wound to shake his shoulder. "Stay with me, Bruvix!"

He doesn't wake, and blood still pours from between his fingers.

This isn't the end.

This can't be the end.

Lowering my head near his lips, I listen for breath. "Elle...Elle-noor," he whispers, so faint I almost didn't hear him, even though my ear is right next to his mouth.

"Hey," I say through tears. I'm trying to smile, trying to put on a brave face because that's what he needs right now, but I can't pretend I'm not scared to death of losing him. "There you are."

Then I turn away to shout, "Help! We need help here!" Grotahk is wrestling with two of the guards and Eduno is currently kicking the shit out of Bzzsil Chi, but upon hearing my call, Drasko races away, yelling for Kaiva.

Bruvix lifts his other hand, guiding my face back toward him, and cups my cheek. "I–I have always s-seen you in the piloi flowers," he mutters, trying to keep his focus on my face, despite it becoming harder for him to catch his breath. "Your softness. Your co-courage."

"Shh," I tell him. "Just rest. Help is on the way. You don't have t–"

"No. P-please," he begs. He tries to pull himself up but can't do much more than slightly lift his head, so I lean down, bringing us closer, mere inches apart. "We shall meet again, Elle-noor, among the flowers."

"Enough of that talk," I scold him. Shaking my head, I pinch my eyes shut, feeling annoyed by his constant pessimistic thinking. He's going to be fine. Kaiva will get here, and we'll take him back to the med tube, and that thing will perform an operation to remove the bullet and sew him back up, and he'll be fine. *We* will be fine. But Kaiva needs to get here before the rest of that can happen. "Where the fuck is she?" I grumble, looking around.

After a few moments, I look down at Bruvix, readying for another battle of hope versus doom. His eyes are open, but his gaze is unfocused. And unmoving.

No.

I put my ear next to his mouth, and I hear nothing. He's not breathing. "No. No, no, no. You are not leaving me," I mutter as my blood-covered hand frantically presses against his throat, searching for a pulse.

Nothing. Nothing is what I find.

"No! You can't leave me," I shout, my voice cracking as a sob wrenches from my throat. "No, Bruvix. Yo-you can't leave. Don't leave," I cry, pressing my face into his neck. At some point, my commands turn to pleas.

Again, I try feeling for a pulse—this time on the inside of his wrist. Maybe his alien body is different in that sense. Yeah, that's all this is. He's just asleep, and I'm going to feel his pulse beneath my fingers because I was merely checking the wrong spot before.

"That's all this is," I say to no one.

When I don't feel it, I try with my other hand.

The tears pour from my eyes when my other hand detects nothing, and soon I'm mumbling incoherently for him to please don't leave me as I press his wrist against my forehead.

When I lift my head, I notice Eduno on his back, and Bzzsil pulling himself to his feet as he pulls a long, twisted blade from the belt of his pants. He doesn't look down at Eduno, though. His gaze is now locked on me. But I don't care. I don't have it in me to care about anything but Bruvix.

I don't know when it happens, but moments pass, and at some point, I realize there is no pulse to be felt because… he's gone. Bruvix is gone.

My big, scarred alien protector has been taken from me.

Tilting my head back, I open my mouth and let my pain come

pouring out in the form of a scream. All my anger, my sadness—I let it all fuse together in my throat, then unleash it into the air.

When all that's left are tears, I press my face into his neck once again and hold him. Just hold him.

Out of nowhere, trees rustle a few feet away, and for a moment I hope it's another one of Bzzsil's guards coming to kill me too. *Take me to Bruvix,* I silently beg as I lift my head. *Take me home.*

But it's not.

Stepping through the tree line is Nanay, followed by the five adult members of her pack. Her lips curl, revealing her sharp, deadly fangs and her blood-red eyes meet mine. She looks down at Bruvix, then back up at me, and… then she leaps.

CHAPTER 28

BRUVIX

*D*ry. My mouth is dry.

I do not care for it.

Smacking my lips together, I attempt to summon some saliva to ease this discomfort. At least, temporarily.

When my eyes open, they land on Elle-noor, fast asleep in the bed next to me. No blankets cover her, and her clothes are rumpled and dirty. Her lips are slightly parted, and her hands are tucked beneath her chin. She is radiant.

It is when I see the fading bruises on her cheek and neck that everything comes rushing back to me.

Death.

Its grasp on me was tight.

Why am I not dead?

Or...perhaps this is the afterlife? Elle-noor is at my side, and is that not what I hoped the afterlife to be like?

Elle-noor's eyes blink open slowly, and a sleepy smile stretches her lips as she rubs her eyes. Then she gasps, trying to stand and rise and reach for me all at once, causing her to fall out of bed. "Fucking fucker!" she grunts as she rubs her backside. Then she leaps to her feet, her eyes wide as she leans in close, the tips of our noses almost touching. "You're awake?" she asks, and before I can respond, "You're awake!"

"H-hello," I croak out.

She turns away, bouncing on her feet. "Kaiva! He's awake!"

I hear Kaiva race down the stairs, and within moments, she is at my side. "Bruvix, my boy!" she exclaims, holding my face in her hands. "We thought we had lost you." Her eyes shine with unshed tears as she looks at the giant white bandage wrapped around my chest. "How do you feel?"

"As if I died."

She chuckles, as does Elle-noor, then asks, "What's the last thing you remember?"

The answer comes easily. "Dying."

Elle-noor's laughter fades, and a frown takes the place of her brilliant smile.

"Why am I not dead?" I finally ask because I am still quite confused.

Elle-noor takes my hand and presses my palm against her cheek. "You were. For about fifteen minutes."

"Nineteen and a half Earth minutes, actually," Kaiva adds.

Elle-noor clears her throat and continues. "The crew carried you back here, and Kaiva got you all set up in the med tube. Then you had surgery. The poison-coated bullet was removed, and your chest was stitched back up, and you've been unconscious for three days."

A cough escapes me, and Elle-noor rushes away, returning immediately with a cup of water. I guzzle it down, and she hands me another. Once that cup is empty, I take a breath.

"And Bzzsil Chi?" I ask, bitterly, as he is responsible for me being dead for nineteen and a half Earth minutes.

"Oh," Elle-noor says, giggling. "He's very dead. Like, 'not even enough parts left to cremate' dead."

"I see," I reply, dipping my chin. Clearly, the crew had a lovely time torturing him and tearing him limb from limb without me, and that realization fills me with envy. Or perhaps they did it to avenge me, which is thoughtful of them, but still. "Who issued the final blow?"

"Final blow?" Elle-noor asks, her brow furrowing.

"Who killed him? Varrek? Ahlvo? Is Varrek well? Have his wounds healed?"

"It was not the crew that killed Bzzsil Chi, my son," Kaiva says, placing a comforting hand on my shoulder. "And yes, Varrek is fine."

I jerk my head back, surprised by her answer. "What does that mean? The crew did not kill him?"

Kaiva's gaze drops to the screen pad in her hand. "All of your numbers are normal, which is very good. You must rest here for another day before returning home. I, uh, I shall leave you two now." Then she gives Elle-noor a nod and hurries up the stairs.

Elle-noor returns my palm to her cheek, closing her eyes as she strokes the outside of my hand.

"Tell me, Elle-noor," I say. It is not that I think she is intentionally stalling, but there is clearly something she is having trouble revealing to me.

"The tr'gorys," she replies, clearing her throat. "The tr'gorys killed him and the other guards. Nanay led the charge. One of the guards tried to kick Stanley, and he responded by ripping his leg clean off. Then the pack focused their attention on Bzzsil, and they tore him apart."

The tr'gorys killed Bzzsil Chi. Even hearing the words in my head, I do not believe them. It does not make sense. None of it. "Wh-what...How did the—"

"I don't know," she interjects. "They just showed up, and even though you were lying there, and I was lying on top of you, they went straight for him."

I rub a hand down my face, puzzled by Elle-noor's words.

Her voice drops into a whisper. "They knew."

"Knew what?"

She shrugs, then shakes her head dismissively. "I don't know. It's silly, really, and you're going to think I'm stupid, but it...it felt like they knew. They knew what Bzzsil Chi had done. That he hurt you, and me. They knew he was the enemy. That we weren't."

"I do not think you are stupid," I tell her honestly. "I would never think that." A smile tugs at my lips, and a chuckle escapes me. "I also do not think a tr'gory would care much about my death."

"Hmm," Elle-noor replies with a smirk.

"What?"

She gently drops my hand on the bed and stands. "Then why have they been sleeping outside the front door every night since we brought you back here?" She tugs open the curtain covering the large front windows, and there they are. The entire pack—Nanay, her four pups, including Stahn-lee, and the five adult males—lying on the ground in front of the door, their big bodies close together but facing every direction, so they can watch for any approaching threats.

Two of the pups wrestle and plop on the ground in a tangled heap of fuzzy black fur, as the other two are sound asleep on either side of Nanay. The five males fan out from there, flanking Nanay from the left and right. She lies in the center, her large head held high. She is not just the new mother of the pack. She is the leader. The alpha.

My jaw hangs open as Elle-noor stands against the window with her arms crossed, a smug smile on her lips. But I am too stunned to banter with her. I do not understand. "Why?"

"I don't know," she says, throwing her hands up. "I honestly don't." She returns to my side and leans down, dropping her pointy chin onto my arm. She tilts her head to the side as she runs her fingers through my mane. "I guess not all beasts are bad."

I lean into her touch, releasing a sigh as she continues running her blunt nails against my scalp. "I guess not."

Then she stops. "So, listen…"

My heart stops beating. I might as well be dead again. She is about to say she cannot be my mate because I did not properly support her pursuit of bonding with the tr'gorys.

"Elle-noor," I begin. I must get this out before she can leave me. "I—"

"I love you."

I stare at her blankly, wondering if I imagined the words coming out of her mouth. "You…"

She smiles. "I love you, Bruvix. I wanted to tell you before everything turned to shit. I wanted to tell you that you're all I need. I'm happy to work in your garden with you, to scrub the clan's dishes after every meal, to check the security feeds with you. I... I don't need anything else. I just need you."

Her words fill me with hope. It is a new feeling for me. "Truly?"

"Truly."

"But that is not what I want for you," I tell her. When her eyes widen at my words, I realize I must clarify. "Your work with the tr'gory is important to you. It fills your dark eyes with wonder. It makes your heart soar. I will not take that from you. What kind of mate would I be if I did?"

Elle-noor's eyes dart between mine, as if trying to assess whether I speak truth. "Are you sure? You'd be okay with me continuing to observe them up close?"

"Yes," I tell her honestly.

I pull myself up, eager to press my lips against hers, but fail to get into a seated position when the ache in my chest becomes so painful that my vision blurs. Elle-noor just giggles and pushes my shoulders back down. "It's okay. I'll come to you, big guy."

She leans in, and her mouth is warm as it moves against mine. Her tongue glides against my lips and I let her in, groaning at the feel of her as her kiss becomes desperate, needy, and her hands stroke up and down my biceps. Bumps cover my skin as her breasts brush against my bare chest, her nipples pebbled and poking through her tunic. My hands flex with the need to grab her and lift her onto my body, making her straddle my aching cock.

My hand gets lost in her soft mane, and I hope it never finds its way out. So soft. Too soft, I've often thought.

Elle-noor is too soft to survive this chaotic, dangerous world.

What a fool I was.

No matter how much fear filled her insides, she carried on. It did not matter what she was facing, whether it was her past, her uncertain future, a violent, aggressive beast standing before her, or a treacherous slaver with a pistol pointed at her skull. She never ran. She never hid. Instead, she fought.

"Xidori kovvari," I mutter against her lips.

Her nose scrunches as the translation enters her mind. "Courageous heart?" she asks.

"Yes."

Because she is the most courageous warrior among us.

EPILOGUE

ELEANOR

"**Y**es! Bruvix, yes. D-don't stop," I moan as his fingers circle my clit faster. "I'm close. So fucking close."

Bruvix slams into me from behind, his fangs scraping the skin behind my earlobe so deliciously that I'm gone. Lost to the sensations of his vibrating dick pumping in and out of me as my pussy holds him in a tight grip. My legs shake as he bites my neck and I cry out, his strong arm wrapped around my middle the only thing keeping me from face-planting into the piloi flower bed. He glides his tongue over my bite mark, cleaning the blood from it. His thrusts continue, but I feel them getting more erratic. He's close.

We can't finish like this, though.

"Wait!" I whimper as I reluctantly push away from his ripped stomach, separating our sweat-covered bodies. I spin around and lie on my back, pulling him down with me. He settles himself between my thighs, and I guide him back inside my body, where everything just feels better. "I need to be able to bite you too, right?"

"Ah," he says, his chest heaving against mine. "Yes. Right."

Bruvix surges forward, and we both let out a moan. "Like that," I tell him when he settles on a rhythm. His eyes are pinched shut and his face is twisted in anguish, but I know that means he's close and trying to make it last for me.

"Hey," I whisper, stroking a finger along his cheekbone. "Look at me."

He opens his eyes, one at a time, and they remain locked on mine, heavy-lidded and swirling with adoration.

I press my lips to his, and whisper, "Come for me." And he does. He throws his head back and growls wildly as his hot seed fills my pussy. I feel it sliding down my inner thighs as I sink my teeth into his shoulder, between his scars. Tasting his blood on my tongue is an odd sensation. For a moment, it feels wrong. But this is how the clan solidifies a mate bond, and I'll do whatever it takes to make Bruvix officially mine.

Eventually, Bruvix stills, and he rolls us so I end up lying on top of him, our bodies still connected. We're covered in freshly tended soil, sweat, and no doubt, petals from the piloi flowers that were crushed beneath us, but I can't bring myself to care. Though I doubt they'll show any sign of wear and tear by tomorrow. They seem to bounce back pretty quickly, these seemingly immortal flowers. He reaches his long arm to the right and tugs a fur blanket over us. "We must sleep now, xidori kovvari."

"Okay," I reply, mid-yawn. "Wow, that was fast."

"Our bodies are eager to complete the bond," he replies with a deep, rumbling laugh. A sound I will never tire of hearing. "When we wake, our minds will be forever linked."

I trace the raised skin of the newest scar on his chest from the bullet coated with poison Bzzsil Chi fired, almost taking him from me. The wound healed within days as is expected with the Trovilians and their naturally advanced healing abilities.

"So glad this week is finally over," I groan, my eyelids getting heavier by the second. "That sucked."

Bruvix laughs again, pulling me closer. "I shall never withhold my cock from you again. If Kaiva had not demanded we wait to ensure my heart could handle it, I would have fucked you the moment I awoke in that flimsy bed."

"Mmm," I mumble, sleep coming toward me with open arms. "I believe you." And I let it take me away.

* * *

An impatient, frustrated howl pulls me from sleep, and though it's incredibly loud, I'm not concerned about the source. I know that howl. Rubbing my eyes, I roll out of the flower bed and stumble over to the edge of the roof. When I look down, I see a hundred-pound pup with red eyes and a wagging tail.

"Hi, Stanley!" I say with a wave.

He barks in response, jumping up with his front feet.

What does he want? More jerky?

Laughing at the grumpiness in my mate's voice, I turn. "Always. But he probably just wants to pl–"

Bruvix stares back at me, grinning from ear to ear as he lounges in the flower bed.

He didn't say that out loud, I realize. "Whoa."

Yes, inara. It worked. We are linked.

Holy shit! I send back. *This is so cool! Okay, I'm thinking of a number betw-*

Twenty-six, he interrupts.

Aah! I mentally scream. *I can't believe this is a thing.*

Do you wish to have me guess the numbers you envision for the rest of the day, Eleanor? Or would you like to go see Stanley?

I wanna go see Stanley, I reply instantly. *Wait, you said my name correctly. I... don't like it.*

I have been saying it incorrectly? he sends.

Yeah, you say it with a pause in the middle. Can you go back to saying it like that?

Elle-noor... he sends. *Yes?*

Yep! I send back. Tying my hair into a low bun, I use a towel to wipe the dirt from my skin. After a few minutes of this, Bruvix and I realize that only a shower will get us clean, and that can wait until later. We throw some clothes on and head outside.

Stanley greets us by jumping up and slamming his giant paws into my chest, and I stumble backward. Then Bruvix steps in front of me and scolds the pup with the point of his finger. "No, Stahn-lee. Jumping is bad."

Stanley's head tilts side to side as Bruvix speaks, and when he's done, the pup lets out a frustrated grunt. Since the attack, our bond with the tr'gorys has strengthened. Nanay greets Bruvix and me with a wagging tail. We've played with the other adult males in the pack, and the pups are always all over us. Bruvix doesn't even seem that afraid of them anymore, which amazes me.

Hungry? I send to Bruvix. Now that we're up, we might as well eat.

Always, he replies.

Before we make it to the meal hall, the screen pad in Bruvix's pocket starts beeping frantically. "What is it?" Bruvix says when he answers.

"Come to my training room," Varrek says, his tone stern. "Queen Ekoya has an update to share."

The comm disconnects, and we run toward Varrek and Chloe's house, Stanley trotting alongside us. I can't imagine what this update could be, but I can't imagine it's good. Bzzsil Chi is dead, so what else is there?

We meet Ava on the way as she steps out from the med room. She greets Stanley with a bright smile and a scratch behind his ears.

"Any update on Nalba?" I ask. "Or Jo?"

Ava nods, but the dark circles under her eyes tell me that neither are fully recovered. "Nalba is okay, but her memory is still wiped. She's frustrated, as you can imagine, but we're working on creating a system using her notes that will hopefully trigger those memories."

"How far back is she missing?" Bruvix asks.

"Well, the last thing she remembers is getting on a ship to leave Trovilia," Ava replies with a sigh. "She doesn't remember anything about Oluura, or how she's spent her time here over the last five years."

My god, that's awful. "And Jo?"

"Jo's doing well, actually," Ava says. "She likes the caves and being with Kate is good for her."

"I'm sure being away from Tibik also helps," I add.

"Mmm-hmm," Ava replies with a look that says, *You don't even know.*

I'm still not sure what went down that night, between Jo and Tibik—why he put up such a fuss over her using her power to take down Bzzsil Chi, and what the dynamics are between them, but a little break certainly can't hurt.

Stanley plops his butt down on the dirt just outside the front door to Varrek and Chloe's, waiting for us to return.

We enter without knocking since Varrek summoned us here. When we reach the second floor and enter his training room, Queen Ekoya of Trovilia is on the screen pad in Varrek's hand, sitting patiently in her throne with her hands in her lap.

Ahlvo, Grotahk, Eduno, and Chloe are here as well, with a sleeping Vahla in Chloe's arms.

"Ah, there he is," Queen Ekoya says when her eyes land on Bruvix. "The undead warrior. Good to see you, my friend."

"And you, Queen Ekoya," he replies in a formal tone.

"This must be your lovely inara, Elle-noor, yes?" she asks.

I step forward and stand next to Varrek. "Hello," I say with a wave. Then I feel rude having not curtsied, so do that too. "Pleasure to meet you."

If she's weirded out by the curtsy, she doesn't show it. Instead, she gets straight to business. "Now, I wanted to congratulate you on the execution of Bzzsil Chi. I am certain it was the best possible outcome for everyone involved. Except him, of course, but no one cares about him."

"Thank you," Varrek replies. "But I must be honest and tell you that we did not kill him. It was the tr'gorys, a predatory creature local to this region of Oluura."

The queen sits perfectly still, and if not for her occasional blink, I would assume the comm froze. "You say a creature killed him?"

"A pack of them," Bruvix adds. "And killed his guards."

Her eyes narrow, and she tilts her head to the side. "You trained these beasts to slay him?" Then she leans in closer. "May I borrow them for a time?"

Everyone laughs at her joke, except for her, which makes me wonder if it was actually a joke.

"I had been building a case against that vile monk slug for several moon cycles before this series of events unfolded, and his death facilitates the move into the next phase of my plan, so I thank you," she says with a smile and bow of her head.

"What plan is that?" Varrek asks.

"I am trying to establish a peace treaty with the king and queen of D'Alluk. Negotiations are precarious after your father slaughtered their males and tried to kidnap their females."

"Yes," Varrek barks out. "I am familiar."

"In order for them to agree to even discuss the treaty, they requested I investigate the disappearance of several D'Allukan females. I suspected they had been sold into slavery but could not confirm who might be the cause. As soon as you alerted me to Bzzsil's death, I had my warriors travel to Nu'Piix to destroy the brothel."

"I assume you found countless unsavory deeds there," Ahlvo replies.

She nods, her eyes wide with excitement. "I did, indeed, as well as the missing females. Every one of them."

"So you freed them? Returned them to their home?" Chloe asks, smiling at the queen proudly. "That's incredible."

"Yes, they were reunited with their families. It was lovely, and all are safe now," she says, placing a hand over her heart. Then her expression turns from relieved to...worried. "There remains one problem."

Varrek purses his lips. "And that is?"

Queen Ekoya shifts uncomfortably in her throne. "Upon entering the brothel, my warriors discovered more human females Bzzsil had captured. Clearly, we have no means of sending these humans back to Earth, so perhaps you could care for them...for the time being."

Ahlvo, Bruvix, and Varrek reply simultaneously with some variation of "Absolutely not!" while Chloe shouts, "Of course, we will!" The three males whip around to shoot frustrated looks at the new mom. But she doesn't back down. "What other option is there?"

"They could be sent to Trovilia, and Queen Ekoya could watch over them," Varrek replies, pointing at the screen.

"Do you think I did not consider that, Varrek?" Queen Ekoya replies tartly. "Now that this treaty is in motion, I must see it to its end. I am traveling to D'Alluk at first light and will remain there until it is done. So I will not be here, and I do not trust anyone else to comfort the humans."

"Yeah, who better to do it than us?" Chloe adds. When Varrek looks as if he's about to argue, Chloe says, "You saved me. Let me save them. Pay it forward."

He sighs, and his shoulders drop. "Fine." He turns back to the screen and asks, "How many are there? And when will you be sending them?"

The queen replies with a slight chuckle. "Expect a remote transport ship to arrive with six stasis pods by tomorrow eve."

"You already sent them?" he shouts. "Why did you even ask?"

"Varrek, I am the ruler of Trovilia," she says flatly. "I need no one's permission to do as I please. But also, I knew Cloh-ee would amend your decision."

"Good to see you, girl!" Chloe exclaims with a wave.

"Farewell, my darling," Ekoya replies. "Kiss that sweet child of yours for me."

The screen turns black, and we stand there in stunned silence. Eventually, Varrek huffs a breath and he and Ahlvo begin discussing logistics. Ava jumps in, offering beds in the med room for them. The conversation gets louder and more frantic, but Bruvix and I remain quiet, our gaze connected.

So, new human females, I send to him.

It appears that way, he replies.

You're not going to trade me for one of them, are you?

I feel his disgust at the idea. *Why would you ask such a thing?*

Just checking. 'Cuz this thing we have? I like it.

I have already told you, Elle-noor. You are mine. I am keeping you. Then his thoughts shift from heated possession to uncertainty. *Um, may I? Keep you?*

I send him every memory of when he's surprised me, protected me, and how he's loved me more than anyone ever has. I want him to know, without a doubt, that his feelings are returned. When he shoots me a smile, and the scar on the left side of his face pulls at his lips, I say, *You better.*

* * *

Thank you for reading KEEPING HIS MATE! I hope you loved Bruvix and Eleanor's story. So what comes next? Have we reached the end of the series?

NO WAY. It's Nalba's turn to fall in love. And our adorable clan cook, Waldric, is ready to make her swoon.

Order HEALING HIS MATE now!

"These aliens are so attractive to readers for a reason - this is exactly the type of personality we'd love to see in reality, and it's gorgeous. We're drawn to it. I dive into every Ivy Knox book knowing that not only will I get a beautiful romance, but I'll also see the best of humanity in the most unlikely of places - on an alien planet, with an alien man who knows how to keep his woman happy in all the right ways." - 5-star reader review

Nalba is known the world over as a genius inventor, but when she suffers a head injury and loses five years of memories, she questions the path her life has taken.

Waking in a bed with an unrecognizable human face looming over her is only the start of Nalba's worst day ever. It turns out she was injured in a recent battle, leaving her with amnesia. Without her greatest asset—her brain—in working order, how is she to know who she is?

Waldric, the clan cook, can't keep away from Nalba the moment he hears she's conscious. He's been crushing hard on her for years, and she barely acknowledged his existence. He's desperate to prove himself a proper mate and vows to win her heart through her stomach. When his freshly baked bread triggers a memory, he jumps at the chance to become her personal chef.

As Nalba uncovers who she was before the accident, she questions whether there may be more to life than striving for greatness through her innovative creations. Perhaps there's room for something more. Or *someone*.

With Waldric filling her life with joy and her belly with decadent treats, Nalba recalls parts of her past long since buried and is faced with an impossible choice: Should she choose love or her career?

Want to find out what happens next? Start reading Healing His Mate now!

ALSO FROM IVY

<u>ALIENS OF OLUURA</u>

Saving His Mate

Charming His Mate

Stealing His Mate

Keeping His Mate

Healing His Mate

Enchanting Her Mate

(This series isn't finished. There's plenty more to come!)

<u>STRANDED ON EARTH</u>

Her Alien Bodyguard

Her Alien Neighbor

Her Alien Librarian

Her Alien Student

Her Alien Boss

ENJOY THIS BOOK?

Did you enjoy this book? If so, please leave a review! It helps others find my work.

Get all the deets on new releases, bonus chapters, teasers, and giveaways by signing up for my <u>newsletter</u>.

FROM IVY

*L*et me begin by saying, Bruvix has totally stolen my heart. Has he stolen yours too? Our grumpy, ale-making hacker has finally found his mate, and I hope you enjoyed their journey as I did writing it. And as soon as he realized she was his inara, he turned into a big, delicious cinnamon roll.

Once I knew that Kate and Bruvix weren't going to work as a pair, Eleanor started taking shape. She's his exact opposite in many ways, which is precisely what he needed. She's the honey to his vinegar, the bright smile to his eternal scowl, and the moment I pictured her face, I saw a fierce, alien wolf-type creature sitting next to her.

Not only was her love of animals the perfect setup to get Bruvix to face his fear, but it was also a great excuse to bring the looming tr'gorys back into the mix. And who can refuse an alien puppy? I mean, come on!

I also knew I wanted a battle scene in which Bzzsil Chi gets killed. He was always going to die, because bad guys never win in my worlds, but I wanted his death to be ruthless and spectacular, and getting ripped apart by a pack of tr'gorys checks both of those boxes.

So where does that leave us? The answer is with a brilliant inventor suffering from amnesia. That's right! It's Nalba's turn to find love, and I think you'll find her story to be quite the tasty tale.

We also have Jo, who has temporarily left the village, and a new group of humans to welcome! Lots more fun to come.

Stay tuned!

Love,

Ivy

P.S. - A special thank you to my amazing editors, Tina and Jenny, who turn my sometimes nonsensical words in to something beautiful. And Mandi, who gave this one a beta read and offered brilliant suggestions to strengthen the bond between Eleanor and Bruvix.

Hugs to my sensitivity readers, Dani Moran and Tessa Villanueva, who helped me honor Eleanor's Korean and Filipino roots.

And to you, my dear readers, for supporting my work and gobbling up my books the moment they go live. I wouldn't be here without you.

RESOURCES

SAMHSA (Substance Abuse and Mental Health Services
Administration Hotline)
1-800-662-HELP (4357)
TTY: 1-800-487-4889
samhsa.gov

Stop AAPI (Asian American Pacific Islander) Hate
Hate against Asian American Pacific Islander communities has risen
during the COVID-19 pandemic.
Together, we can stop it.
https://stopaapihate.org/

RAINN (Rape, Abuse, & Incest National Network)
1-800-656-4673 (call or chat)
rainn.org

National Suicide Prevention Hotline
1-800-273-8255 (call or chat)
suicideprevention.org

National Domestic Violence Hotline
1-800-799-SAFE (7233) (call or chat)
thehotline.org

Ivy Knox has always been a voracious reader of romance novels, but quickly found her home in sci-fi romance because life on Earth can be kind of a drag. When she's not lost on faraway worlds built by her favorite authors, she's creating her own.

Ivy lives with her husband and two neurotic (but very cute) dogs in the Midwest. When she's not reading or writing, she's probably watching *The Good Place, What We Do in the Shadows,* or *Fall of the House of Usher* for the millionth time.